Little Mishaps & Big Surprises

CJ MORROW

Copyright © C J Morrow 2018

All Rights Reserved. No part of this publication may be reproduced or transmitted in any form or by any means, electronic or mechanical, including photocopy, recording, or any information storage and retrieval system, without permission from the author.

This book is a work of fiction. All characters, locations, businesses, organisations and situations in this publication are either a product of the author's imagination or used factiously. Any resemblance to real persons, living or dead, is purely coincidental.

Cover artwork: Lyubickaya Lyudmila/Shutterstock
Design: © A Mayes

ISBN: 172077823X
ISBN-13: 978-1720778233

DEDICATION

To my best friend, Maxine, who *enjoyed* a
Moroccan spa treat with me.

Also by CJ Morrow

Blame it on the Onesie
A Onesie is not just for Christmas
Mermaid Hair and I don't Care

Never Leaves Me

The Finder
The Illusionist
The Sister

One

As I drag my wheelie-case along Strand I can't help smiling. I love this time of year in London: seven in the evening, in the middle of winter. The shops are shut but people are still around, some waiting to catch friends for dinner, others on their way to a West End show. There's a sense of anticipation in the air, excitement, thrill.

It's 28th December and I've made a lucky escape. Soon I'll be back in my lovely room in my delightful flat in Covent Garden. Not, you understand, actually in Covent Garden, but in a hidden alley off a side street you've probably never noticed.

The air smells cold and I can see my breath. A lonely snowflake drifts across in front of me. Snow. That would be nice, especially since I intend to squirrel myself away for a few days and just chill out. I've stocked the fridge with wine and food and I've promised myself some *me* time. I've earned it over Christmas and my vile train journey from Swindon has increased my need for peace and harmony.

Oh, I know they have to do maintenance on the tracks, and I know that public holidays are the best time to do this, but my journey has taken twice its normal hour and I'm tired. The train-replacement coach they laid on from Swindon to Reading would have been tolerable had it not been for the large, creepy man who insisted on sitting next to me and squashing me against the window. Only as we got off did I realise there were spare seats aplenty elsewhere. But he never spoke to me, so I suppose that's a positive, and I made sure that I went into a different carriage when we finally got on the train.

From Paddington to Charing Cross Tube Station took a fast twenty minutes and now I'm nearly home, trundling three days of dirty clothes and the Christmas presents from my family along the street.

If it wasn't dark I would probably be walking past St-Martin-in-the-Fields church, but further on the backstreets are more deserted and darker and a girl can't be too careful.

From Strand, I take a sharp right and see the bright lights of Covent Garden. Every year we have a different Christmas display, one year it was barrels stacked in the shape of a Christmas tree, another year a giant reindeer; it's something different every year and it always makes me smile.

I veer off and scrabble down the side street. It's definitely getting colder and more snowflakes are falling even though they fade away as they hit the pavement. I wonder if it will settle? In Swindon and in Aston Bassett it was raining when I left. Here the ground is dry so if enough snow falls it might stay. A blanket of snow would look so pretty on my favourite cobbled streets.

Down the alley and I reach my front door; solid and wooden, innocuous with its faded green paint, you'd never notice it if you ever walked past. I love that about London; the hidden places. You could live here all your life and never discover them all. I always marvel at the vastness of London after I've been to visit my parents.

Key in the door, up the stairs, clomp, clomp, clomp – my case on the treads. The optician below is shut, my flatmates are away, so I'm disturbing no one. I'll be alone. Solitude. Just what I need after Christmas with my family.

As I round the top of the stairs the smell of toast hits me, it even makes my mouth water – as though I haven't had enough to eat after four days of my mum's cooking.

Is someone here?

The kitchen to my right and the bathroom straight ahead, are in darkness but as I start up the next flight of stairs, my case clomping behind me as a warning – because a squatter, or worse a burglar, might just think there were several of us coming up the stairs – I notice a chink of light coming from the living room.

I have a horrible feeling, a twisted sinking feeling in the pit of my stomach. I know I'm not alone but I wonder which of my flatmates is here. I could just carry on up to my bedroom, ignore whoever it is. But I don't. I balance my case on the bottom step of the next flight of stairs and turn back just as the living room door opens slowly, almost tentatively.

'Hi Charlie.' It's Yan's sleepy face that greets me. 'You're back early.'

'Hi. No. I'm not.' I hadn't actually told Yan or CeCe when I would be back; it's none of their business. 'When did you get back?' I fight to control my irritation.

He grins, glances to his left. I follow his eyes and see CeCe flopped on the sofa; her face too is pale from sleep.

'We never actually went home,' she says, stretching her arms out in front of her; she reminds me of my mum's cats.

'Ah.' Realisation dawns rapidly. I can't believe this has happened again. They have become a couple. Right under my nose. Oh shit.

'Would you like a drink? We've got wine on the go.' Yan opens the door wider so that I can step into their secret, cosy nest.

'Yeah, why not. It is Christmas.' I force a smile as CeCe jumps up and gets a wine glass from my old painted sideboard, and Yan pulls a bottle of white out of an ice bucket on the coffee table.

'Ice bucket. Wow.' I try to keep my voice light.

'Yeah. Should still be cold.' Yan pours wine into the glass that CeCe holds in her tiny little hands before passing it to me.

'Pinot?' But I know the answer.

'Yeah.' CeCe looks sheepish. 'We borrowed one. We owe you.'

'What the hell,' I say as I knock it back and grab the bottle for a refill. There's plenty left so they haven't drunk much. Then I notice the empty bottle of red on the floor, *my* red – no wonder they were sleepy.

'Have you eaten?' CeCe asks. 'We had toast earlier; I could do you a slice. If you're hungry.' She smiles the smile of the guilty, caught red-handed and I wonder if they've had my pâté or soft cheese to go with their toast and wine.

'No, you're all right.' I flop down onto the sofa, as does CeCe; there's only room for two. Yan sits on the arm of the chair in front of us.

'So, you didn't go home for Christmas?' I take another large gulp of the wine, my wine.

They shake their heads in unison.

'Why not? I thought you were.' They were both supposed to be away until the thirtieth, or that is what they told me. I wonder how long they have had this planned.

'Chinese don't really celebrate Christmas,' CeCe says, her eyes cast down.

'My dad was going to my brother's, so…' Yan's voice trails away and he shrugs.

'So how long has this been going on?' I smile my encouragement.

'What?' They cast furtive looks at each other, exchange shy smiles.

'You two.'

'Um, about a month.' Yan doesn't even look at me.

'Yeah, beginning of December. When my iPad stopped working and Yan fixed it.'

'Oh, I see.' I don't, because I didn't know anything about CeCe's iPad or Yan's ability to fix it because I thought he was a builder not an IT specialist. I take another gulp of wine and we sit in awkward silence.

Finally, Yan breaks it.

'Did you have a good Christmas with your family?'

Was it good? Hard to say, really.

I arrived on Christmas Eve, just before eleven, and it cost me fifteen pounds to get a taxi from Swindon station to Mum and Dad's place in Aston Bassett. Fifteen pounds. I could have called them, I know that, but it would have meant a thirty-minute wait before they even got to me, and that's assuming they can find their keys and the traffic obliged. I suppose a sensible person would ring them from Reading and give them the half-hour warning they need to arrive on time. But, I've done that in the past and then the train has been delayed and Mum has sat in the car park seething about wasting her time when she could be getting on with the Christmas baking, so I don't bother anymore. I don't even tell them what time I'll arrive.

I burst into their place without knocking and they pretended they were excited to see me and I pretended I was so glad to be home, even though their house has never actually been my home. Then, once my stuff was stowed away in the granny annex where I have to sleep, it was sleeves rolled up so I could help Mum with the Christmas food – we make what seems like hundreds of mince pies and sausage rolls that no one really wants to eat. As with every year, it was non-stop prep until the *proper guests* arrived late afternoon.

The proper guests are my brother Joe, his wife Marlene and their children Benjy and Kiki. I adore my niece and nephew so it's always a delight to see them. However, I have to control my irritation because no one ever suggests that Marlene helps with the cooking.

At just turned forty, Joe is eighteen months older than me and I love that he is also much taller than I am. At six-foot-two he makes me my five-foot-nine feel quite petite. We have the same thick, dark hair and dark eyes, as well as the same build which on Joe looks manly and strong and on me looks ungainly. But, such is life. There is no mistaking us for anything but brother and sister; one idiot I once went out with even asked if we were identical twins. I declined his offer of a second date.

We get our height from Dad, he's as tall as Joe;

Mum, however is barely five-foot-four. When we pose for family photographs, I like to stand between Dad and Joe so that I look normal. I look like a giantess if I stand next to Mum, or Marlene, who is even shorter than Mum. I like Marlene, I really do, but we don't have a lot in common.

Marlene is German and uses that to excuse her sometimes blunt turn of phrase. The first thing she said to me on Christmas Eve was typical of her.

'Darling, you're looking a bit loose. You should do a class with me. I will create one just for you. We start tomorrow.' *Loose* is Marlene's euphemism for fat and flabby. Marlene is a gym instructor; she has toned muscles where I didn't even know muscles existed. She's wire-thin and super bendy and at thirty-six and a mother of two has the body of a twenty-year-old. I hate her for that sometimes.

'Not over Christmas, eh,' Joe cut in, watching me shuffling and smiling before trying to decline her offer.

Marlene narrowed her eyes at him before she turned to me. 'I write out some exercises to take home. You do them. Yes.'

'Thanks Marlene,' I said, but we both knew full well that I wouldn't. I don't think I've even brought them back to London with me. Oops.

Benjy and Kiki were then hovering, fresh from the smothering welcome of my parents and it was my turn to hug them to bits.

'Benjy, Kiki. Happy Christmas. You've both grown so much.' I hadn't seen them since the summer and they seemed to have leapt up inches.

'It's Ben now,' Benjy said, his tone flat.

'Oh. Okay. Ben.'

'He's so grown up now he's at secondary school.' Marlene's tone screamed annoyance. Ben, flicked his eyes in her direction before disappearing upstairs to claim the top bunk before his sister got any ideas.

'Are you still Kiki?' I bent down to hug my niece. Her real name is Catherine, but Benjy – excuse me, Ben – couldn't say it when she was born, calling her Kiki instead and it stuck.

'Yes Charlie.' She hugged me tight and whispered into my ear. 'You're my favourite auntie.' A running joke as Kiki has no other aunts because Marlene has no siblings.

I couldn't help noticing a smell when I hugged Kiki and it took me a second or two to realise what it was. Dog.

'Joe,' Marlene started, 'tell your Mum and Dad about Herman.'

Joe cast Marlene a look then smiled at Mum.

'Is he all right? He's not, you know…'. Mum glanced at Kiki and stopped speaking.

'He's fine, but we've had to bring him with us. I hope that's okay.'

'Um, well.' Mum wasn't at all pleased about Herman coming with them. 'Where is he?'

'In the car. Joe thought he should tell you before we brought him in.' Marlene laughed. 'I said you wouldn't mind. You love animals, Penny, don't you? He can sleep in the kitchen.'

It's true, Mum does love animals; when we were growing up we had every pet going, iguanas, mice, fish, rabbits, hamsters. We never had a dog, though, and that wasn't accidental. Mum has two cats now, William and Harry; she calls them her princes – for obvious reasons.

'I'm not sure how the princes will react. The kitchen is their domain.'

Right on cue William flipped through the cat flap and wound his body around Marlene's legs.

'So cute.' Marlene wiped the cat and his hair from her legs as she struggled to keep an inane grin on her face.

'Herman can sleep with us, Mum. He's so old now he doesn't do much except eat and sleep.'

'Not upstairs.' Mum's shoulders rose in horror. 'We don't have pets upstairs, never have and you know that Joseph.' She used his full name, his telling-off name.

'Right. So where can he sleep?'

'In the annex.'

'But I'm in the annex,' I said. I don't mind Herman but he is an ancient Golden Retriever and he smells.

'You're in the bedroom; he can go in the kitchenette.' Mum turned and walked out of the room, and that was that.

'He won't bother you,' Marlene said, smiling sweetly. 'He's no trouble. It's a big annex, plenty of room for two.'

I suppose Marlene is right.

Mum and Dad moved out of Swindon, where Joe and I grew up, after Joe left for university and I left for London, not long after the *Iain incident*. It seemed to us both that they moved so we wouldn't, or couldn't, move back in with them. They had said they were downsizing, but after six months they decided that Dad's Mum, Granny Suze, would move in with them so they built the annex. It has two bedrooms, a large geriatric shower room and a sitting room with a kitchenette at one end. Granny Suze died five years ago and the annex has become handy extra space. Every Christmas I sleep in the granny annex because there are only three bedrooms upstairs, one for Mum and Dad, one for Joe and Marlene and one with bunks for the kids.

One year I suggested to Mum that it made more sense for Joe and Marlene and the kids to use the annex, but she said she didn't want to clear all her crafting stuff out of the smaller annex bedroom. So, I always go in the annex; the bonus is I have the bathroom all to myself.

Joe was despatched to haul a reluctant Herman out of the car and as they entered the kitchen William arched his back and started hissing.

'Shush cat,' Marlene said, her authoritarian voice silencing him instantly, which caused Mum to wince visibly. 'Shoo, shoo,' Marlene continued and chased William through the cat flap and out into the garden.

'I'm not sure this is going to work.' Mum glared at Herman who, by then, had slumped down on the floor and was eyeing the cats' feeding bowls.

'Put him in the annex, Joe. Give him his dinner in there.' Marlene issued her orders before sloping off to the sitting room.

No one said anything else but hackles had risen. Families, eh?

After tea, which consisted of copious ham sandwiches – from the Christmas ham – accompanied by the sausage rolls and at least two each of the mince pies Mum and I had made earlier, the kids watched TV and Mum and I cleared up. Dad busied himself in his workshop – God knows what he was doing – and Joe and Marlene went up for a rest. It's all right for some.

Once we'd gone through the charade of hanging up the stockings, purely for the benefit of the kids, of course, even though they both know that Santa isn't real, Joe suggested a trip down to the local. Mum didn't want to go, neither did Marlene, which was just as well as someone needed to stay home with Ben and Kiki. So Joe, Dad and I went; just like old times.

To be strictly accurate there aren't many old times. I think, since Mum and Dad moved to Aston Bassett, we've probably been to the pub on Christmas Eve three times. The pub was quite empty by the time we arrived, the fire was burning low and it looked as though it was being allowed to die.

'Bit quiet for Christmas Eve,' Joe commented to the barman when he ordered our drinks.

'No food tonight, so not many in. Full house tomorrow, Christmas dinner's never been so popular. That's why we're closing early.'

'Early?'

'Ten.'

It was already nine-thirty, we didn't have long. As soon as Joe came back with the drinks and told us this, I went straight back and ordered another round. I was on white wine, they didn't have my favourite pinot, so I was drinking the house white. Dad and Joe were on pints of bitter. We managed to squeeze a third round in before we were ushered out.

Three large wines in half-an-hour is quite a feat, even for me, and I really knew it once we stepped outside and the cold air hit me. Dad and I felt momentarily dizzy so Joe and I linked arms with Dad and the three of us giggled our way home.

Marlene had already gone to bed when we got back, and Mum was waiting to ply us with cheese and biscuits before bed. This was followed by more mince pies and a final chocolate orange split between Joe and me. I felt quite sick by the time I went to bed, especially after we had a nightcap – just a tiny port.

You would think after all that alcohol that I would have slept well, but I didn't. Not, I hasten to add, that it was my fault. It was Herman's. I've never really been bothered by snoring, either my own or anyone else's – I've never been with a man long enough for that to become a problem – but Herman's snoring penetrated the deepest parts of my brain and gave me a headache.

'That's what you get for drinking so much.' Mum arched her eyebrows at me the next morning as I fumbled in the kitchen for coffee and paracetamol.

'No. It was Herman's snoring that kept me up all night. It was God awful.'

'Yes, he is old, he does snore,' Marlene quipped, sipping a green smoothie at the table. She was wearing her jogging gear and had, apparently, done 5k that morning, as had a reluctant Joe. 5k on Christmas morning, what the hell?

I wanted to tell her to shut her face but it's not nice to start a row at Christmas, so I said nothing at the same time wondering where I could buy some earplugs on Christmas day.

The kids were allowed to open some of their presents after breakfast and Ben and Kiki were delighted with my gifts. For Kiki, some great little clothes from a fabby London kiddie boutique which I knew she would love, and a game for Ben's new PS something or other, which Marlene and Joe had bought him. Marlene had emailed the exact details so I knew it was the correct one and the look of delight on his face confirmed it. Phew. It's so easy to get these things wrong.

The rest of us waited until after dinner, which I helped cook while Marlene, Joe and Dad sat on their backsides in the sitting room. To be fair Dad did ply us with drinks – no alcohol for me and Mum until dinner was ready and special juices he'd had to order online for Marlene. Joe just refuses to drink that stuff – good for him – he opted for canned beer with Dad.

Dinner was great, Mum is a great cook and I'm a good, if reluctant, kitchen helper. After we'd stuffed ourselves, and the dishwasher, we all retired to the sitting room for the grand present opening. There's an order to these things in our family and only one person at a time opens their presents while everyone looks on and oohs and aahs accordingly.

We make the kids wait until last, that way they pay attention to everyone else, even though they only have a couple of presents left that they've not opened earlier.

Mum always starts; she opened everything so slowly that I wanted to rip it from her hands. Then Dad, then Marlene, then Joe, then, finally, me.

I'd taken a couple of my presents down with me, my Secret Santa from work and the present my best friend Gen had given me. Gen's present was perfume, the kind she knows I'll never buy myself because it's too expensive. Joe and Marlene had bought me a designer top, Mum and Dad had given me theatre ticket vouchers, which was what I had asked for, and Ben and Kiki had given me new pyjamas, pale blue with snowmen on them.

'I'll wear them tonight,' I grinned, holding them against me for size. 'Thank you.'

My last present, the last one of the grown-ups, was my Secret Santa from work. I felt confident it would be rubbish, the limit was ten-pounds, so it was likely to be a joke present, they usually were. Last year, I had a mug which said *I'm so sweet* when empty but as soon as hot liquid went into it said *I'm a bitch*. One trip through the dishwasher fixed that, it's now permanently stuck on *I'm a bitch*, which makes me smile when I see Yan drinking out of it. I dragged out opening my Secret Santa just to tease Ben and Kiki who were itching to get to their own presents.

'Come on Auntie Charlie, hurry up.' Ben was spinning one of his few remaining presents between his fingers, the paper crinkling as he spun.

'It'll soon be your turn,' Mum admonished. 'Just have some patience.'

All eyes were on me as I slowly unwrapped the package. I wanted to delay the moment when everyone groaned – which was guaranteed. I'd warned them it would be something cheesy, I explained that it was my Secret Santa from work, so they knew what to expect.

I removed the wrapping paper to find an innocuous box. I slowly screwed up the paper and tossed it towards the bin bag that Dad had brought in to collect all the rubbish.

'Auntie Charlie,' whinged Kiki.

I grinned as I slowly opened the box, lifting the lid and discarding it.

'What's that?' Kiki asked as an eight-inch dildo slid out from the bottom of the box.

'Oh my God,' I yelled, scrabbling to catch it before it hit the floor. But I didn't. It was Herman who, having slumbered in the corner most of the day, had suddenly come to life. He clamped the dildo between his teeth and it began to vibrate.

Joe, jumping up, tried to wrestle it from Herman's jaws. Marlene started hitting Herman across the back and shouting 'drop, drop.' But Herman wasn't letting go of his prize.

'Is it for Herman, Auntie Charlie?' Kiki's innocent voice filled the room. 'That's nice of your friends to think of him.'

'What's he got? What is it?' asked Dad who hadn't seen it properly before Herman got his jaws around it. 'Is it a bone?'

I shouldn't have laughed, I know, but I couldn't help it.

While I laughed, Marlene and Joe wrestled Herman as Dad and Kiki looked on bemused; but it was Mum and Ben's reaction which was priceless.

'Disgusting,' said Ben, who at eleven evidently knew what he was looking at. 'You're an old person.' He shook his head at me and blushed.

I cringed with shame and annoyance. I am not old.

'Charlene,' shouted Mum. Oh dear, she was using my full name, my telling off name. 'Do something.'

I jumped up and between the three of us, my brother, his wife and me, we bundled Herman into the kitchen and Joe finally got the dildo out of his dog's mouth. He handed it – covered in Herman's drool – back to me.

I stepped back. 'No thanks.'

'Okay.' Joe flung it at the bin but Herman leapt into the air and caught it as it flew past him.

It was Marlene who tempted him to drop it a second time with the lure of a mince pie or two.

'I thought he wasn't supposed to have rich food,' I

said to Marlene once the furore had died down. The dildo was finally in the bin and Herman was on his third mince pie.

'He's not supposed to eat plastic and batteries either,' she spat at me. 'But he would have.' She shook her head in disgust as we slinked back to the sitting room so the kids could open their final presents.

'It wasn't my fault. I didn't buy it,' I snapped back as I sat down.

'That's enough, Charlene,' Mum said, as though I were a child.

I bit my tongue and nodded at Ben to open his presents.

Everything after that was an anti-climax – excuse the pun. We ate and drank more than we needed or wanted and slept in front of the TV until bedtime. Joe and I did manage a sly snigger about it in the kitchen when we were making coffee but other than that no one mentioned Herman and the dildo again.

That was Christmas day, done and over for another year. I was tired and even Herman's snoring from the annex kitchenette didn't keep me awake. But his howling woke me up from the deepest, sweetest sleep.

'Shut up, Herman,' I yelled through the wall.

He howled more. It went on and on and I waited for Joe or Marlene to come and sort him out. But no one came even when the howling got louder.

Finally, I hauled myself out of bed and yanked open my bedroom door.

The smell nearly knocked me off my feet.

I flicked the light on and Herman stopped howling, instead wagging his tail in delight at seeing me. He'd had diarrhoea all over the kitchenette; thank God the floor was tiled and not carpeted.

'Urgh,' I gagged putting my hand over my mouth and nose. I could taste it.

Herman seemed to take this as his invitation to jump up at me, knocking me over. I slipped in his mess and he had obviously paddled in it because I had poo paw prints on the front of my brand-new pyjamas.

'You've ruined my new pyjamas,' I screeched. 'You big shit.'

Herman hung his head in shame and started whining.

Clambering to my feet, stumbling and slipping on the dog diarrhoea, I flicked open the bathroom door and nudged Herman inside. Luckily, the bathroom is a wet room, specially kitted out for Granny Suze, and as I sprayed Herman's feet and his backside clean, I also peeled off my pyjamas before taking a quick shower too. Thankfully, Mum had put dark towels in the bathroom for me, and after drying myself and Herman I used them to mop up his mess in the kitchenette while he yelped in the bathroom.

Mum uses the annex kitchenette as a makeshift laundry room, which was particularly helpful as I loaded my pyjamas and the towels, as well as Herman's sleeping blanket into the washing machine and set it going on the hot wash.

He whined a bit when I let him out of the bathroom but that was mainly because his beloved blanket had gone, but after a good sniff around he settled himself down to sleep and I was able to go back to bed. After tossing and turning, I finally managed to get back to sleep myself, even though the stench of dog diarrhoea lingered in my nose.

When I told Marlene about it all the next day she had no sympathy but made a face which screamed *serves you right*, raising her eyebrows and half smirking at me, as though it was my fault.

'Marlene seems to be blaming me for your dog shitting everywhere last night,' I told Joe when he walked Herman and I went with him.

'Yeah. Just ignore her.' Joe laughed.

'It's not funny. I had to wash all that lot in the night and then again in the morning after Mum declared them not clean enough. The tumble dryer's on full pelt now. My lovely new pyjamas were in there too. I fell in the shit; I had to have a shower in the night.' I was really annoyed with everyone for not taking this as seriously as I thought they should. No one had apologised or empathised.

'How's work?' Joe said, changing the subject.

'Yeah. Fine. You?'

'Yeah. Same. You working between Christmas and New Year?'

'Yes,' I said, smiling. We both knew I wasn't but I always tell Mum and Dad that I am so I can make an early escape.

'I wanted to leave early too but Marlene wants to stay for New Year.'

'That's so she can sit on her bony arse while Mum waits on her.' I said this laughing and Joe joined in as we both knew it was the truth.

When we got back Mum had folded all the dry towels and left my pyjamas on my bed. I held them up to me; they had shrunk and the colour had faded.

'Shit bag,' I muttered under my breath.

'Who is?' Kiki's little voice came from behind me.

'Oh nothing. Shall we have a go at that crochet kit Nanny bought you?' I'm crap at crafts so it would be as much of a learning experience for me as Kiki.

'No. I don't really like that sort of stuff. Can I play with your makeup instead?'

An hour later Kiki and I both looked like clowns and Marlene's pinched face when she saw us made me laugh out loud.

'I'll never get that off,' she hissed.

'At least it doesn't stink like dog shit,' I whispered out of Kiki's earshot.

'Ha bloody ha. Come on Kiki, bathroom.'

Boxing Day dragged on. Too much food, too much time together. Marlene, once she'd cleaned Kiki's face, wanted to go through the exercises she had prepared for me. To keep the peace, I obliged in the living room while Mum gave helpful hints and Dad kept dodging from side to side in an attempt to watch *The Great Escape* on TV. He's seen that film so many times he must know it off by heart anyway.

A reluctant Herman was dragged around the block before bed in an effort to ensure that there wouldn't be repeat of the previous night. I told Joe that if there was they would be cleaning it up themselves. All six of my nearest and dearest had insisted that they never heard Herman howling. How convenient.

I wore my – by then – very snug, new PJs and went to bed early. Herman, bless him, didn't disturb me at all, neither howling nor snoring. I had a blissful night's sleep.

It was daylight when I awoke, rested and happy and not just because I'd slept well, but also because I was going home, my home, London. Mum had mentioned something about lunch but I'd told her I needed to get back early and was catching a train around eleven. I'd already persuaded Joe to take me to the station so Mum couldn't delay my leaving. And, I'd checked the live departure boards on my phone and a train was definitely running, not a coach replacement, not at that time.

I showered and dressed and packed my wheeliecase ready to go home. I assumed that one of the kids had taken Herman into the main house because I still hadn't heard a peep from him. Only as I opened the door into the kitchenette did I see that he was still there.

'Hey, poo poo,' I joked, nudging him with my foot, 'wakey, wakey.'

Herman didn't grunt his disapproval, or snore or even acknowledge my toe poke. Herman didn't move.

I stood over his inert body for several minutes willing him to wake up. Deep down, I knew he wouldn't.

I stepped over his body and let myself into the main kitchen, closing the door behind me. Kiki and Ben were sitting at the table eating cereal, Joe was feeding bread into the toaster and Mum was sipping coffee while standing at the sink and staring out at her garden.

'Morning.' I sounded much cheerier than I felt. I wondered when would be a good time to break the news about Herman.

'Hey, Sis,' Joe smiled at me. 'Toast?'

'No. You're all right, I'll sort myself out.'

He took a plateful of toast to the table and the kids attacked it with chocolate spread laden knives.

'So German,' Mum muttered to herself as she turned to watch them.

'Mum,' I hissed.

I helped myself to muesli and coffee and sat down with Joe and the kids. I felt guilty just sitting there, knowing, but I wanted to catch Joe alone.

'Where's Marlene? Out jogging?'

Joe rolled his eyes. 'In bed. Headache.'

'Mummy's always got a headache,' Kiki said. Out of the mouths of babes.

'That's not true,' Joe said. 'Now eat up your toast. Then we can take Herman out for a walk if you like.'

Both Ben and Kiki groaned.

'Okay, I'll take him. Fancy it, Charlie, before I take you to the station?'

I glanced at Kiki's little face and smiled at Joe. 'Yeah.'

Ben and Kiki stayed at the table much longer than I expected or wanted them to. We'd all finished and Mum came over and removed everyone's plates and started to stack the dishwasher but still the kids lingered.

Joe got up, went into the hall, came back with his coat and mine and started hunting around for Herman's lead. The kids still sat at the table playing a convoluted, and rowdy, game of *I Spy*.

Joe whistled for his dog. 'Where the hell is he?'

'Um, Joe, could I have a word please?'

Suddenly, there was silence and everyone looked at me. Joe frowned, Mum raised her eyebrows and the kids just stared at me.

'What's wrong?' Ben asked. He looked worried, scared almost. So much for me attempting to be discrete.

'Joe.' I yanked his arm and pulled him into the annex, shutting the door behind us.

'Wake up, boy. Come on. Walkies.' He prodded his dog but it was pointless. 'Oh fuck. Marlene's going to go ape.'

'It is upsetting. I think it was peaceful though, if that's any consolation.' I patted my brother on the back as he sniffed back his sorrow.

'Yeah, she wanted him put down before we came, but I wouldn't let her. I'll never hear the end of it. Oh fuck it. Couldn't you hang on, boy?' He turned to open the door back into the main kitchen. 'Don't let the kids in here until I tell Marlene.'

'What's going on?' Kiki's little voice asked as I followed Joe.

'Just got to talk to Mummy a minute.' Joe leapt up the stairs.

We all heard her scream as Joe broke the news. Kiki started to cry even though she didn't actually know why, but Ben had worked it out.

'Herman's dead,' he announced. 'Isn't he?'

I nodded and squeezed both kids' shoulders as Kiki wailed and Mum marched into the annex. She didn't look happy when she came back.

Upstairs Joe and Marlene were shouting at each other and while we couldn't hear every word, 'I fucking told you so,' came loud and clear from Marlene's mouth.

'What now,' Marlene yelled as she stomped down the stairs. 'What will we do with him?' She appeared in the kitchen red and angry and trailing a silk robe, and Joe, in her wake. They disappeared into the annex while we all waited in the kitchen.

Dad came in the front door, rushed through to the kitchen carrying the newspapers he'd just been out for and frowned at us.

'What's going on? I could hear shouting half way down the road.'

'Herman's died,' Ben said causing Kiki, whose crying had subsided into sobbing, to start wailing again. I sat down and pulled her onto my lap, hugging her.

Marlene flung open the door and burst from the annex.

'Benji, take your sister up to your room. Go and tidy, please. Adult talk here.'

Ben stood up, grabbed Kiki's hand and dragged her away, but not before he managed to say, 'It's Ben, actually.'

'Go,' Marlene yelled, pointing towards the stairs.

'Chill,' Ben mouthed behind his mother's back.

'What will we do with him?' Marlene looked around the room for an answer before muttering something in German and narrowing her eyes at Joe.

'Call a vet?' Mum offered.

'Call a vet. Is this vet a miracle worker?' Marlene threw her arms up in the air.

Mum flinched and stepped back, pressing herself against the sink.

'I suppose we could bury him,' Dad said. 'In the garden.'

'Oh,' Mum keened.

'The cats are out there.' Dad shrugged. 'Several of them,' he added.

'But he's enormous, where could you put him?'

'Behind the compost heap is the only place I can think of without digging up flower beds or the lawn.' Dad was being very pragmatic.

'Mmm.' Marlene cocked her head while she considered it.

'Couldn't you take him home and bury him in your own garden?' Mum obviously didn't want him in hers.

'What? No, Penny. It has to be done today. We are staying until New Year.' Marlene folded her arms and pursed her lips.

Mum nodded and forced a thin smile. She knew she was beaten.

'Come on then, Joe,' Dad said. 'We'd better make a start before that forecasted rain starts.'

'Marlene,' Joe said as he followed Dad out to the garage. 'You sort the kids out.'

Mum and I watched from the kitchen window as Dad and Joe – hobbling as his size eleven feet were squeezed into a pair of Dad's old size ten wellies – dug a giant pit behind the compost heap.

An hour later, the seven of us stood in the pouring rain under an assortment of Mum's colourful umbrellas while Marlene recited a prayer in German and we sang *All Things Bright and Beautiful* over Herman's body. Kiki had cried herself out by then, but Ben, his sorrow now manifesting, bawled all the way through the funeral.

And I had long since missed my train.

We went back inside leaving Dad and Joe to backfill Herman's grave. Mum put the kettle on.

'I blame those mince pies.' Marlene said as she shooed Ben and Kiki into the living room.

'Well, you gave them to him.' I couldn't resist it.

'We had to get that disgusting thing off him.' Marlene shuddered and grimaced.

'That wasn't my fault. I didn't buy it.'

'Still yours,' Marlene muttered, turning away.

'Joe said you wanted Herman put down before you

even came,' I spat back.

Marlene let out a long sob and ran upstairs.

'Coffee or tea?' Mum said, deadpan.

A couple of hours later it was Mum who drove me to the station; Joe was busy consoling Marlene over Herman's death.

I groaned when I saw the coaches lined up in the rain outside the station. Mum leant in to give me a hug.

'Have a safe journey,' she said.

'And you have a fabulous holiday,' I replied. I'd quite forgotten that Mum and Dad were going on a round-the-world cruise in January.

'If that lot ever go home,' Mum muttered. 'I could do with the time and peace and space to pack.' She half laughed.

'Tell 'em to bugger off, Mum.'

I grabbed my case from the boot and we kissed goodbye.

Yan and CeCe's eager faces are waiting for me to tell them all about my Christmas. Shall I regale them with tales of the dildo, diarrhoea, dog death and funeral? Perhaps not.

'Yeah, it was great,' I say, smiling and helping myself to a third glass of *my* wine.

Two

I toss and turn in bed chewing over the Herman incidents in my head before I focus on the Yan and CeCe situation. It can only mean trouble. For me.

If I'm honest I'm quite pissed off about it. I felt confident that they would not be attracted to each other. Ever. Physically like chalk and cheese, their personalities and backgrounds, and their cultures are very different. I thought they had no common ground.

When CeCe came to live with us Yissy was still here. We were an all female household and I loved it. We had nail varnish nights and prosecco nights, and movie night was always a romcom. CeCe had never seen Bridget Jones's Diary – how could that be? She had explained that her father was a Chinese patriarch who didn't approve of decadent western films. She, perversely, became addicted to all things Bridget Jones.

We had fun, us three girls. Then Yizzy started making noises about being homesick. I tried to persuade her it would pass; she'd only lived away from her parents in Birmingham for six months. Sadly, she wasn't convinced. Her parting shot – a backhanded compliment – was to say that even though I'd been a great substitute mother, it just wasn't the same. I preferred to think of myself as a big sister. Big in every sense, not only older than

CeCe and Yizzy but also considerably bigger; neither of them made it past five-foot in the growing race.

It was Yizzy who suggested Yan as her replacement; a friend of a friend who, having split up with his live-in girlfriend, needed somewhere new fast. I agreed to interview him just to please Yizzy but I had no intention of letting him move in; I wanted another female.

In my role as house-mother, a term coined by my best friend Gen, I interview all new tenants. As a tenant myself that might seem odd, but I've lived here for seventeen years and, though I say it myself I'm good at choosing tenants. In some cases, too good. Out of the eighteen I've chosen over the years, twelve of them have ended up as couples. That includes Michael and Sebastian, who were gay, not that I had picked up on that fact when I first met them, but I don't think Michael knew either at the time. Their wedding, five years ago, was the best I've ever been to. And, the campest: doves, a marching band, white horses and a pink marquee.

Now I have to contend with CeCe and Yan's burgeoning love. I'm astonished that they have become an item. When Yan first came to see the room, it was CeCe who answered the door. She showed him upstairs to the sitting room where I was waiting and, preceding him, made faces indicating her horror – she actually stuck her tongue out in disgust. Yan is big, not fat, just big. He's six-foot-six and made of muscle. He works for a big building company and spends his days humping heavy stuff around in West London mansions. He's second generation Polish, has a cockney accent and I liked him immediately, not least because he made me feel small and feminine. The fact that he horrified CeCe was a bonus as far as I was concerned – no romance there. How wrong was I?

I managed to tackle CeCe about when Yan took our glasses down to the kitchen.

'I thought you didn't even like him,' I said, remembering her tongue gesture on first seeing him.

'I know,' she said, tilting her little head. 'But, Charlie, love changes everything.'

What could I say to that? I'd like to think that it won't be a problem; that we'll carry on just as we have for the nine months since Yan first came to live here, but experience makes me fear otherwise.

I have the large bedroom with the en-suite bathroom, complete with bath and separate shower. The other two rooms – Yan and CeCe's rooms – are half the size of mine and they share a bathroom two floors down, next to the kitchen. Oddly, that's never a problem when people are single; they trundle up and down the stairs in their bath robes and just get on with it. But, once they become a couple everything changes, they want to share a candlelit bath – there isn't one downstairs, only a shower. They want to share a bed – only single beds will fit into their rooms. Soon, suggestions are made for a room swap; I have a king size bed, so much better for two people. It's my own bed; I bought and paid for it myself. I'm not swapping it for an old single bed.

I'll never move out of my room, I've earned it. I've lived here all these years, even if I didn't start out in the big room.

It was my best friend Gen who asked if I was interested in moving. She wasn't my best friend then, we just worked together and had bonded over our stupid names. I thought Charlene was cringey but it was nothing compared to Genevieve. She already lived in the flat – we've always called it a flat even though it's on three floors – and a single room was coming up vacant soon. At the time I was sharing a room in Camden with another girl who I really didn't get on with and the prospect of my own room was very alluring. Even more so when I found out that it would cost me only fifty pounds a month more but save me money on travelling to work. I jumped at the chance.

Gen and I had the smaller bedrooms and Anand and Shilpa, the owners, had the large room with the lovely en-suite, the one that is now mine. I look back on those two-and-a-half years when the four of us lived together with nostalgia; it was the best of times. Shilpa cooked great vats of curry, Anand played guitar and Gen and I giggled and danced and cemented our friendship with cheap plonk and evenings spent dying each other's hair.

Then, suddenly, everything changed; Gen got herself a very serious boyfriend, Ralph, and within months they were talking marriage and children. Ralph had saved a substantial deposit and wanted to buy, but it meant moving across London where houses were more affordable. Three children later and they're still together, and their more affordable house is now worth nearly a million.

Then Shilpa announced she was pregnant, wanted to move back to Wembley where her family lived and wanted a garden. I panicked, imagining myself suddenly homeless, but Anand and Shilpa decided that they would keep the flat and let me have the large room cheap providing I looked after all the tenancy issues.

So, it's me who ensures the council tax and utility bills are paid and that we get the best broadband deal, and it's me who gets the washing machine repaired, or replaced. It's me who selects the tenants – though Gen has joked that I'm more like a dating agency. And, it's me who has been doing this for years, so I am not moving out of my big room no matter how romantic it might be for my flatmates. And if that sounds selfish, well maybe it is.

I don't know what time I finally fall asleep but it's late when I wake up and I'm starving. I peer out of the window where there is no evidence of the previous night's snow but there's a ground frost which twinkles in the weak sunlight. It looks magical.

As I trundle down two flights of stairs to get some breakfast I hear giggling. My worst fears are confirmed when I enter the kitchen, Yan and CeCe are sitting at the little table feeding each other spoonsful of cereal. I suppress a groan. This is such familiar territory. I am to be the interloper in my own home. The gooseberry. Again. I hate this.

The whole situation is probably exacerbated by the fact that I haven't had a serious relationship myself, or any relationship actually, for quite a few years now.

'Morning,' I chime, trying to ignore their antics.

'Hi Charlie,' CeCe sings. 'Did you sleep well?'

'Yes thanks,' I lie and open a new box of my favourite sultana bran, which thankfully, only I eat. We have a system for food which works on the principle that everyone buys and eats their own food. No sharing or borrowing unless it's previously agreed. The exception to this rule is milk, which we do share.

I glance over at the amount of milk CeCe and Yan have slopped onto their cereal and hope they haven't used it all. I yank open the fridge and breathe a silent sigh of relief; there's more than enough, they've obviously bought more since I've been away.

After cereal and coffee, which I consume standing up as there are only two chairs at the table, I load my dishes into the dishwasher. The lovebirds are still at the table, staring into each other's eyes and slowly drinking tea.

I check the fridge to see what of mine they've eaten. The pâté has gone, so has most of the soft cheese as well as a pair of little chocolate puddings I was looking forward to, and the cream to go with them. I sort through the shelf getting more and more irritated before checking my wine. They've had four bottles. Four. I didn't even know they liked wine, neither of them has shown any interest in it before. Yan usually drinks beer and CeCe drinks Chinese herbal infusions that stink the whole flat out.

'Sorry,' CeCe's high-pitched voice says, suddenly she's standing behind me and peering over my shoulder, which she can only do because I'm bending down. 'We ate some of your foods.'

I turn to face her; she is smiling so sweetly.

'And my wine,' I add.

'Sorry. We'll replace. I'll go to Tesco soon.'

By Tesco she means our Tesco Metro which is not where I bought all my goodies.

'It all came from M&S,' I say as sweetly as I can.

I watch her face drop. We have a great M&S food hall in Covent Garden, it's even closer than Tesco but CeCe hates it. She used to work there and believes she was discriminated against because she's Chinese.

She left under a bit of a cloud after accusing management, her fellow workers and even customers – I think there might have been a misunderstanding. She complained, got nowhere and now refuses to go in there.

'Why don't I go and replace what you've taken and you can reimburse me later.'

'Good idea,' Yan says, putting his and CeCe's dishes in the dishwasher. 'In fact, here's some cash, you spend it on what you like. Sorry we ate your stuff.' He pulls the money out of his back pocket then thrusts fifty-pounds at me.

'Um, okay. If there's any change I'll give it to you later.' I'm hastily adding up the cost of the wine and the goodies and doubting there will be any change. I glance over at the table and notice milk slops are already pooling. I pick up the dishcloth ready to wipe it up.

'Yeah, whatever,' he smiles, takes CeCe by the arm and urges her towards the stairs.

'Sorry,' CeCe sings again, grinning at me.

I feel like throwing the dishcloth at both of them.

'Hey,' I call up the stairs after them. 'We'll need to sort out the party stuff later too.'

'Yeah, whatever,' Yan calls back without even turning.

I clench my hand around the dishcloth to prevent myself from hurling it.

I hate *whatever*.

The M&S food hall is surprisingly empty but I suppose the usual office workers aren't in here today getting their lunch. Most of the Christmas food has been reduced, which is great for me, I buy a few lovely things I didn't see before Christmas. But, I cannot find the yummy little chocolate puddings so have to settle for a rather large cheesecake, and cream.

Unlike the food, the wine has not been reduced and when I've finished, the fifty pounds Yan gave me isn't quite enough, I have to add another four pounds. I'll let him off that.

'Don't look at me like that,' a woman's voice says as I fumble my goodies into my *bags-for-life*. I take no notice as I know she isn't talking to me and I carry on packing.

'I said, don't look at me like that.' The voice is louder this time and, though her English is good, her accent is more pronounced: Eastern European, I think.

I'm tempted to look up but her tone is so belligerent that I really don't want to provoke her. I've learned it's best to keep your head down and walk away in these situations.

'Hey you,' she calls again. 'I know who you are. I know where you live.'

Around me there's a palpable silence, so, probably like everyone else at the tills, I chance a glance.

She's staring at me. Right at me and she's taking steps towards me. Aside from her shouting she looks respectable, she's early thirties, nicely dressed in smart jeans and warm jacket and she's carrying an expensive handbag. Very expensive. Her hairstyle suggests she is high maintenance. She's also very slim and well-manicured – she's pointing one purple tipped finger at me.

I should run, I should grab my bags and run.

The purple finger jabs the air in my direction.

I should run, abandon my bags and run.

Nobody else speaks. Not even the check-out operator to whom I have just handed over fifty-four pounds. Sod M&S loyalty points, where is a security guard when you need one?

'Yes, you,' she yells again.

Will no one come to my rescue?

'I don't know what the fuck he wants in you. Look at you. Big lump.'

Help. I'm frozen to the spot, my fingers clutching my shopping bags which are still resting on the checkout.

She staggers closer, then closer still.

I smell the familiar perfume of gin on her breath. It's only twelve-thirty; she must have been at it some time to be this drunk.

She starts to speak and jabs her finger in front of my nose between every word.

'Don't,' jab, 'you,' jab, 'think', jab…

'Everything all right, madam?' A deep voice cuts across her jabbing. A security guard. Hurray. Thank you, M&S, I knew I could rely on you.

I open my mouth to speak but Mrs Purple Tips beats me to it.

'I'm just sorting her. I'm telling her she can't take a husband and live with it,' she says, her accent getting stronger with every word.

The guard looks at me.

I shrug. I shake my head. Why should I have to explain myself?

'Well, keep it down please, madam.' He offers her a smile.

'Are you telling me what to do? Who the fuck is you?'

'Madam, please.'

'What's your name? What's your fucking name? I report you.'

I should take the opportunity now and go, get out while I can.

Stupid me.

'Hey,' I say, trying to diffuse the situation. 'I don't know your husband. You've got the wrong person.'

She turns her attention back to me; a look of relief passes over the security guard's face.

'Well, you would say that, wouldn't you? Fucking dog.' Her eyes, with their fake eyelashes, sweep over me as her mouth twists into an ugly shape.

Oh God.

Another step towards me, her head tilted up towards my face and I'm breathing her exhaled gin.

The guard is on his radio but I cannot hear what he's saying. I'm thinking, hoping, praying that soon this will be over and I will be out of here and on my way home.

'Fucking dog,' she yells again.

Then she vomits all over me. It misses my face but only because she's shorter than me and her head has dropped down, but her vomit covers my coat and my boots.

I find myself gagging at the smell of it.

She falls to the floor, knocking her face against the side of the checkout as she falls, her purple-tipped fingers twitching in the air.

The check-out operator rips off several sheets of blue paper roll and thrusts them at me. I attempt to wipe myself down.

Another security guard appears, quickly followed by a first aider. They're soon calling an ambulance.

I know I should stay. I know they will want me to tell them what happened for their accident book, but I don't want to get involved. I don't want to stand here in my vom-covered coat stinking and gagging. Anyway, Mrs Purple Tips seems to be recovering now.

I take my bags and sneak away while the attention is all on her, I justify my escape by convincing myself that there are enough people here to help.

I should have run away in the beginning.

The five-minute walk back home seems to go on forever, every person on the streets of Covent Garden is looking at me before stepping aside and grimacing. I know it looks as though I have puked all over myself, that I'm the gin-soaked drunk.

Thank God, the kitchen is only one floor up. I dump the bags and pull off my coat before stuffing it into the washing machine, grateful that's it's a puffa coat and fully washable. I use wet wipes to clean off my boots.

It wouldn't be so bad if there had been even a grain of truth in her accusations. Me, a husband stealer; I should be so lucky.

I unpack my M&S goodies, although the shine has gone off my treats now. I put the white wine in the fridge – I must remember to hide it before the party – and keep the red wine back to hide in my room.

The street door bangs. CeCe and Yan come giggling up the stairs.

'Hey,' Yan greets me. 'Ambulance up the road.'

'Oh yeah?'

'Yeah, outside M&S. Carting some woman away. Apparently, there was a fight in the food hall.'

'Really? Are you sure?' This cannot possibly relate to me.

'Yeah. Mistress versus wife. Got really nasty. Split lip and broken nose.'

'That can't be right,' I say.

'Yeah. Even in your beloved M&S food hall.' Yan laughs. 'Got it from the horse's mouth. Went to school with the security guard, he was out supervising the ambulance.'

CeCe, who until this point hasn't said a word, now chips in. 'See, M&S is a bad place.'

What can I say to that? Nothing.

'What's the smell?' Yan sniffs the air. 'You're starting early.' He nudges CeCe and together they laugh at me. It's starting already: them against me.

'Ooo Yan, tell Charlie about the party shopping.' CeCe jumps up and down like an excited puppy.

We've agreed that CeCe will organise the food, taking a trip down to Iceland in Waterloo to pick up some of their party packs and that Yan will organise the booze, mainly because he wanted to choose the beer and neither CeCe nor I care about beer. We've set a budget and chipped in an equal amount of money each. We've even factored in getting taxis back so no one has to carry all that food or drink on the tube.

My job is to organise the flat and decide on the theme; this year it is children's TV characters. It's always fancy dress for New Year's Eve and I've created the invitations. We're allowed to invite twenty people each, safe in the knowledge that only half will turn up, even if they do tend to bring a few strangers with them. We set a start time and tell people not to be late because we lock the door; that way we don't have any gatecrashers.

'Yeah, we've done it online. Delivered to our door on New Year's Eve,' Yan says, swaggering.

'Between eight and ten am,' CeCe adds, grinning to show how pleased she is.

'Okay. Cool. Is that just the food?'

'No, food and drink. Bit more expensive but saves everyone a load of hassle, especially humping it home. You owe me another twenty quid.' He puts his hand out for the cash.

'What? You spent an extra sixty pounds? Where did you get it? Fortnum and Masons?'

'Sainsburys,' CeCe answers. 'Better quality than Iceland.'

'Is it?' I don't attempt to hide my annoyance. God knows how much they've bought.

'I'll give it to you later.' And I'll be deducting the four-pounds from my M&S replacement shop too. I pick up my handbag and red wine and march upstairs to my room.

I stomp into the bathroom to wash my hands again but I can still smell the gin-vom. So, I change my clothes. Very annoying, I've only had these jeans on an hour-and-a-half.

My phone pings as I open my wardrobe looking for something else to wear. A message from Gen makes me smile.

Gen: *Hey you. Fab family Christmas? xxx*

Me: *Not really. Will tell you when I see you. xxx*

Gen: *Missing work? Lol*

Me: *You must be joking. Ha ha. Missing you though.*

Gen: *Same here. Really looking forward to NYE party. xxx* She follows the message with lots of wine glass emojis.

Gen and I work for the same company just down the road in Holborn. It's great because it's only one tube station away or, a brisk ten-minute walk – I usually walk, it's cheaper and easier.

I've been there almost eighteen years now, continuously; Gen has been there for nineteen, on and off. She's had three babies so has taken maternity leave. The company we work for is a call centre, but, and I always have to stress this to people, we're not sales, we're inbound. We provide customer services for lots of smaller companies who don't want to run their own customer service department. It means that we have to acquire a lot of knowledge in a short time whenever we get a new client. It can be quite a challenge.

I'm a team leader; I have to ensure my team of twenty know their stuff. And, of course, as team leader, I have to know it better than anyone else. I also do the hiring and firing for my own team. It used to be easy; when I first started most of the people I worked with were like me: British. Now we have more Eastern European and Indian employees than British. I'm not a racist, but it can be quite tricky. While everyone has very good written English and can speak the language well, sometimes their accents, which do sound more pronounced on the phone, can cause a few problems. When we have a client whose customers are, not to put it too delicately, of the older generation, they think they are speaking to someone in a foreign call centre. That's usually when I have to step in and take over the call.

Gen isn't a team leader, like me she started as a customer service administrator but when she came back after her first maternity leave she was promoted to team leader – before me, who hadn't had a break. I remember feeling aggrieved about that, even though Gen is my best friend. So, I was thrilled when I got promoted when she was on her second maternity leave. Then, she came back and was promoted again. I've given up feeling pissed off about it. Gen is now part of the senior management team and I'm not, but we're still best friends.

Since it's now two in the afternoon and the middle of winter, I'm tempted to put my pyjamas on instead of more clothes. Then I remember that I have to pop round to our next-door neighbours and put an invitation through their door. We do this every year because we know the party is going to be rowdy. Every year we invite them, every year they never come. I've never seen our neighbours in all the years I've lived here. Were it not for the occasional noise from next door I would be convinced no one lives there.

I pull on a cosy pair of leggings, my furry boots and another coat, and grab the invitation I printed out at work before Christmas. On my way out, I pass Yan and CeCe in the kitchen, they're cooking themselves some lunch.

'Hey,' I call, just so there's no misunderstanding. 'Don't eat any of my goodies.'

'We won't,' calls CeCe, her voice irritatingly high. 'We have our own goodies.' They press their heads together and giggle. Yuk.

I step outside and notice how much colder it has already become since I came back from M&S. I can see my breath in the air when I exhale. I trip along the alleyway and round to the front of our building and locate next door's front door. It's very showy. Dark wood with a glass panel running down the middle from top to bottom. The glass is marked with a checked-pattern, some squares opaque, some clear. This means I can see straight into their hallway. I'm so pleased that our door is hidden and solid, affording us privacy and anonymity.

I push the invitation through the door and watch it skid across the white, polished tiles. Could they be marble? I imagine how cold that must feel in this weather.

Without actually pressing my nose against the glass I peer right in. White stairs lead up to the flat which, like ours is above a shop. While we're above an independent optician, this flat is above Baglatari, one of those very expensive shops that sell handbags. The kind of handbags I will never be able to afford.

In the flat hallway is a folded bicycle. It's pushed towards the far wall and comprises gleaming chrome and white leather. It looks like a sculpture especially chosen to complement the décor.

Back in my own flat I slam the door so Yan and CeCe know I'm back. I find them still giggling in the kitchen. Oh double yuk. So, I haul myself upstairs, dump my coat, retrieve my bottle of red and head into the living room. I get myself a wine glass from the sideboard, pour myself a liberal amount and slump on the sofa.

How very different this flat must be to next door. We have a sofa and four mismatched armchairs, as well as a table which Yan made out of scaffolding planks. I have to say that when he first suggested it I was a little sceptical but now I love it. It's proper shabby chic and goes really well with my sideboard. I found the sideboard in a skip around the corner, one evening, when a neighbouring property was being modernised. Being the biggest I had climbed into the skip and manoeuvred it to the edge so that Gen could catch it before it fell to the ground. Looking back, I don't know how we did it. I think wine may have increased our strength.

I jumped out of the skip while Gen groaned and complained that it was heavy, and then together we managed to get the sideboard out. We carried it home, it took us ages, lifting, dragging and stopping to get our breath. It's solid wood, oak I think, so very heavy. When we weren't puffing and panting we were laughing and we had quite a few odd looks.

'How the hell will we get this up the stairs?' Gen called as we approached our front door?

'Oops, hadn't thought of that.'

A couple of lads, also fuelled by alcohol, had appeared in the alleyway and helped us. I think they might have stayed the night. That was in the days before Gen and Ralph. Anand and Shilpa had loved it, especially after I had painted it a soft blue with the pale green undercoat showing through in places.

I can't imagine anything so kitsch being in the flat next door.

Three

I spend the next day or so avoiding Yan and CeCe and enjoying my M&S goodies. I also tumble-dry my coat, which, despite gin-vomit woman's best attempts is none the worse.

New Year's Eve arrives, as does the party food and drink. They've also bought paper plates, and plastic wine and beer glasses; no wonder the total bill was so high. But, I have to admit this will save on washing up and breakages, so I decide to give Yan the full twenty-pounds.

CeCe hides herself in the kitchen sorting out the food and pondering over what time the mini-quiches and burgers should be heated up while Yan and I rearrange the living room.

We push Yan's table to the back of the room and move the sofa and chairs so that there is space in the middle to dance. It's usually just me and Gen who dance while everyone else tries their best to avoid or ignore us. We're normally waving our wine glasses at the same time, so sometimes sloshing occurs. The very large, and ancient rug beneath our feet bears its wine stains very well; the heavy pattern is able to absorb both red and white wine as well as beer without complaint. Gen always says it's the alcohol that has preserved it for so long; it should be in shreds with all the wear and tear it's been subjected to.

When we've finished I get the balloon pump out and blow up twenty balloons. Then it's getting ready time. We've told everyone we've invited that they need to be safely inside our place by nine pm. After that we lock the door. It's rare that anyone arrives before eight, but I like to be ready early.

I take myself off for a nice soak in the bath in my en-suite bathroom – a luxury I will never cease to enjoy. I lock my bedroom door behind me so I won't be disturbed. When Anand and Shilpa lived here there was no lock on the door, but Gen and I knew never to just barge in or assume we could use their bathroom.

That courtesy did not to seem continue once they left. I remember coming home from work one evening to find my door ajar. Even though there was no lock, I always closed the door behind me. As I entered the room I heard my toilet flush. I froze. I thought I was alone in the flat because no one had replied when I'd called out a hello as I came in.

My bathroom door burst open and Ozzie, who worked in Zizzi on Strand and originally came from Birmingham, leapt out, closing the door behind him.

'Uh, hello.' He was as startled to see me as I was him.

'What are you doing?'

'Bathroom,' he said looking behind him.

'Yes. But it's mine. Yours is downstairs. I made that clear when you moved in.'

'Yeah. But, you know, caught short.' He sauntered towards my bedroom door.

'Don't do it again.' I had my hand on the bathroom door.

'You might want to leave it a while.' He grinned

and was gone.

I gagged when I entered the bathroom. The offending turd was still floating in the toilet. I retched as I flushed it away, though it took several attempts before it went down. I sprayed air freshener about, followed by perfume. I kept the door closed and the extractor fan on for half an hour. Even after that I swear I could still smell it.

Later that week I had a locksmith round to fit a lock on my bedroom door.

Never again.

After my bath I dry my hair; I don't take too long to style it as my costume will cover my head. I'm going as Bungle, the bear from *Rainbow*, a childhood favourite. Yan and CeCe are Teletubbies. I'm not sure who will be the hottest inside their costumes, all three are furry creations. Yan and CeCe have hired theirs but I bought mine on eBay and I'll resell it on eBay when I've finished with it. When I tried the head on I could see through some gauze near the nose but not very well. I also noticed that the body smelled a bit fusty and sweaty. I've sprayed it liberally with *Neutradol* and hope that my body heat doesn't reactivate the second-hand pongs. It's been airing on my wardrobe door for two weeks.

Despite wearing a bear-head I take some time to apply my makeup, fancy dress or not, this is still party. I take the odd sip from the glass of red I've poured earlier.

There's a knock on my door and I jump up to answer it. A little red Teletubby stands before me jumping up and down. CeCe. Behind her Yan is dressed as a purple Teletubby and waving.

'Hello,' I laugh.

'Say our names, say our names,' CeCe's muffled voice squeaks.

'Um.' Of course I know what the Teletubbies are but I don't know their individual names. These aren't from my childhood, I'm too old. 'La La?' I venture.

'No, silly. I'm Po and Yan is Tinky Winky, and we won't answer to anything else.'

'Okay. I'll try to remember.'

'Where is your costume?'

I point at my wardrobe.

'What is that?'

'Bungle.'

CeCe shakes her head and puts her hands out in a questioning manner, a very Teletubby gesture.

'From Rainbow,' I clarify.

She shakes her head again.

'Paint your whole world with a rainbow,' I sing. 'With Rod, Jane and Freddie and Zippy and George.'

CeCe shakes her head again and Yan shrugs his great purple shoulders.

'Never mind. He's a big, friendly bear who's prone to mishaps. And don't call me Bungle. I'm still Charlie inside.'

CeCe performs a theatrical nod and she and Yan waddle off, attempting to hold hands through their furry paws.

How sweet.

I pull on some suitably cool underwear; my sports bra – not that it's seen much action in the gym – because it has ventilation holes around the cups and a comfortable pair of cotton knickers. I think my Mum might have bought these for me many years ago. I pull on a pair of greying sports socks which I think once belonged to my brother and decide I will wear my brown ankle boots once I have the costume on.

I start to climb into Bungle. I chose this costume not just because he was a favourite of mine but also because he was tall, like me. By the time I have the body on I am starting to feel hot and bothered and I haven't even got the head and gloves on yet. Thank God we agreed to turn the heating off; with so many costumes often layered over normal clothes we know everyone will be hot.

As I am fanning myself my phone pings.

Gen: *So so sorry. We can't make it. Ring me if convenient.*

I dial Gen's number.

'I'm so sorry,' she says, sounding as though she is about to cry. 'We've all got d and v. I don't know if it's something we've eaten, probably the curry Ralph made yesterday with the week-old turkey, or a bug.'

'Oh no.' I'm sorry for Gen and also disappointed that my best friend, my partner in criminal dancing, won't be coming.

'I'm so pissed off. I won't get to wear my George outfit.' Gen was coming as George, the pink hippo-thing out of Rainbow. Ralph had been persuaded to come as Geoffrey, Rainbow's human presenter, and Gen was preparing to coax him into a blonde mop-like wig and a stripy jumper. He's a reluctant fancy-dresser, is Ralph.

'I'm so going to miss you.' I sound like I'm whinging, because I am. It's seems that this last week has been all crap and vomit.

'I'm so sorry. It started last night. The kids were first and fourteen-year-old boys are not the best at making it to the loo in time. Honestly, there was shit and puke everywhere. I'm so cross with him. I've been washing bedding all damn day. I didn't start with it until lunchtime. I'm not as bad as Ralph and the kids but I can't come and infect you and your guests.'

'Course not. I'm sorry you're all so ill.' I am, and Gen is right, she can't come and infect my guests, but I love partying with her; it takes me back to my youth. 'I hope you're better soon,' I add before we say goodbye.

Great. I'm so sad now. I've invited other people, of course, but none is as much fun as Gen. There's several coming from work, and one of them *might* be the perpetrator of the dildo-dog-murder for all I know. I wonder if I should attempt to get to the bottom of that or not mention it at all. Who knows, with a few drinks in them, someone might confess.

The sound of the doorbell means our guests are starting to arrive. I pull on the Bungle head and push my hands into the gloves which give me paws. I examine myself in the mirror through the gauzy eyes. I look quite impressive.

'Paint your whole world with a Rainbow,' I sing again as I leave my bedroom, closing the door behind me and wobbling down the stairs to the sitting room.

'Hi Charlie,' someone calls and I turn to see a few of the girls from work. They're dressed as fairies. Incredibly sexy, tiny, cute fairies, their legs on full display beneath their pastel, floaty mini-skirts and their gossamer wings. I'm not sure which TV programme they're from, but what the hell.

I wave and I feel like a great, big, stupid brown bear. Why didn't I choose something more glamorous?

Time for wine, I think.

A few hours later and I don't care what I look like.

I've discarded Bungle's head because it's very difficult to eat and drink and chat otherwise. I'm dancing alone with my wine glass in the middle of the rug while everyone else is, as predicted, avoiding me.

The sexy fairies have found equally sexy Morphs – several young men in form fitting body suits of various colours. They've already formed couples and are hugging each other and their drinks. Tinky Winky is sitting on the sofa with Po on his lap. The food has gone down well and there actually isn't much left, which is really good because we usually end up eating the stuff for days, then throwing it out. Maybe paying more was worth it. Judging from the noise coming up the stairs there are a lot of people in the kitchen, which is where the action always is at parties, because that's where the alcohol is.

Po jumps up and puts the TV on. Jules Holland is presenting his *Hootenanny* – pretending it's live when we all know it's pre-recorded. It's nearly five to midnight. Tinky Winky starts herding us downstairs – the reluctant fairies don't want to go but Yan won't take no for an answer.

Soon everyone is outside waiting for Big Ben to strike and the fireworks to start. One of the big advantages of New Year's Eve in Covent Garden is that we can see and hear the fireworks. It's bitterly cold outside and, for the first time tonight, I'm grateful I'm wearing a furry bear suit.

The countdown begins and we all join in. Big Ben starts to strike and suddenly it's a new year. The fairies and the Morphs start kissing with more enthusiasm than a new year deserves. I turn to go back inside and bump into Zippy.

'Zippy,' I yell, laughing.

'Bungle,' a muffled voice says from behind the zip.

I watch mesmerised as Zippy puts a hand up and slowly undoes the zip.

'Hello,' a male voice says. Is that a trace of an Australian accent I detect? 'Happy New Year.' He reaches out and pulls me towards him.

Suddenly I find my head inside Zippy's cavernous mouth and kissing is taking place. And, I rather like it. Fireworks are going off all around us and, oddly, inside my head and even my body.

The kiss seems to go on for ages, almost too long. Certainly long enough for me to note that Zippy is quite a bit taller than me.

Finally, our mouths unlock. I pull back. But I'm stuck; my hair horribly entangled in Zippy's zip mouth. I yell.

'What's wrong?' the Australian asks.

'I'm stuck. My hair is stuck on your zip.'

'Um, right.' When he starts to laugh, so do I. Taken out of context that comment could sound quite lewd. 'Keep still,' he adds as he tries to untangle my hair. But he can't see what he's doing any better than I can.

I yank my head back and consider that losing a few strands will be a small price to pay for unlocking us. It doesn't work and it hurts like hell. I squeal – like a girl.

'Okay, calm down,' he says, hugging me.

We're so close, our faces merely an inch or two apart and yet we cannot see each other at all.

'What's your name?'

'Charlie. What's yours?'

I think he answers but I don't hear it because a particularly loud firework goes off with a bang right at that very moment.

'Well, pleased to meet you Charlie?' He leans in, not that he has to lean far, and kisses me again. Really kisses me, and it's very nice.

'And you,' I mumble when our lips finally part.

'So, you live in London?' He does that Australian thing where the end of the sentence goes up making it sound like a question, which I suppose it is.

'I live here. It's my party. Well, mine and my flatmates.'

'Cool. Was it you who invited me?'

'I don't think so. I don't know you, do I?'

'I'm staying next door. There was an invitation put through the letterbox.'

'Then, yes, it was me.' I laugh. This is a first. 'I've never met anyone who lives in that flat before. I invite them every year. You're the first one to come.'

'I don't live there.' His voice sounds as though he's smiling but, in the pitch black of his Zippy head it's hard to tell. 'I've just been staying there for two nights. I needed somewhere in London to camp out. Friend of a friend of a friend thing. The owners are away, apparently they always go to Switzerland for Christmas.'

'Oh. Well. You're still very welcome to my party.'

'Thank you, Charlie.'

'You're welcome.' I want to add his name but feel it's too late to ask what it is now; that moment has passed.

He leans in and kisses me again. Oh God, I'm enjoying this.

'Is that you in there, Charlie?' Yan's voice says when there's a break in the fireworks.

'Yes,' I yell. 'I'm stuck. My hair is caught on the

zip.'

I hear Yan snigger before he speaks. 'Okay, let me see.' He fumbles about with my hair and twists my head around, which means Zippy's head twists too.

'Ow,' we yell in unison.

'Sorry, I can't see. We'll have to go inside to get some light.'

'We can't see where we're going,' I yell.

'Can't you get a torch, mate?' Zippy says.

'Have we got a torch, Charlie?' Yan asks.

'No,' I lie, thinking about the one in the top drawer of my bedside table, alongside personal things I don't want Yan to see.

'Inside it is then. Come on, I'll guide you.' He starts to manoeuvre us and I feel myself beginning to fall.

'Whoa,' yells Zippy, gripping me to him. 'That isn't going to work.'

'Shall I get some scissors then, and cut you out?'

'No.' I imagine what Yan, the builder, would do to my hair, not even thinking about the mess he would make of it.

'Only trying to help. Shall I just piss off?'

'No,' Zippy and I yell.

'Look, you walk backwards and I'll walk forwards. I'll hold you. You won't fall. We'll take it easy.'

'Okay.' I'm oddly comforted and convinced by his words.

Guided by Yan, we start our slow journey towards our front door. When we reach it, Yan calls out encouragement.

'Half way. Just the stairs to do now.'

'We can't do the stairs, Yan,' I yell. 'Sorry,' I say to Zippy, realising that I must be blasting his eardrums.

'Can't you do it here? It should be light enough.'

'I'll try,' Yan says. 'But I need to be above you to see. Budge up.' He pushes past us and Zippy and I – already too close for strangers – are squeezed together even more. I can feel that Zippy is quite pleased to be with me.

Yan starts yanking at my hair again. I yell my discomfort while alternately apologising to Zippy.

After what seems like forever we are finally free. Our heads pop apart.

'There you go Bungo,' Yan says, laughing.

'Bungle,' Zippy and I say together before laughing ourselves.

'Whatever,' Yan says, disappearing up the stairs and calling out for Po as he does so.

'Him and his girlfriend are Teletubbies,' I explain to a frowning Zippy.

'Bit after my time,' he says.

'Me too. Drink?' I gesture upstairs towards the kitchen.

I don't know how many drinks it takes to get him on the rug dancing, but we're soon smooching and swaying together and exchanging life stories. He tells me that his mum is English and his dad Australian and he spent a lot of his adolescence travelling between the two countries. Now he spends most of his time in Australia.

'So, did you visit your mum for Christmas? Is that why you're here?'

'Yes, I did. I love Oz, I love the warmth and the sun but I like an English Christmas.'

'What? Cold and snowy?' I laugh.

'Well, more cold and drizzly, but yeah.'

'Where's your mum live?'

'The middle of nowhere,' he laughs, grabbing me and whirling me around. 'What about you? You don't sound like a London girl?'

'I'm from the middle of nowhere too,' I laugh. Two can play that game.

'Cool.' He leans in for another kiss, but I dodge him.

'Don't you want to take your head off?' I ask. 'I don't want to get stuck in your zip again.' We both giggle; our silly innuendo making us sound like characters in a *Carry On* movie.

'I'm a bit worried about losing it.'

'What?' I shout as suddenly the music is turned up.

'I don't want to lose my head,' he shouts, just as the music is turned back down again.

A roar of laughter goes on around us.

'What do you mean?'

'I've hired this costume, it wasn't cheap and I don't want to damage it or lose it.'

'Okay. I know where you can put it where it will be safe.' I take him by the hand and lead him upstairs to my bedroom. I open the door and stand back so he can go inside. 'It should be okay in here.' I lean in and flick the light on.

He steps over the threshold then turns back to me, his hand extended. I'm still wearing the bear paws and watch as his Zippy hand grabs my paw. He pulls me into my bedroom and pushes the door closed behind us.

As he pulls his Zippy head off, I see his face for the first time. He has a kind face, not drop dead gorgeous, but nice. The kind of face a woman could trust. He's probably my age and his skin is lightly tanned, his eyebrows and lashes bleached. A pair of soft, blue eyes twinkle at me. Or, at least I think they twinkle, but it could be the wine.

He rubs his hands through mid-brown hair.

'Bloody hot in there.' He puts Zippy's head on my chaise longue

'Tell me about it. I abandoned Bungle's head hours ago. I couldn't drink anything. At least you could put stuff in your mouth with that big zip.'

'Yeah. Even if some of that stuff got stuck.' He winks then moves in closer and pulls me to him and we kiss.

It is so much better without the Zippy head.

When our mouths finally part, he smiles.

'I like you Charlie.' His voice sounds husky.

'I like you too.' I whisper back. I wish I knew his name, but saying, *what's your name again* now, seems wholly inappropriate.

He spins round, presenting his back to me.'

'Could you unzip me, please?'

'How did you get into this?' I pull at the zip until it slides down but it requires a lot of tugging to get it going.

'Bit like a wetsuit,' he laughs, kicking off a pair of ankle boots before shrugging off Zippy's body and flinging it on the chaise too. Underneath he's wearing shorts and a vest. Around his neck is one of those watertight bags that surfers use. I laugh, I can't help it. 'I know, not exactly party wear but it was hot in there.' He lifts the bag necklace off. 'Had to put my key and phone somewhere.'

I nod in agreement, smiling, and then freeze in horror.

'Your turn,' he says, fumbling around for the fastening to release me from Bungle.

Oh God, he's going to see what I'm wearing underneath. I start to resist his undoing of me but it's too late. Bungle falls from my shoulders.

I cross an arm over my chest and try to cover my hideous old knickers with my other hand. I feel my face redden as I look down in embarrassment. Bungle's body is pooling around me on the floor; I can't step out of him because I still have my boots on, though what I really want is to pull him back on. Why or why didn't I wear decent underwear?

Because I never thought something like this would happen.

'Okay,' he says, stepping back. 'I don't want to force you into doing anything…' His voice trails away.

'It's not that,' I say.

'Oh. Then what?'

'I'm not really dressed for seduction.' God, this is so cringeworthy.

'And I am?' He laughs. 'We could just pretend we've met at the gym after a hot and sweaty session.'

'Cheese,' I call out.

'I know. I'm not one for chat up lines.'

'No. You're not.'

'Seriously, do you want me to go?'

I look him up and down, I'm appraising him and I'm not trying to hide it. He's hot. His body is tight and taut – he obviously *does* spend time in the gym.

'No. Stay.' I smile. 'I have wine.' I nod towards my dressing table, my wine glass from earlier sitting next to a two-thirds full bottle.

'Cool,' he says, bending down to pull off my boots and uncouple me from Bungle.

We take turns sipping wine from my wine glass

and after that, much of what happens is a lovely, funny, fun and quite blissful blur.

'Charlie, Charlie,' a husky voice whispers in my ear.

I turn over and groan. It's pitch black and I am so tired.

'Charlie, I have to go now.'

'Go where?'

'I have to get the plane back home.'

'Back home where?' What is he talking about?

'I did mention it earlier but I'm not sure you fully understood. The reason I was staying next door was because I'm flying back to Oz. My father's ill, very ill.'

'Sorry to hear that,' I mumble. 'How will you get to the airport?'

'I've got a taxi booked. It's costing me an arm and a leg, it being New Year's Day. I've got to go now.'

'There's a fold up bike next door, you could use that. Save you money.' I open my eyes and reach over to flick my bedside lamp on.

'That bike isn't real.'

'What?'

'It's a sculpture.'

'Ha ha.' So I was right. 'Oh God. Are you going like that?' He's standing in front of me in his underwear and shoes.

'No. Obviously I need to get some clothes on. I'll just nip next door and get my stuff.'

'Oh, right.'

'I just wanted to say if the circumstances had been different I'd have asked you out on a date.'

I snort. Date. That all seems a bit after the event. 'Okay.' I hear myself snort again.

'I really like you, Charlie.' He leans in and kisses

me on the forehead.

'Cool,' I mutter.

'Hey,' he says. 'Will you do me a favour?'

'Yeah.'

'Will you take my Zippy suit back to the hire shop? I've jotted down the address.'

'Urgh.'

'Please. There's a big deposit on it.' He says it in that questioning Australian way that makes it sound tempting.

'Okay,' I hear myself agree.

'Bye,' he calls from the door.

'Yeah, bye.'

Four

When you have a hangover you really appreciate the proximity of an en-suite bathroom.

Daylight is sneaking its way through the gap in the curtains and burning a line on my forehead. I groan and drag myself towards the toilet. I hate being sick but it's the best cure. Well, that and food. I know it doesn't work for everyone, but it does for me.

I want coffee and cereal, followed by toast with lots of butter. And, when my head stops spinning I'll go down and make that. Until then, I'll try to sleep it off. I rinse my empty wine glass, fill it with water, drink, then crawl back into my bed. I lie there waiting to feel better. That's when my eyes alight on Zippy's head smiling up at me from my chaise longue.

Why the hell is that still here? Didn't Zippy skip off hours ago, some bullshit story about a sick dad in Oz? All men are the same in my experience, lovely when they want something and arses after they get it. Shame, because Zippy did seem rather sweet and he had a kind face. And, from what I can remember, hazy though it is, we had a good time in bed. Oh well, it's not as though I'll ever see him again, and that suits me just fine.

Maybe I can sell Zippy on eBay when I sell Bungle. I'll make a bit of money and actually come out on top; that'll make a nice change, me winning where a man is concerned.

I've never had a lot of luck with men. Gen says it's because I either pick duffers or, if they're not duffers, I don't give them a second chance. I don't see why I should give anyone a second chance. We only get one chance to make a first impression – or so the cliché goes – so make an effort. Anyway, as I tell Gen every time she introduces me to one of Ralph's weirdo friends, I don't need a man to complete me. Gen thinks it's a shame that I haven't met Mr Right and don't have any children; she thinks I'd make a great mum. I've told her, just because I play nicely with her children and can even have a pleasant and sensible conversation with her teenage son – which she apparently can't – doesn't mean to say I should be popping out my own.

My mum says that not all women are cut out to be mothers. I think she means me when she says that, but sometimes she has a wistful look on her face and I wonder if she's referring to herself. Unless, of course, she's trying to console me; after all, Mum was there during the *Iain incident* and, even if I never confided in her, she's since worked out a lot of the detail.

Iain was my first serious boyfriend. Actually, to be honest, he was my only serious boyfriend; every man I've met since has never lasted more than two or three dates. I suppose I don't really trust men and, invariably, they live down to my expectations. Zippy proves my point.

Iain and I went to the same school, though we hardly knew each other there. We got together at an-end-of-exams party one of my friends was holding. We were sixteen. I was looking forward to going to college to do my A' levels and Iain was starting a plumbing apprenticeship in September. We had the whole summer and our whole futures ahead of us and we were in love. Deep, deep love. I thought it would last forever. With his thick, wavy hair, his dark seductive eyes, his generous lips and, the fact he was much taller than me, he was my perfect man.

We spent every hour we could together over that summer, on our own, with friends, even with our parents sometimes. As long as we were together we were happy. We talked about a future, a home, holidays, a dog, a life. Iain was savouring his last few weeks of freedom before starting full-time work and I was enjoying time with no study and just my Saturday evening waitressing job. It paid well and the tips were good. Mum and Dad approved of it as they thought it kept me out of what they called *Saturday-night-trouble*. They believed that every teenager in Swindon went out on Saturday nights and drank too many alcopops, took drugs and did God knows what.

Iain and I were already doing *God knows what*.

Iain started his job, I started college and our love grew deeper. This was serious, really serious. Mum started to get twitchy, Dad frowned his concern from the sidelines.

Christmas came and we'd been together for six glorious months. Iain turned up with a ring on Christmas day. I opened the box and he saw the twinkle, the hope, in my eyes.

'It's not an engagement ring,' he said.

'I know,' I lied, crestfallen.

'Just a friendship ring.'

'Oh. Just friendship.'

'Well, no, you know, lovers and stuff.'

'Yeah.' I pushed the ring onto my right-hand ring

finger.

How gauche we were. How young.

How stupid.

We were both turned seventeen. We were comfortable together. We were a couple. He went out with his mates when I worked Saturday nights; it suited us both. It allowed him to let of steam without me watching; even then I knew how immature seventeen-year-old boys could be.

Except I didn't.

It was late January when I realised I must be pregnant. I desperately checked my dates, prayed it couldn't have happened. I wasn't one of those stupid girls; we'd been careful. But, not careful enough.

I let the knowledge fester for a week before I told him. I hadn't told anyone else, I wanted him to be the first to know. He came round one evening when Mum and Dad were out, he'd been drinking. Lager, he said but it smelt stronger than that to me.

'You can't be,' he said, the blood draining from his face.

'I am. I've done the test.'

'Oh for fuck's sake. You can get rid of it, can't you?'

I shrugged, biting back tears, saying nothing. This wasn't how I had imagined it; I knew he'd be shocked but then I thought he'd be delighted. Inside, I was. I wanted to have Iain's beautiful baby.

He began pacing around my parents' lounge, punching his fist into the palm of his other hand.

'It ain't mine, is it?'

'Of course it's yours.'

'No. I've been very careful.'

I started to shake, then to cry.

'I knew it. It's that tosser Rory's, isn't it?'

'Who?'

'That Rory from the restaurant. I've seen how he looks at you.'

'He doesn't. I hardly know Rory.' Rory worked behind the bar, he was twenty-five and not in the least bit interested in me. I hardly had any contact with him; I was under eighteen and not allowed in the bar area.

'Yeah, right. I've seen when I've walked past when you're working there. I've seen you flirting with him.'

'I don't. I never have.'

'You're a slapper,' he roared, pushing past me, grabbing his jacket from the chair.

'But, Iain,' I called, running after him.

At the door he stopped, turned back to me. I thought he was seeing sense but then I saw his ugly, angry face.

'Bitch,' he hissed.

Then he punched me in the stomach. It took my breath away. I fell to the floor, doubled over in pain. He left, slamming the door behind him. He didn't even look back.

I dragged myself up to my bedroom and lay on the bed, sobbing. I couldn't think straight. I had hiccups from crying so much. When Mum and Dad came home I pretended to be asleep.

I awoke in agony the next morning. I was bleeding and aching all over. There would be no baby. Iain had got his wish. My bed was covered in blood, thank God the mattress cover had done its job. I stripped the bed and bundled the bedding up and waited until I was alone in the house.

Mum and Dad both went to work before I left for

college and it wasn't unusual for us not to see each other at breakfast. After they had gone I crept downstairs with my bloodied bedding and stuffed it in the washing machine.

I made toast and sat on the sofa eating it slowly, after two bites I stopped eating. There was no point in anything anymore. I had lost my baby and my boyfriend all at once.

I took two paracetamol and crawled back to bed; I didn't even bother to remake it, just climbed in without any sheet or duvet cover.

I decided I would tell no one about the baby; I was confident Iain never would. I would be up and dressed as though I'd been to college when Mum and Dad came home and no one would be any the wiser. Joe was away at university so I'd never have to explain it to him either. Iain and I had just broken up, it happens. Everyone would understand that and, I suspected that my parents, especially Mum, would be secretly pleased.

If only Mum hadn't come home at lunchtime; how was I to know she was having a half-day? I never heard her come in, I never heard her downstairs; I was fast asleep in my unmade bed. But, when she came upstairs singing at the top of her voice – something I'd never heard her do before – I awoke and froze.

She was bustling around in the airing cupboard, moving from room to room, she burst into mine with a pile of clean washing for me.

'Oh,' she said. 'What are you doing here? And what's happened to your bed?'

'Don't feel well,' I said, trying to keep my face below the covers.

'Oh dear. What's wrong?'

'Stomach ache, you know. I've put my bedding in the washing machine.'

'Tedious period pains? I'll bring you up a hot water bottle when I finish this.'

I muttered my thanks and Mum left the room. Ten minutes later she was back with more paracetamol and the promised hot water bottle.

'Here,' she said, thrusting a glass of water at me. 'Sit up and take these.'

'Thank you. Can you just leave them for me please?'

But she wouldn't be deterred. She reached in and put her hand on my forehead.

'You seem very warm. Too warm. Sit up and let me see you. Come on.'

I hauled my sad self up and Mum saw my tear stained face, my swollen, red eyes.

'Is it that bad?' She sat down on the bed.

'Yes,' I murmured as she fed me the tablets and watched me drink the water. She pushed the hot water bottle under the duvet.

'Have you had any lunch?'

I shook my head.

'I'll make you a sandwich. Why don't you come down and lie on the sofa, you can watch TV.'

'Um, I don't know.'

'I'm going out,' she said, 'so you can watch what you like.' She smiled and walked away. 'Cheese and pickle okay?'

'Okay.'

Mum left me on the sofa, a fleece blanket covering me, my sandwich and the remote control on my lap. Two hours later I went back upstairs. She had remade my bed, using a thick blanket in place of a mattress cover. I climbed in and snuggled down and slept.

'Are you coming down for tea?' Mum's voice woke me up. It was dark outside. 'Your dad's gone out so it's just you and me.'

'Okay,' I muttered. 'In a minute.'

Downstairs Mum had laid the table for two. We ate pesto pasta together in silence.

'I had to put your bedding on to wash again, it was quite badly stained,' she said as she took the plates off the table.

'Sorry,' I muttered.

'Not to worry. It's all clean now. Unusual for you to be so bad with your periods.' She went into the kitchen. 'You seeing Iain tonight?' she asked as she returned with a tub of ice cream and two bowls.

I shook my head and looked down at my spoon.

'Just as well if you don't feel well. Two scoops or three?'

I didn't answer, just kept staring at my spoon.

'You can see him tomorrow when you're better.' She put a dish with two scoops of ice cream in front of me.

My head down I just stared at it. I could feel the tears coming; my throat ached with fighting them back.

'Do you want some more paracetamol?'

I nodded; it would mean that she would leave the room and I could take a deep breath and not cry.

'I'll get them when you finish that.' She nudged the bowl closer to me.

I picked up my spoon, pushed it into the ice cream then lifted it to my mouth. The howl came out as I tried to eat.

'What's wrong?' Mum's alarmed voice asked. 'Is it still that bad?'

I shook my head as snot dribbled out of my nose.

'Come on, what is it?' She felt my forehead, put her arm around my shoulder.

'It's Iain. We've broken up.'

We never spoke about it again, not properly anyway. But, over the years Mum said the odd little thing and when Joe's children arrived I saw how she watched me with them, or maybe I imagined it. I never told her how Iain had punched me or accused me of sleeping with someone else. More fool me, I still loved him and I didn't want Mum and Dad to think badly of him. For a little while, I even thought that we might get back together. Looking back, I must have been mad; I should have reported him to the police. At the very least I should have told Mum and Dad.

You live and learn.

Three months later I jacked in my college course and came to London. My parents weren't happy but there wasn't much they could do to stop me. Later that year Mum and Dad moved to Aston Bassett, and, as they say, the rest is history.

I don't think I'll ever trust another man again.

Zippy's stupid face is still grinning at me as I get up and pull on my dressing gown. I fling my Bungle body over it so I can't see that stupid grin before I stumble down two flights of stairs craving my coffee, cereal and toast.

Zippy's stupid body is sitting at the table eating my cereal.

'I thought you had a plane to catch,' I snap. 'I thought you had to leave early.'

'Going soon,' the reply comes. 'Just eating.'

I scrutinize Zippy's face without the mask. He's Chinese. I don't remember that. I shake my head and put the kettle on, glancing back at this stranger who I have slept with. Wow, I must have drunk a lot.

I make my coffee before opening the fridge for milk. There is none.

'God's sake,' I mutter under my breath. 'No milk.'

'So sorry,' Zippy says, grinning. His bowl containing my cereal is swimming in milk. Greedy arse.

I don't reply but open the cupboard to hunt for the long-life milk I keep for emergencies. It's usually right next to my cereal. Except my cereal box isn't there. I fling open a few more cupboard doors. No cereal. I'm angry now and getting angrier as I flip open the recycling bin to see the empty box in the bottom.

'You ate all my cereal? Really?' I cut open the milk carton and pour some into my coffee.

'So sorry.'

'And what was all that bullshit about you having to leave early?'

Zippy stares at me with confusion in his eyes.

'Forget it.' I wave my hand at him. Maybe I dreamt it in my alcohol induced stupor. 'I wished you hadn't eaten all my cereal though.'

The front door opens and CeCe and Yan come in giggling. Are they going to be giggling all the damn time?

'Hey Charlie,' CeCe says, smiling. 'Great party.'

'Yeah.'

Yan puts a Tesco bag on the worktop. He pulls milk from it and a box of cereal – Tesco's version of my cereal – and a loaf of bread.

'Sorry my cousin ate all your cereal.' CeCe takes the box from Yan and hands it to me. 'I've bought you another.'

'Thanks.' I take the box and stare at it.

'They didn't have your usual brand.' CeCe smiles sweetly at me.

'Well, thanks anyway.' I put the box down and pick up my coffee.

'Sorry my cousin is so greedy. He's like that.' She gives her cousin a playful slap around the head.

'Your cousin?' I suddenly have a flashback to the things her cousin and I did. I shudder; I must have been wearing some strong wine glasses last night.

CeCe's cousin has finished his breakfast and is now standing up, shaking hands with me and saying goodbye to CeCe and Yan. Then he's gone, clutching Zippy's head which he's retrieved from under the table. He must have moved ninja-like to get upstairs and retrieve the head from my room without me noticing. My hangover must be worse than I thought.

'He's so much shorter than I remember,' I voice my confusion.

'Is he?' CeCe frowns at me but follows it up with a smile.

'Yeah.' I sigh and examine my new cereal box. 'Much.' I'm sure that we stood mouth to mouth when I got my hair stuck in his zip. It's just as well I'm doing *Dry January*, I obviously drunk far, far too much wine last night. My body could do with a break.

After Yan and CeCe giggle their way up the stairs I open the cereal box CeCe gave me and peer inside. It looks the same as mine, it smells the same as mine, so, almost begrudgingly I pour myself a bowl, splash on some fresh milk, not the UHT stuff I had in my coffee, and sit down in the chair Zippy vacated.

After I've eaten a second bowlful I have to admit that I think it tastes better than my premium brand. I'll probably buy this again as, no doubt, it is cheaper.

After another cup of coffee and my toast, I start to feel more like my normal self. I'm glad Zippy's gone and I'm glad he didn't make a big show of affection when he left.

After a shower, I pull on some warm clothes then check my phone. A message from Mum wishing me a happy New Year, another from my brother. I reply to them both, then read a message from Gen.

Happy New Year. Hope your headache isn't too bad. Lol. We're all feeling a lot better this morning. Did you meet any interesting men? Lol Lol. xx

I reply: *Happy New Year. I don't need a man to complete me.* xx

She comes back instantly: *Course you don't. See you at work tomorrow.*

I send a thumbs-up emoji in response.

Work. I'd almost forgotten about work. After today everything will be back to normal. A new year maybe, but nothing's really changed since last year. I still work at the same place I have for years and years, I'm still a team leader, we still do the same work. Inbound, not sales.

I don't make New Year resolutions anymore, it's almost impossible to keep them. Once, when I used to smoke, I resolved to give up. By noon on 3rd January I was smoking again, and by the end of the day I'd more than made up for my two days of abstinence, smoking the equivalent of four days' worth of cigarettes. They say the best time to give up smoking is when you go on holiday because everything is different. That's what I did, several times over several holidays and in the end, it worked.

Despite not believing in resolutions I do always look at my life at this time of year, assessing what is new and different from this time last year. Invariably, nothing has changed. And, this year is no different. Not that I'm complaining; I'm happy, I love my life, I do. I love where I live; I love my job – most days. It could be so much worse; I could still be with Iain, married maybe, bringing up our child, or children. And taking a beating whenever Iain drank too much.

Life could be so much worse.

I make my bed, tidy my room and find Bungle's head wedged under my bed along with my balled-up underwear from last night. I have no recollection of removing it, just standing like a fool before Zippy in washed out old tat. I hang Bungle's body on its coat hanger and hook it over the wardrobe door again. I'll take some photos and put it on eBay later.

As I turn back to the chaise I see Zippy's grin.

'What the…?' I'm frowning as I pick it up. Underneath, his body is neatly folded and there's a note on top.

Hi Charlie
It was great meeting you. I had fun, hope you did.
Please return Zippy to the hire shop,
there's a big deposit on him.
Many thanks
Oliver, aka Zippy
x

It's followed by the address of the costume hire

shop which is just off Tottenham Court Road.

'Two Zippies.' I drop Zippy's head back on his body, grateful that I haven't slept with CeCe's cousin.

So, my Zippy's name was Oliver, not that it matters now, I'm not going to meet him again. Unless I go to Australia, which is highly unlikely.

'Charlie, Charlie.' There's a knock on my bedroom door.

'Yeah,' I call as CeCe pokes her head into my room.

'We're getting a Chinese; do you want to share?'

'For lunch?'

'Yeah. Well, late lunch.' She giggles again. Stop giggling.

'Yeah, okay. Thanks. Are you ordering online? If so, I'll just have what I always have.' I might as well, I don't feel like cooking. 'CeCe,' I call just before she closes the door.

'Yes?'

'Did you and Yan clear up the party this morning?'

'Yes. No.' She giggles again. 'Yan did. But he said most of it was rubbish, just plastic cups and paper plates. No food left.'

'Cool. Thank him for me.' I'm pleased we won't be eating party food for days unlike previous years.

'Okay.' And she's gone.

My mouth is already salivating at the prospect of chicken chow mien and vegetable spring rolls.

After our Chinese meal, which we eat sitting at Yan's big plank table in the sitting room, I excuse myself and disappear back into my room. I have some serious *internetting* to do.

First, I take a few photos of Bungle and get him

on eBay. I put a long date for bids on him as, I suspect, the need for fancy dress costumes will be somewhat diminished now. I'm tempted to put Zippy up but remember the large deposit on him. That is likely to be more than I could get for him on eBay.

Then, I get onto the serious business of booking a holiday, well, a mini-break, for me and Gen. It's her fortieth in February and we're having a girly-break. It's my treat and I'm picking the destination; it'll be a surprise for her. We have agreed the date which is the week before her birthday because Ralph is treating her and the kids to *Centre Parks* for her actual birthday – which doesn't sound like much of a treat to me, all that riding around in forests and too much fresh air.

Years ago, Gen mentioned that she'd like to go to Marrakech and I know she has never managed to get there. So, that's what I'm going to book.

An hour later and it's done. We fly out of Heathrow on a Monday morning and come back on a Thursday. I've chosen a lovely hotel – a riad, a prince's palace, no less – right in the heart of the Medina. It has a spa, a pool and a jacuzzi and the hotel photos look amazing. I've paid for a superior room inside the actual palace rather than in the modern addition. Gen and I are sharing a room but, because it has a separate sitting room, we shouldn't get on each other's nerves too much.

I'm excited when I message Gen and confirm the dates and tell her it's booked. She puts the dates in her diary, then we arrange to meet for lunch the next day.

Gen looks flustered as she catches up with me outside our office. We work in Holborn which really isn't that far from home for me at a quick pace, and we have been known to skip back to my place sometimes. But, ideally, we need more than an hour and I don't think we should start the year off with extended lunch breaks, even if Gen is a senior manager.

'Where shall we go?' I ask.

'Somewhere away from here. I need wine.' She grimaces.

'Already,' I laugh. 'The year has only just begun.'

'Yeah, and don't I know it?' She rolls her eyes then strides out in the direction of our favourite little hideaway, Ken's. It's down a backstreet, then down an alley and only *those in the know* know about it. Which means no one from work does.

'Hey girls,' Ken calls as we slip in the side door. 'Usual table for two.'

'Yes please,' Gen answers, 'and bring two glasses of pinot.'

'Just one, Ken,' I correct. 'Make mine a tonic water. Oh, and a tuna panini.'

'Yeah, panini for me too, please.'

Ken scuttles off as we push ourselves into our usual table at the back of Ken's tiny establishment. There are only four tables and, today, only one other is occupied. Fortunately for us most of Ken's business is grab and go from a window at the front and he does a roaring trade at lunchtime.

Gen waits for her wine to arrive then takes a big gulp before she speaks.

'That bastard Bryan Smith.' She shakes her head.

'Urgh, that creep.'

'Yes. That creep.'

'What's he done now?'

'His job, I suppose.' She sighs and takes another mouthful of wine. She glances round at the occupants of the other table before leaning in closer to me. 'I had a meeting with him this morning and he was insinuating that come appraisal time not everyone will be getting a good one.'

'What? I thought, as a company, we were performing well. That's what was said at the Christmas party.' Now it's my turn to shudder. Bastard Bryan had made a lewd comment to me then tried to rub his hand over my leg as we sat at the same table. He was, as usual, talking non-stop crap as he did so. I don't know how I got put next to him; Gen thinks it was his doing. I'd slapped his hand away and glared at him, while he continued to spout his crap and lecture anyone who was within hearing range about his favourite subject – himself. He didn't miss a beat even though I know I slapped his hand hard. Afterwards, I almost wondered if I had imagined it.

'Yes, that is what he said. Lying bastard.'

'I suppose there will be a few underperformers.' I mentally run through my team trying to work out if I have any.

'No, not a few. Most.' Gen corrects.

'Most. How can that be?'

'Quite.' She purses her lips. 'That's why I'm so bloody angry. We've been arguing. He basically told me to shut up.'

'Oh God. Rude bastard.'

'Yeah.' She shakes her head.

Ken brings our paninis and we eat in silence for a few minutes.

Gen takes a deep breath and a big gulp of wine. 'Anyway, never mind about work, tell me about the party.'

'Nothing to tell really. I did have a nice time with Zippy.'

'Zippy. Zippy. There was a Zippy? Oh,' she whines. 'We would have had the complete set. Bungle, George and Zippy, and Geoffrey. Bloody kids bringing that bug into my house.'

'Actually, there were two Zippies.' I then tell Gen how I thought I'd slept with CeCe's cousin.

'Trust you,' she laughs.

I tell her about Herman's horrible demise and the part the Secret Santa dildo seemingly played in it.

'That's horrible. Any idea who gave it to you?' Gen turns her mouth down in disgust.

'Could be anyone. There are over a hundred people at work and, I think, everyone took part in the Secret Santa.'

'Bastard Bryan Smith,' Gen declares. 'Especially after he groped you at the Christmas party.'

'Eugh, no. He wouldn't.'

'Yeah, probably sent Bev out to get it.'

We snigger together at the thought that Bev, Bastard Bryan's loyal PA, could have been sent out on such a task.

'She'd do anything for *my Bryan*.' We put our heads together and snigger over our lunch. Bev *does* do anything for *my Bryan*. She's been his PA for years and moved down from the head office in Nottingham with him when he came to work in the London office eight months ago. She worships the ground he walks on. If ever there was a case of unrequited love, Bev has it bad. Not that she stands a chance with *my Bryan*; we've all seen the photo that he keeps on his desk showing his glamorous wife and two small sons. He keeps the live versions safely ensconced in Leeds, his home town.

'Well,' I continue, 'whoever sent it has the death of Herman on their hands, not to mention the puke and poo. Oh no, that was me, all over my hands.' We laugh again, covering our mouths in an attempt to keep the noise down as other customers have now joined us.

Our lunch break passes too quickly and we're soon on our way back to work, excitedly talking about Gen's birthday treat.

'Tell me where it is,' she implores.

'No. You'll enjoy it all the more when we get there.'

'Thanks for lunch,' she says, as we part. 'I knew you'd cheer me up.'

Five

Mum's message arrives and I jump. Not just because I'm semi-daydreaming at my desk but also because I haven't realised that half of January has already gone. There's a picture of her and Dad on the balcony of their cabin, they're wearing coats and scarves and holding up champagne glasses.

We're off to sunnier climes, says Mum's message, followed by sunshine emojis.

Me: *Have a great time.*

It's drizzling outside today and the sky is grey. I prefer cold and clear with a chance of sunshine, or snow. I almost wish I was going with Mum and Dad but they won't be back until April. I smile to myself as I wonder if work would allow me to take three months off. Even without pay, I doubt it.

'What's tickled your fancy?'

The voice jerks me back to reality as Bryan Smith's belly bulge moves directly into my line of vision.

'Sorry?' I say.

'I saw that secret smile from afar. I wondered what had amused you?'

'Oh nothing. Just pleased to be here, Bryan.' I pause. 'Like you.'

'Mmm,' he says, managing to make it sound lewd. 'Like you, too.' His voice is low and melodious and I doubt anyone near me will have heard him. He sidles away, his feet skating along the carpet.

I sit and stare and watch him disappear down the office and out through the doors. I grab my phone and message Gen.

I think Bastard Bryan has just come on to me.

Gen replies instantly: *Vom, vom and double vom. What did he say?*

Tell you when I see you. Lunch?

We're in our favourite lunch place again but today it's full and we have to wait a few minutes for a table to clear. I have to keep my voice down as I tell Gen the juicy details of what went on. As I recount it, it sounds quite tame, lame even.

'Maybe he thought you were coming on to him.'

'Oh God, do you think so. When I said *like you*, I meant that I was pleased to be at work and so was he. I didn't mean I liked him. I don't want him thinking that. He's an odious fat turd.' I say this, expecting Gen to laugh, but she doesn't.

'Just avoid him. That's the best thing to do. That's what I'm trying to do.'

'Not easy when he creeps up on me.'

'I know. I know.' Gen sighs and grimaces.

'Have you had any more meetings with him?' I'm almost afraid to ask.

'Oh yes.' She glances around the other diners to confirm no one from work is here, then leans in. 'Don't repeat this, but he says that only thirty-percent can have good appraisals. The rest must be average or below average or put on warning.'

'But that's not fair. How can you put a number on it? I agree people who aren't good enough should know that, but they should be helped. Seventy-percent can't all be average or below.'

'I agree. That's why I've been arguing with him. Average is no pay rise. Below average is being helped to improve and think yourself lucky you still have a job, anything below that means good bye.'

'Oh.'

'Yes.'

I think for a moment, mentally running through my own team.

'I think I have only one average in my team and that's because he's still learning the job. The rest are good and some are very good.'

'We're not having a very good grade anymore.' Gen glances at the door as new people arrive.

'Does that mean no bonus?' The very goods always get a bonus.

'That's exactly what it means.'

Now it's my turn to sigh. 'I suppose this has come from head office.'

Gen shrugs and leans in closer until she is almost whispering in my ear. 'I think it is entirely Bastard Bryan's idea and, I suspect *he'll* be getting a hefty bonus for implementing it and saving the company money.'

'No. Surely not. What makes you think that?'

Gen raises her eyebrows and shakes her head. 'Can't say,' she says, quietly. Then I remember that on the days Gen doesn't lunch with me she lunches with Zoe, head of HR.

'I'd better be good then.'

'I think you'll be fine with Bastard Bryan.' She half sniggers but I don't join her.

'Don't say that. I'm not being nice to him for a pay rise.'

'No. Me neither.' Gen suddenly looks close to

tears. Catching my shocked look, she takes a deep breath and forces a smile.

'What's wrong?'

'I don't think Bastard Bryan rates me very highly. He particularly doesn't like that I challenge his ideas.'

'Bastard,' I hiss, because I really don't know what else to say.

'Yep. What are you having?'

We both order paninis but neither of us finishes them.

'Shame it's Dry January,' I comment as we leave. 'Could have done with wine today.'

'Still doing that?' Gen asks but her voice sounds distant as though she's thinking about something else.

'Yeah.'

'Cool. Thank God it's Friday, eh?'

'Yeah.'

Saturday morning and the sun sneaks in through the curtains. I jump up and see that it's frosty outside. That's so much better than grey and damp. It makes me want to go out, not that I need anything; I picked up a few items from Tesco Metro and M&S on my way home from work last night.

Then I see Zippy smirking at me, he's still folded on my chaise longue. Maybe today's the day I take him back to the costume hire shop. I could do with that big deposit, like everyone else I've spent too much over Christmas and it's a long time to payday at the end of January.

What the hell can I put him in? I start hunting through my cupboards and drawers. Somewhere in this room is an Ikea bag. That would definitely be big enough, and strong enough. It's not a blue Ikea bag, the ones you buy at the tills to carry away your purchases. It's a yellow one, the ones you do your shopping with and are supposed to hand back. Mum and I stole it on a trip to Ikea in Bristol. It wasn't intentional, but amid the confusion at the tills of shuffling all the things we had bought – that we really didn't need but had to have – we somehow walked away with the yellow bag.

We were too embarrassed to take it back when we realised and, secretly we were a little bit pleased at having got one over on Ikea. Naughty, that.

I find the bag rolled up in the bottom of my wardrobe, underneath my boots. It's perfect in size though crinkly and a bit brittle from overuse. A pristine blue one would have been better for my purpose today.

I stuff Zippy's head and body into the bag and attempt to twist the handles together to stop him from overflowing. He's surprisingly heavy when lifted. Part of me is thinking I can't really be bothered. Another part of me is thinking that I want him out of my room. Another part of me is thinking that I could still eBay him, even though I've had very little interest in Bungle. The final part of me is thinking about the deposit; I really could do with that. And, I did promise I would return him. A promise is a promise even if it is given while still under the influence of too many wines and too little sleep.

After breakfast I put on a thick jumper, my puffa coat, woolly hat, scarf, gloves and my extra grip boots and haul Zippy down the stairs. I've decided not to go by Tube, the walk will do me good and it's a nice morning. I've calculated that it will only take me twenty to twenty-five minutes to reach the shop.

Thirty minutes later and I still haven't got there. I'm sweating in all my clothes due to having hauled Zippy about and he seems to be getting heavier by the minute. I pull out the piece of paper with the address on and check my location. I've passed the shop. Damn it. I've been looking and I haven't seen it. How can I have missed it? I retrace my steps until I find the correct number. There is no shop.

I drop Zippy in his crinkly yellow bag onto the pavement and step back to survey the shop fronts. I'm looking for number 121, but 121 is a lingerie shop – not the kind of lingerie I would buy, I hasten to add. I stand with my hands on my hips while I think about what to do next. One thing is for sure, I am not hauling Zippy back to my flat. I glance around for a bin; there are none. I glance across the street just in case the number is wrong and scan the shop fronts; no fancy dress shops.

I'm seriously considering just leaving Zippy where he has landed and casually walking off when I spot the door. It's narrower than a normal door and painted a dull black. A small sign stuck just above the handle says *Lookers Costume Hire and Fancy Dress.*

I grab Zippy and try the door, it gives easily and opens onto a tiny hall from which leads a very narrow flight of stairs. The door is so narrow that I have to turn sideways to walk through and I have to manoeuvre Zippy in after me. I have to take the stairs sideways too. I kick the door closed behind me and am plunged into darkness. I fumble about on the wall; I'm convinced I saw a light switch. Finally, I find it; a big timer button that puts the lights on. I bang it and am illuminated.

I'm puffing and panting by the time I reach the

top. There seem to be more stairs than I would expect and they are steeper than normal and I'm sure that each step is higher than usual. There's a half-glazed door at the top of the stairs, writing across the glass reads *Lookers*. There is a curtain on the other side of the door which prevents me from peering in. There's no landing so I lean from the top step and try the door handle. It's locked. I rattle it to no effect.

Damn it. There is no space to turn around on the stairs so I will have to go down backwards, and kick Zippy down the stairs in front of me, or is that behind me?

Oh, why did I bother?

I start to back down the stairs, it's precarious enough but then the light goes out. I'm stranded in the darkness and I'm starting to get very hot again, there seems to be no air on these stairs. I feel sweaty around my hairline.

Am I panicking?

I think I might be.

'Calm down,' I say to myself as I start to pant. 'It's only stairs, it's only dark.' This is ridiculous.

After a few pants and deep breaths, I calm myself. I'm ready to recommence my descent. I push Zippy behind me and kick out my left leg trying to find the step below, in the process Zippy slips from my grasp and hurtles down the stairs. That's one way I suppose.

I drop down on my hands and knees and attempt to go down again. The carpet feels gritty and dirty beneath my hands; I try not to think about it too much and wonder if I have a pack of wet wipes in my bag. This time it's a lot easier without Zippy. I will be so grateful when I get to the bottom and get out of this weird place.

Finally, I reach the bottom and step on Zippy's head.

Suddenly the light goes on and a voice speaks.

'Well, what have we here?'

I look up to see a small man with a long white beard peering down at me from the top of the stairs.

'I'm trying to find the fancy dress shop.' I try desperately to untangle myself from the Ikea bag handles.

'Then you've come to the right place. Come up. Come up.'

I repeat the stair climb again and it's not any easier a second time. When I reach the top, I fall through the half-glazed door then pull myself up to my full height and force myself to smile at the little man.

'Those are some strange stairs, aren't they?'

'Are they?' he says. 'I never use them myself. Now how can I help you? Are you after a wizarding outfit? Hermione perhaps?'

'Err, no, thanks.' Do I look like a Harry Potter fan?

'Oh. Harry?' His voice sounds hopeful.

'No, thank you. I want to return this one.' I pull open the Ikea bag to show Zippy's inane grin.

'Ah, Zippy. Welcome home. We've been waiting for you.' He raises a single eyebrow at me. 'We've been ringing you and leaving messages but you haven't responded. You're very overdue.'

'Well, I didn't hire him. The person you've been leaving messages for has gone back to Australia and left Zippy with me. Maybe he's not getting your messages, that's probably why you haven't had any response. From him, I mean.'

'Mmm. Remove him from the bag please.'

I decant Zippy onto the counter and wait while the little man examines him closely – which seems to take a very long time. I take the opportunity to look around the shop; it looks like it has been here for centuries. All the surfaces, including the walls, are scratched wood. Racks and rails laden with fancy dress and costumes suitable for TV dramas are lined up and covered in clear plastic. Finally, satisfied, he speaks.

'He seems fine.'

'Yes. He is.'

'There's just the little matter of the overdue fee.'

'What?'

He pulls a calculator from under the counter and begins tapping out numbers.

'An extra ten days at twenty pounds a day. That will be two-hundred pounds.'

I laugh. He's joking, surely.

'Alright, I'll give you a special discount. One-hundred pounds.'

I realise that he's serious.

'You must be joking.'

He tilts his head at me and smiles. 'Very well, but you drive a hard bargain. Because I like you I'll increase the discount. The final overdue fee is ten pounds.'

'Okay. That seems fair. Deduct it from the deposit please.'

'Mmm.' He pulls a large bound ledger from beneath the counter and starts to thumb through the pages. He reaches for a pen – I half expect it to be a quill – makes some alternations in the book and smiles at me before slapping it shut. 'Done,' he says.

'Good. Okay, how much is the deposit?'

He opens the book again, thumbs through the pages, runs his finger down a column and looks up at me. 'One-hundred-and-fifteen pounds. That's with the late fee taken into account.'

'Cool. Thank you.'

He slaps the book shut and I wait for my money.

'Is there anything else I can help you with?'

'No, just the deposit please.'

He puts the ledger back under the counter and looks at me as though I am stupid.

'The hundred-and-fifteen,' I prompt him.

'Yes. It will be refunded to the original hirer's credit card.'

'What?'

'Credit card. It was paid by credit card.'

'Of course it was,' I mutter, turning to leave and mentally preparing myself for the strange skinny stairs. No wonder Zippy was so keen for me to return it. Bloody cheek.

Gen laughs and laughs when I recount the story later on the phone.

'It was like a visit to Hogwarts or something. And to think I trundled that bloody costume all the way there for nothing. And it got heavier with every step.'

'Did you really think he was gifting you the deposit? You're hilarious.'

'I know. I suppose it was rather stupid of me.'

'And greedy,' Gen adds, sniggering.

'Yes, you're right. But you know how it is after Christmas, spent too much and a long old January. And no bonus to look forward to either.'

'Shush,' Gen says. 'I told you that in confidence.'

'I'm in my bedroom at home; I don't think anyone

is listening.'

'Hope not,' says Gen sounding less amused now. I hear her sigh before she changes the subject. 'Got any plans for the weekend?'

'Yes, I'm going to see a show tonight.'

'Ooh, which one?'

'Les Misérables. Again.'

'Um, why?'

'Cos I was asked.'

'Oh, I see. More information, please.'

'Just a guy I know.' I say no more.

'And,' Gen urges.

'Well, that's it.'

'Well I need more. You know I have to live vicariously through others now that I have husband and children. So, come on.'

In the end I have to come clean and tell her that my friend, Anton, had a couple of tickets and was let down by his boyfriend who had to work late. So, I'm going in his place. I know she would much rather I had met, what she calls, *a lovely man*.

'Have fun,' Gen says, sounding disappointed. 'And keep looking for him.'

'I've told you, I don't need a man to complete me.' I don't. It's true. And the Zippy-costume-deposit fiasco has put me off going out with straight men again until at least Easter, if not well beyond.

Six

The rest of January disappears in a flurry of light snow and slushy puddles and there is no more mention of appraisals, bad or otherwise. They take place twice a year and the next one is due in April, so Gen says we shouldn't assume the problem has gone away.

I've managed the whole month without any alcohol and, I'm happy to report that I don't seem to be missing it as much as I feared.

February sidles in and soon Gen and I are embarking on her birthday treat. I've had to tell her which clothes to bring, but, until we reach the airport she still doesn't know where we're going.

'Oh. Wow,' she says as we join the queue for the plane to Morocco. 'Oh. Wow. Thank you so much.'

'I hope it lives up to expectations.'

'It will, it will.' She almost jumps up and down; a nearly forty-year-old woman as excited as a child. 'I've always wanted to go to Marrakech. Always.'

I give Gen the first of her birthday presents once we are in our seats, belts on and taxiing down the runway; a Marrakech guidebook. She spends most of the flight studying it and reading out points of interest to me.

'Where are we staying?' she asks, an hour into the flight.

'Where would you like to stay?' Only after I've said

this do I realise the folly of it.

'Well, I'm sure wherever you've chosen will be wonderful. But, ideally it won't be one of the big chains on the outskirts.' Once the words are out of her mouth she winces, also realising *her* folly.

I feign a look of disappointment.

'It'll be fab,' she says, reaching for my hand. 'Wherever you're taking me will be fab.'

I nod slowly, hoping that it will be fab while also feeling quietly confident; if the hotel's website is a true representation then it will be better than fab.

We land and pick up our luggage.

'Ralph usually does this,' Gen mutters as she hauls her heavy suitcase off the carousel.

'How much stuff have you got in there?' I laugh, frowning at the size of her case.

'Well, I wasn't sure what I would need.'

'But I told you.'

'Yes, well, I like to have a choice of what to wear.' She glances over at my suitcase which is half the size of hers. 'And you can always borrow from me if you need to.'

'I doubt that.' I laugh and pat her on the back. We both know that nothing Gen wears will fit me, not even her knickers. While I am tall, Gen is average height, while I am what my mum has always referred to as ample, Gen is average. Were it not for her ginger, corkscrew curls, Gen would blend into any crowd.

Outside the airport we join the long queue for a taxi.

'The guidebook says agree a price before getting in,' Gen says as we reach the front of the queue.

'Okay.' I step back and let Gen do the haggling

and soon we're bouncing around at high speed in the back of a big old Mercedes and heading for the Medina.

As we approach the city boundary arch I wonder if the taxi will fit through it. We slow down and it feels as though the taxi takes a breath and pulls in its sides before we squeeze through. Gen and I both do the same – as though it will help.

We slide swiftly down narrow streets which are more like alleyways, or even tunnels, with their high stone sides and cobbled roads. We pass tiny workshops where every type of business is conducted, from welding to leatherworking to cooking. Scabby, skinny donkeys pull carts across in front of us and seem only to escape our passing taxi's bumpers by chance.

The driver has his window down and the pungent – and not always pleasant – smells and sounds of the Medina gush in and knock us sideways. I'm overwhelmed by the stench of everyday life here, food and sewage, animal dung and aromatic spices. Suddenly we pull up to an abrupt stop outside a studded wooden door set in an acre of drab stone wall.

The driver glances back at us with a look of expectation on his face.

'This it?' I'm afraid the door doesn't look very promising.

He gabbles something that sounds vaguely like the name of our hotel then gets out of the car. The boot goes up and he pulls out our suitcases and dumps them in front of the door. Gen and I get out.

I glance up and down the street, despite it being the middle of the day it's dark. The walls are high and the sky above, though bright blue, seems alien and distant.

'Just like I imagined.' A broad smile lights up Gen's face. 'Thank you so much.'

I force a small smile in response; I'm really not too sure about this place now. Any of it. A whiff of manure, both animal and human, drifts up to my nose and I have to suppress a gag.

As I fumble around in my purse to pay the fare Gen knocks on the hotel door. I pay the driver the agreed fare but he waits expectantly. I fumble again and pull out two dirhams which I hand over. I'm grateful that someone at work had some spare currency they didn't want because it means I have some coins. He looks at his hand then my face, shrugs his shoulders, mutters something in Arabic and gets into his taxi before roaring away. It's only as I approach the now open door that I do a hasty conversion of dirhams to pounds on my phone and realise I have just tipped the driver the equivalent of sixteen pence. No wonder he seemed both confused and ungrateful.

I step through the door which is immediately slammed shut behind me and breathe a sigh of relief. The hotel reception is an elegant cave-like room, the floor covered in terracotta and blue tiles, the walls painted a soft orange, ornate furniture is lined up around a large colourful carpet which vaguely reminds me of the rug in my living room.

'Isn't it cool?' Gen waves a large iron key at me. 'I've signed us in; they just need your passport.'

I grimace at the prospect of handing over my passport but realise I have little choice.

'When will I get that back?' I ask the receptionist,

noting how aggressive I sound yet unable to rein it in.

He doesn't answer but smiles at me and waves us towards his colleague who, dressed like a waiter from another century, stands at another door. I grab my suitcase but the receptionist calls out to leave it.

'I don't like my suitcase being out of my sight,' I whisper to Gen as we are escorted out of the reception area and into a large tent.

'It's fine. Don't worry so,' Gen says through a happy smile.

'Please.' Our waiter waves his arm towards the long, carpet covered benches which line the edges of the tent. We step onto layered floor rugs before taking a seat.

A woman with smiling, dark eyes lays a tray holding a small, ornate silver teapot and tiny, green glasses onto the coffee table in front of us.

'Vodka shots?' Gen giggles quietly into my ear. 'In a Bedouin's tent. Isn't it fab?'

'Mint tea.' Our waiter begins to pour and we watch as he ladles sugar into the glasses before handing them to us.

'Mmm, lovely,' Gen says, smiling.

'Sickly sweet, though.' I take one sip then put mine back on the tray.

'Drink it,' Gen says. 'It's part of the experience.'

'I will. It's too hot.' I'm desperate to see my passport and my suitcase again. I don't feel comfortable here but I can tell from Gen's body language as well as her words that she is loving every minute.

Another woman appears with a plate of tiny cakes.

'Ooo, look baklava. Yum.' Gen helps herself to a sticky square.

'That is sweet too.' I almost wince.

'What's the matter with you, you love sweet stuff.' Gen nudges me gently.

'Since Dry January, I've gone off it a bit.' I take another honey-coated cube; it's still sickly sweet. 'Not having alcohol seems to have affected my taste buds.'

'Well, it's not Dry January anymore.'

'No. Thank God. And, I've been saving myself 'til we got here.'

'But we're well into February.' Gen frowns at me.

'I know. But, well…' I laugh and take another sip of mint tea. Letting it cool hasn't made it any more appealing. 'I've got into the no alcohol habit, and I've lost weight too, so that's a bonus.'

'Well, I hope you're not going to be a bore on our holiday.'

'Course not.'

The receptionist appears with our passports and hands them over.

'Mesdames,' he says, directing his smile at me. I feel churlish and ashamed and try to hide it by replying in French.

'Merci monsieur.' I instantly regret it as he then assumes I speak French and responds with a long sentence.

'Um,' I mutter, but Gen, whose French is excellent, jumps in and answers for me.

'What did he say?' I mutter all the while watching his retreating back.

'Hoped you had a safe journey and wished you well for your stay here.'

'Oh,' I say as we are led along a soft terracotta path towards our room. We pass a shimmering swimming pool, its blue water twinkling out an invitation. On all sides orange trees laden with fruit send out their sweet, delicious scent making the odour of sewage almost a distant memory. The birds in the trees are tweeting away, the air is light and I'm starting to feel confident again about my choice of hotel.

'This is so lovely. Where did you find it?'

'Good old internet. I'm so grateful that it's as lovely as it looked online.'

We pass the modern rooms with their patio doors opening onto the public path and carry further on. Gen turns and frowns at me. I don't want to tempt fate by promising anything, so just shrug.

Up a few curving steps and we stand before another studded, oak door. Our waiter, who, I realise probably isn't a waiter at all but another receptionist, unlocks the door and ushers us inside.

'Oh wow,' Gen says, almost jumping on the spot.

We're standing in a large sitting room; two sofas surround a coffee table which is almost groaning under the weight of a bouquet of flowers and a fruit bowl big enough for a banquet.

Our receptionist leaves us to explore and, as he leaves, indicates that we should read the hotel's welcome booklet.

Gen picks it up but doesn't look at it, instead running into the next room where two double beds sit side by side. She rushes through to the bathroom and I follow her to find a deep, tiled, sunken bath and a separate humungous shower cubicle.

'Look,' she squeals, rushing towards the large sideboard also in the bathroom. 'Robes and slippers. Can this get any better?'

'I'm so relieved you like it.'

After we unpack we agree to explore the hotel,

which doesn't actually take us very long. I've explained to Gen that we should have a guide to explore the Medina. We go to Reception to enquire and suddenly we have one arranged for tomorrow. I'm a bit nervous about the cost as this whole holiday is my treat for Gen's birthday, but once I've done the conversion calculation on my phone, I'm pleasantly relieved.

We agree that next on our agenda is lunch in the hotel's restaurant, which, it seems is also inside a tent, a very elegant one, but still a tent.

'That was lovely,' Gen says, after we've eaten our fill of French cuisine, we've agreed not to have wine with lunch because we'll be having it with dinner. She then asks how my parents are enjoying their holiday.

'I got a message in the middle of the night, they were just heading out of Honolulu and are going to Tonga next. It came with a photo of them on their balcony; they look really well.'

'Must be amazing, a world cruise. I'd like to do that when the kids are older.' Gen pauses for a second or two. 'Actually, much older. As in moved out. I wouldn't want them left alone in my house.' She laughs.

I stop for a moment and think about whether I would like to go on a world cruise. 'I don't think it would be much fun on my own,' I muse, unintentionally aloud.

'You won't always be on your own.'

'I think I might. Not, I must add, that I mind. I don't need a man to complete me.' I'm trotting out my mantra and Gen raises her eyebrows in response.

'Anyway, I think there are lots of people who holiday alone. On those cruises you team up with them.' Gen gives me a sheepish look. 'And other holidays too.'

'You seem to know a lot. Have you been investigating?' I'm joking but can tell from Gen's face that she isn't.

'Well, you know.' She shrugs. 'You don't really go away unless it's with me, do you? And that's not very often.'

I realise that she's right. We've been on a few short spa breaks and I once went on holiday with Gen and Ralph and the kids when they were little, but I just ended up babysitting so Gen and Ralph could go out for dinner.

'I'm quite happy,' I say, sounding defensive.

'Course you are.' Gen smiles brightly at me.

I am. I really am.

We leave the tent restaurant and saunter back to our room. It's incredibly warm, the sun is high and the pool is calling us. So, it's bikinis and flip-flops on as soon as possible.

'Do you think this is okay?' Gen asks as we sit down on sun loungers.

'Yes, we're staying here.'

'No, I mean us, scantily clad.'

'We're not scantily clad; we've got our swimming gear on.'

'Yes, but, this is a Muslim country. You know…' her voice fades away just as two German girls, half our age, saunter past chatting away, in string bikinis which leave little to the imagination. 'There you are then.' Gen laughs. 'We look positively overdressed against them.'

Dinner that evening is more lovely French cuisine

and Gen chooses a light Chablis to go with it.

'Is this okay?' I ask as I lift the glass to my lips. 'It smells odd.'

'Does it?' Gen inhales deeply. 'No, it smells fine to me.' She takes a large mouthful. 'It tastes good too.'

'Must be me,' I laugh. 'Dry January has put me right off alcohol.' I take a sip myself and wince at the taste. 'I think I'll let you have this bottle.'

'I can't drink all that on my own.'

'I'm sure the hotel will put it by for tomorrow evening.'

But they don't need to as Gen does manage to drink the whole bottle by herself.

'I shouldn't have had all that wine,' she says the next morning as we're getting ready. It's ten-to-eight and we're skipping breakfast because the guide is arriving at eight.

'Have some water.' I pass her an elegant glass bottle; three appeared in our room while we were at dinner last night. Maybe they thought we would need it. 'I'm starving, it's a shame we're missing breakfast.'

'Don't talk about food.' Gen pulls on jeans and slips her feet into her Sketchers. We've been advised to dress conservatively out in public, but we'd have done that anyway as it's not particularly warm this morning, despite the early morning sun.

Our guide waits for us in Reception, he's tall and good looking. Too good looking really and I can't take my eyes off him. He has the most incredible skin; so flawless that I wonder if he is wearing makeup. I fight the urge to touch his face. He reminds me of *Omar Shariff* who I'd seen in *Dr Zhivago* when I was channel surfing at my parents' over Christmas.

He introduces himself but, as is the norm for me, I don't catch his name and even if I did, I can't get *Omar* out of my head. Especially when he explains that although he's lived in Morocco for most of his life, he's actually Egyptian.

He takes us on a walking tour of the Medina, explaining customs and even a little about the Islamic religion. He makes it clear that he doesn't approve of extremism, in fact he's very vehement about it. Gen and I feel embarrassed and wish he would just change the subject.

As we continue our walking tour Gen is like a kid in a sweetshop – a very trusting one. I'm more wary, conscious of men's eyes on us and grateful we have *Omar* with us.

We trek around some sights of interest, they pass before my eyes and are instantly forgotten, a tomb here and statue there. Fortunately, Gen is the culture vulture and constantly refers to the guidebook I have given her.

We find ourselves in the central square, the world famous Jemaa el Fna, with its snake charmers and con-artists in equal measure.

'Is that real?' I whisper to Gen as a cobra sways out of a basket and darts its forked tongue in my direction.

'It is,' Omar says, urging us away. 'And you cannot always trust them. Come, come.'

We wander past the immense carts of oranges and nuts, and head towards the Zouk. Gen performs a little jump for joy and rushes inside ahead of us.

'Madame, no. No,' calls Omar. 'Wait.'

We catch up with a puzzled Gen.

'Madame, please, stay with me. You will be lost.'

'Okay,' Gen says to Omar, then whispers to me, 'that's so he can take us to his cousin's carpet shop.'

'No. Stop it,' I hiss.

We pass stalls selling spices displayed in precarious mini-mountains, their colours so vibrant they dazzle. Every stall keeper invites us in with promises of good health and free offers.

'Asda price,' one calls after us, patting his back pocket. 'Lovely jubbly,' he calls again, grinning as we pass, laughing.

Gen buys herself a leather handbag in one of the Zouk shops and I, for reasons that aren't exactly clear to me, buy myself a leather pouffe. It's just the outer and will need stuffing when I get it home, but at least empty it will fit in my case.

'That's lovely,' Gen says, running her hands over the fine tooling on the pouffe's surface. 'Such lovely colours, gold and black and that lovely vibrant blue.'

'I love it.' I clutch it to my chest. I do love it, but I don't know what I'm going to do with it, there's not much need for it in our flat and anyway I wouldn't want Yan's giant hooves on it. 'I'll keep it in my bedroom.' Probably in the wardrobe, I admit to myself, but I have to have it.

We turn a corner in the Zouk and arrive at a carpet shop.

'Told you,' Gen sniggers.

I glance back and see that we are deep within the Zouk and I feel claustrophobic but realise that I wouldn't want to chance escaping on my own because this place is like a maze.

An hour later after we have drunk more sickly-sweet mint tea and simultaneously smiled and shaken our heads, we are outside minus any carpets.

'They were lovely,' Gen tells Omar, but we just don't have the need for them like you do. All are floors have fitted carpets. Except in Charlie's place, and she already has a carpet just like that, don't you?'

'Yes, I do.' I think of the old wine-stained living room rug with its elaborate pattern and, while it's true that the design is similar the quality is definitely not.

Omar shrugs, he doesn't appear bothered. It's as if he's had to take us there as part of some secret agreement, but he doesn't care if we buy or not.

My stomach rumbles and Gen laughs.

'Hungry?' Omar asks.

'Very. We missed breakfast,' Gen tells him, seemingly forgetting that she couldn't have faced it anyway.

'I take you somewhere lovely. Somewhere tourists don't go.' He sets off at a pace that makes Gen and I scuttle along behind him.

We turn into streets that have certainly seen few tourists and arrive at a large, blue-tiled, restaurant. Omar pushes open the door and is greeted warmly by the owner. A lot of Arabic words and laughter are hastily exchanged and Omar ushers us to a table. We're the only women in here but the other customers, having glanced up when we first arrived, seem disinterested in us.

Clean plates are put before us.

'Where's the loo?' Gen asks. 'I want to wash my hands.'

Omar beams his approval and nods towards the steps in the corner.

'Me too.' I jump up when Gen does.

We totter down some precarious steps and find toilets, one for men and one for women.

'That makes me feel a bit better,' I say as Gen pushes the door open. 'At least women do come in here.'

Gen raises her eyebrows in reply and closes the door. I wait patiently outside. She smirks when she comes out.

The toilet – if you can call it that – is a hole in the ground surrounded by tiles and two feet marks.

'Urgh.'

'I took my jeans off and hung them on that hook,' Gen says.

I do the same then balance precariously either side of the hole. I wee for England, well I would, wouldn't I? Some of it splashes back up and lands on my trainers. Thank God I took Gen's advice about the jeans.

Hands, and shoes, washed and we head back up to the restaurant to find food spread out on our table.

'Oooo, lovely.' Gen sits downs and starts to tuck in. I'm slower but have to admit that the selection of chopped meats, diced tomato with onion and flat breads is rather lovely.

'Very good,' I say to Omar who waits expectantly for our verdict.

He smiles his pleasure.

'Wow,' Gen says after I've paid. 'What an authentic experience. Thank you, Omar. Thank you, Charlie.'

'Cheap too.' I push the extra notes I had expected to part with back into my purse.

After lunch Omar asks if we'd like to go out to the *Menara Gardens*.

'Yes, yes,' Gen says, flicking to the correct place in her guidebook.

'I call a taxi.' Omar pulls out his phone and makes a call. Three minutes later a beaten-up Mercedes screeches to a halt in front of us. Omar leans in and has a speedy conversation with the driver. I'm not sure if it's just the way they speak or if there is actually an argument going on but there does seem to be a disagreement which lasts quite a while.

Eventually Omar nods then turns to us, a smile fixed on his face.

'Is this the part when we're sold into white slavery?' I joke to Gen in a whisper.

'Yeah, and they were arguing about how small they will have to dice up the camel to pay for us two old bags.'

We giggle together and Omar frowns at us. I hope he hasn't heard.

'Mesdames,' he says, almost bowing. 'My cousin is taxi driver, he already has passengers but has agreed to take us for just sixty dirhams if we share. I have agreed. It is a good price.'

'Okay,' Gen says, dashing towards the taxi.

Omar opens the rear door and gestures for me to get in. I glance inside and see two large Moroccan men. One of them, somewhat reluctantly, gets out of the car and lets me get in. I'm just thinking that isn't too bad when he climbs back in next to me. I am squeezed between the two of them. They both turn and face away from me as though I smell.

Gen, who is still standing outside, leans in and winks at me.

Omar opens the front passenger door and waves Gen inside. I suppress a little resentment; I'm bigger than her and she would have fitted in the back better than me. She sits in the front passenger seat then turns around and beams at me. Oh well, I suppose it is her birthday treat.

'No, no,' Omar calls to Gen. 'Move over.'

'Move where?' Gen turns her head towards the driver who sits tapping his hands on the steering wheel.

'You're small. You sit in middle.'

'But that's the gear box.'

'Yes. You move over.'

'But I'll be in the way.'

'It will be good. Move over.'

Now it's Gen's turn to be reluctant and mine to be grateful that I'm in the back as she shifts over to sit on the centre panel, her legs nudging the dashboard. Omar jumps in and, before he's even slammed the door shut we tear off, belting around corners as we all lean left or right. I'm squashed by shoulders and thighs and I can't say it is enjoyable.

We pull up outside the gardens and Omar and one of the Arab men tumble out, closely followed by me and Gen.

'That was interesting,' Gen laughs as Omar has another conversation with the driver.

'Horrible.'

'Oh come on. When was the last time you were sandwiched between two men?'

'Don't be disgusting.'

'You can pay the driver when he takes us back,' Omar tells us as we watch the taxi hurtle off.

'No other passengers, I hope.' I can't face that prospect again.

'No others,' Omar says without a hint of a smile.

The day which started out quite chilly has turned into a warm afternoon with the sun burning down on us.

'I'm hot now.' Gen peels off her jacket, folds it up and stuffs it into her shoulder bag.

'Me too. Even that cold wind isn't cooling me now.' Not helped by the taxi ride from hell.

'Yes.' Omar stares off into the distance. 'We are a cold country with a hot sun.' His voice is solemn with wisdom. I struggle not to snigger.

'We're a cold country with no sun,' Gen quips. 'Especially not in winter.'

Omar frowns a look of puzzlement and leads us towards the lake and pavilion.'

After an hour around the gardens Omar calls for the taxi again. Thankfully, it's just the driver inside when it arrives.

'I will take you somewhere lovely for final visit.'

'Cool,' Gen says. 'We love lovely.'

The taxi's tyres screech up outside a cake shop.

'Oh yes,' Gen hollers, leaping out of the taxi.

'You can pay now,' Omar smiles at me. 'We walk back to hotel from here.'

I pull out dirhams and pay the man. Whatever the normal price is, I don't know, but the hundred dirhams I pay for our two journeys seems cheap.

Inside the cake shop the smell of honey is overpowering. I'm not sure whether I like it or not. The cakes are displayed in glass cabinets around the walls.

'Pick three each.' Omar points to the sticky squares, says something fast in Arabic after we have chosen then ushers us towards the back where the tables are. There are a few women in here but no tourists. We sit at a table and wait.

'Can you hear that sound?' Gen says as the ubiquitous pot of mint tea is put on the table.

'Yeah.' I am aware of a soft humming but I'm not paying much attention because all I'm thinking is how nice a coffee would be. But I know better than to ask for one in a place like this; it'll be a thimbleful of black tar.

The cakes arrive. Then we know what the humming sound is, or was, for now it has changed to buzzing.

'Bees,' Gen screams, batting them away as they swarm around our sticky treats.

I glance around the other tables to see bees buzzing around every one yet the other customers take no notice at all, neither moving out of their way or attempting to swipe them away.

Omar doesn't react either, just picks up one of his cakes and begins to eat.

'I better not get stung. Quick, eat up.' She bats another two bees away and forces a cake in her mouth whole.

'I don't think I can,' I say as I lift mine to my mouth and smell the sickly sweetness of honey. I put it back on the plate.

'You don't like?' Omar seems astonished.

'I'm sure it's lovely.' I don't want to cause any offence. 'But it's too sweet for me.'

He looks at me as though I am mad then glances at Gen who has scoffed all her cakes and is now starting on mine.

'What?' She frowns. 'I just want to get away from the bees.'

Five minutes later we're outside, the mint tea untouched, the cakes eaten and the bill paid. Omar seems bewildered. He walks us back to our hotel and I pay him.

'Mint tea?' The receptionist waves towards the tent.

'No, thank you,' we chorus before heading for our room.

'No one batted an eyelid, that's what I found so weird.' Gen and I have been giggling about the bees and the taxi journey since we came back. We're showered and changed and ready for dinner, and we're looking forward to it. Tonight, is Moroccan night.

'I doubt they do Moroccan wine.' Gen studies the wine menu before finally picking a French one, which is all the hotel seems to offer anyway. 'I'd prefer a Pinot Grigio,' she whispers.

The wine arrives before the food, I've asked for only a small glass but as I hold my glass up to my mouth the smell overwhelms me. I hate it. I take a sip. It tastes worse than it smells. I glance at Gen who is sipping and enjoying.

'Is it okay?' She feels some kind of responsibility because she chose it.

'I'm sure it is. It's just me. Dry January has killed my desire for alcohol.'

'Maybe I should do it next year.' She giggles. 'You'll have to try harder, I can't drink a whole bottle on my own again.'

'You don't have to; they will keep it for tomorrow.' I roll my eyes at her.

First course is pigeon legs, two each.

'Is there actually any meat on these?' Gen holds one aloft.

I look and shudder. 'Don't know, don't care,' I mutter.

She takes a nibble on hers. 'Quite nice.'

'Have mine.' I push my plate towards her.

Gen nibbles a little off the legs and puts them back on my plate.

The next course is rice soup.

'Where's the soup?' Gen giggles as we peer into our bowls of murky water to see sparse grains of uncooked rice floating around. 'Tastes a bit like dishwater.'

I push my rice grains around the bowl and wait for it to be taken away.

The tagine that follows is lovely, a lamb and vegetable concoction that smells as good at it tastes. The weird ice cream we eat for desert is also okay, though I don't manage to finish mine.

Then it's entertainment time. A belly dancer appears. She's beautiful, with smooth, youthful skin the colour of caramel and dark hair in a long, swishy ponytail. She's wearing an azure blue outfit; Arabian pants and skimpy crop top adorned with jangling discs. Between her forefinger and thumb she tinkles tiny little cymbals as she gyrates her waist around the tables. She looks like a genie from a bottle.

The middle-aged European men on the table near us ogle her under the watchful eye of the band which plays her accompanying music. Band is probably a generous word for an ancient, scrawny man sitting cross legged playing drums and an even older man playing a small guitar and singing. When he hollers out his notes I can see his teeth – all three of them.

'I'm not too sure about this,' Gen says. 'It doesn't seem to fit with what we've come to expect of a

Muslim country.

'No.' I watch the drum player scowl at the European men.

It all feels uncomfortable and rather embarrassing and we're grateful when it finishes.

I still haven't drunk my wine.

'We could take the bottle back to our room,' Gen says once our table is cleared so that all remains are the ice bucket and the bottle.

I wince. I don't mean to.

'I think it's quite nice.' Gen looks hurt.

'I'm sure it is. I just can't get back into wine. It's been like this for weeks now.'

'What are you like?'

She calls the waiter over to have the wine saved for tomorrow, glances at her own empty glass, then grabs mine and stands up.

I'm grateful I won't have to pretend I like it and, as I check the time, I'm sorry it's not later because I would just like to go to bed.

'I'm quite tired after today's excitements,' Gen says, linking arms with me as we weave our way through the orange trees and back to our room.

Half an hour later we're both in our spacious beds with books balanced on our laps. I fall asleep without even turning the pages.

Seven

What are we doing today?' Gen is as bouncy as *Tigger* and just as irritating.

I, on the other hand, awake groggy and can still taste last night's dinner on my own breath, including the pigeon legs that I didn't eat. I dash for the bathroom.

'You okay?' Gen's face is crumpled in concern when I return after being sick.

'Something didn't agree with me. But I'm fine now.'

'You sure?'

I nod.

'Breakfast?'

'Yes, I'm actually quite hungry.'

After breakfast Gen asks again if I have anything planned.

'It's our last full day,' she opines. 'Let's not waste it. We could go out without a guide now we know where to go. We could go to Jemaa el Fna square again and see the snake charmers properly. Omar pulled us away yesterday.'

'I don't think so.' I follow my objection with an involuntary shudder.

'It wasn't that bad. Was it?'

'Let's just say that I'm glad we had a guide and I've

no desire to repeat any of it.'

'You're such a wimp.' Gen leans over and pats my knee.

'Was that his name, Omar?' I'm amazed I actually got it right.

'I don't know. I couldn't understand what he said his name was,' Gen confesses. 'He just reminded me of Omar Sharif.'

I start laughing. 'Me too.'

Gen joins in and we giggle like kids for far too long.

'Enough. We have plans.' I stand up, decisive and commanding. 'And they don't involve anything dangerous either.'

I outline the plan for the day. In the morning we're booked in for a facial at the hotel spa, followed by a little light lunch. In the afternoon we're back in the spa for a luxury manicure and pedicure.

Gen is almost jumping for joy.

'How much is this all costing?' She eyes me cautiously.

'Don't worry, it's my treat.'

'That's what worries me. You've paid for everything. Everything, flights, hotel, yesterday's treats. I think I have to pay for today.'

'No, really. I've budgeted for this.' It's true, I have. This will be my main holiday this year, not just because it's costing an arm and a leg but because, and I hate to admit this even to myself, Gen is right, I haven't really got anyone else to go on holiday with. 'I insist. And if you mention it again I will cancel the lot.' I look Gen sternly in the eye.

We pass the pool on our way to the spa; the sun is up and it is twinkling on the water. It's much warmer than this time yesterday.

'That looks inviting.'

'Probably a bit cool yet. We can sunbathe after all our treatments.'

'Yes, it'll be nice to grab ourselves a bit of vitamin D before we go back to damp England.'

We arrive at the spa and smile at the receptionist. She's young and beautiful with flawless skin and perfect makeup. This is good, and bad. Good because she's a great advert for the spa, bad because it makes us feel like a pair of old crones even though, officially, we're both still in our thirties.

She smiles as she ticks us off her appointment sheet and shows us through to the treatment rooms; Gen is ushered into one and me into another. We're handed menu cards to choose our facials.

'I'm having the rose oil one,' Gen calls through the open door.

'Me too,' I laugh, having already decided that would be my choice as well. It sounds so inviting and luxurious.

My facial therapist arrives with her assistant and the door is closed. It's a squeeze with the three of us in the room, and unusual. In the UK it's usually just me and the beauty therapist.

She examines my skin without speaking, frowning as she pulls my face around and pinches my cheeks. Finally, she speaks. But not to me, to her assistant, who nods.

'Madame,' says the assistant as she tries to take away the menu card that I am still clutching in my hand. I grip it tighter.

'I want this one.' I point at the rose oil facial.

The assistant conveys my choice to the therapist

who frowns and forms her mouth into a straight line. A lot of speedy Arabic is exchanged.

'Non, madame,' the assistant says, managing to wrestle the card from my hands. 'Non.'

'But that's what I want.'

The therapist, evidently understanding, shakes her head vehemently and starts covering me with a blanket, a move designed to pin me down. She pulls my hair back into a towel and wraps it tightly out of the way. She mutters something to the assistant.

'Madame,' the assistant addresses me. 'Is not suitable for skin.' She pokes a finger into my cheek. 'Is for ...' she strokes her own youthful face.

I get the message. No rose oil for me. I'm too old. I lay back and surrender myself to my fate.

The process is similar to at home, cleansing, steaming, massaging, it's all very nice until we get to the face mask part. This is when I should have been having the rose oil mask, breathing in the lovely aroma and feeling calm and relaxed. Instead I'm having something else, and I don't know what it is, I can't even see because I have cotton wool pads glued to my eyes.

I hear what sounds like an egg cracking followed by whisking in a bowl before a cool gloop is spread thickly over my face and neck. It smells suspiciously familiar.

I'm left in the room alone. This is fairly standard, usually they play some soothing music which invariably includes tinkling bells, today's music is a little less soothing, but not unpleasant.

I lie there for what seems like an hour. My face and neck start to tighten as the mask dries. It gets tighter and tighter and then I feel the urge to sneeze. I try to hold it back, but cannot.

The mask pulls and cracks. I feel little flakes slide down past my ears.

The therapist and her assistant return and there's more speedy Arabic.

'Madame,' says the assistant. 'You have spoiled.'

The therapist tuts and picks at a few flakes.

'Sorry,' I mutter, wondering just who the hell the client is here.

Twenty minutes later I'm clean and creamed and thrust out into the reception where I find Gen sitting waiting for me.

'You been waiting long?'

'Seconds,' she says. 'Your skin looks amazing.'

'So does yours.'

'My face feels a bit stiff,' I say, trying to smile.

'Me too,' Gen says, fishing in her purse.

'No, I'm paying and it's going on the hotel bill.' I try to push her purse back into her bag.

'I'm paying the tip,' she says.

I turn to see my therapist and her assistant waiting expectantly before smiling when Gen gives them a handful of dirhams each.

We turn to leave but not before the receptionist grabs us. She checks our appointment times for the afternoon then asks if we would like any other treatments. She thrusts a brochure at each of us.

We scurry off to lunch as quickly as we can, giggling without much facial movement as we go along.

'I had egg white,' Gen says, once we're out of earshot. 'I saw the egg shell.'

'I think I did too. I heard the egg crack. I wasn't allowed the rose oil.'

'Me neither. I think we're too old.'

'Bloody cheek.'

In the lunch tent we sit by the open door and watch the pool. The German lovelies are out again parading in their string bikinis and the waiters all look out as they pass the door. Other guests are also taking advantage of the warmth.

'It's a cold country with a very hot sun today,' Gen muses.

'Mmm, we'll do that later.'

'Let's hope Buddha of the Pool has gone by then.'

'Who?' I lean out a bit further to see who she means. The man is completely bald and his torso and limbs are also hairless. He is semi-reclining against his sun lounger with his legs crossed in front of him. What finishes off his Buddha impersonation is his very large, very rotund belly.

'Sixty-six weeks pregnant,' Gen deadpans as I guffaw and pull my head inside as he turns to see where the laughter is coming from.

We arrive at the spa again with ten minutes to spare. The receptionist books us in and asks if we want any more treatments. We have left the brochures she gave us in the dining room without even looking at them. Undeterred, she whips another one out and proceeds to flick through it with us.

'For you, madame,' she points at me and then at a picture of eyebrows.

I peer at it. Micro-blading, it says. The English description explains how it's a semi-permanent eyebrow tattooing process. I glance in the mirror at my eyebrows, I'm actually quite happy with them as they are. I don't want thick, inky-black arches.

'No thanks,' I say, smiling and handing the brochure back.

'Madame.' My facial therapist suddenly appears. She grabs the brochure from the receptionist and thrusts the micro-blading page under my nose. 'Madame,' she implores, stabbing at my eyebrows.

'No. Thank you.' I force a smile as Gen sniggers into her hand.

The therapist scowls and wanders away, no doubt to whisk up some more egg white for her next unsuspecting victim.

Gen and I enter a vast room that doubles as a hair salon and a nail bar. Gen is whisked away to the hand desks while I am ushered into a chair, I assume, for my pedicure.

'Shoes, madame,' another beauty in her twenties says.

I slip my feet out of my flip flops.

A foot spa is produced, it's not dissimilar to the ancient one my mum has at home. It's plonked in front of me and the girl leaves, appearing a minute later with a bucket of water. She pours it into the foot spa. I lift my feet to put them in it.

'Non, madame.' She wags her finger at me before trotting over to a shelf to grab a bottle. She comes back with *Dettol* and proceeds to tip some into the water. Dettol. The disinfectant. I'm sure my mum washes her cats' bowls out with it when they've been ill. The water in the foot spa turns a milky white. Where is the lovely smelling, foaming foot soak I have in London? 'Madame,' she says, pushing the foot spa closer to me.

I lift my feet and immerse them in the white water. Initially, they sting, after that, it's okay.

To pass the time I look around me, wondering if they wash the hair in Dettol too. A woman, a fellow guest I assume, is having her hair blow-dried. Every stroke of the brush yanks her head back sharply and I see her wince. I wonder why she doesn't say anything, and then remember my own experience with the egg white. Resistance is futile. I catch her eye and she flashes me a complicit grimace.

Fifteen minutes later my feet are pulled out of the foot spa and examined for flaws, that is, calluses and corns. Words are muttered in Arabic and a metal foot file that resembles a giant cheese grater is produced. It's my turn to wince now, but I do add a few ouches in for good measure.

'Sorry, madame.' She isn't sorry at all.

Gen, meanwhile is sitting with her back to me at the nail bar. She doesn't know what she's got coming.

I'm sure we'll laugh about it later.

The nail technician working on Gen calls over something in French to the girl working on my feet. There then follows a lot of conversation, spoken in French with some Arabic thrown in. The tone is angry, actually, bitchy is a better description.

My French is poor but even I can tell that they are slagging off their boss. Big time. From the back I can see Gen's shoulders going up and down; she's suppressing laughter. They're not to know she speaks good French.

This continues throughout my pedicure and Gen's manicure. I'm plunged in and out of the delightful Dettol several times until it's time to paint my toenails. Once they are finished they look good, although the choice of polish – pale pink or dark pink – isn't what I would normally choose. I notice that the girls working here all have crimson talons themselves. No boring pink for them.

Gen and I swop. We exchange a few sniggers as we pass.

'Dettol for you,' I whisper.

'And you.' Gen crinkles her eyes at me.

I can hardly believe that my hands are now being plunged into Dettol. Using it for feet is one thing, but hands.

I'm at the fingernail painting stage when the manager of the spa comes in. She's older than the others but just as flawless in skin and makeup. Her eyebrows are micro-bladed.

The girls, who have not stopped complaining about her to each other are suddenly silent.

'Bonjour Madame,' they chorus.

She nods her reply.

Now we're sitting in stony silence as our treatments are finished.

Gen tips the girls when we leave and thanks them, in perfect French, for an entertaining afternoon.

I smile as though I understood every word too and we leave them staring open-mouthed at us.

'Did you get most of that?' Gen says once we're outside.

'I got that they hate their boss.'

'And some. They were calling her a fat, lazy cow who has long lunches and doesn't do any treatments but takes the lion's share of the tips.'

'Oh dear. Anything else?'

'No,' laughs Gen. 'Just that, over and over.'

We've been so long in the spa that the sun is going down and there is a chill in the air. We won't be sitting around the pool.

'Probably just as well, what with our old crinkled faces, better to keep them out of the sun.' I pat Gen's arm as though we are two old dears.

'I think if my feet or hands touch water again they will dissolve.'

'Dettol,' we say together.

'I'm sure we'll laugh about it in the future.' I grab Gen's arm and march her back to our room where we both slump on our beds, exhausted from doing nothing, but having plenty done to us. I have to admit though that our hands, feet and faces do look good.

We're up early the next morning to pack. As I bend over my case trying desperately to force it shut – why do cases shrink when you're packing to go home – I feel last night's rather nice dinner sitting in the back of my throat. I rush to the loo to be sick.

'Okay,' Gen asks when I come back.

'All this rich food.' I roll my eyes. 'It doesn't really agree with me.'

'No. Do you want to skip breakfast?'

'No. I'm starving. Why? Do you?'

'No. Not at all.' Gen smiles at me. 'I don't have a hangover if that's what you mean, it was only half a bottle.' Gen finished off the previous night's wine as again I couldn't even stand the smell of it.

'Cool. Let's go.' I'm out the door and down the path and Gen is trotting behind me. 'I'll have to find a new drink, I've gone right off wine.'

'You have, haven't you?'

After breakfast, of which I've eaten plenty, we're back in our room killing time until the taxi arrives.

'How are you feeling now?' Gen asks.

'Fine.'

Gen smiles and continues to look at me.

'What?'

She shakes her head but still stares at me.

'What?'

'Have you been sick much, before here, I mean?'

I think for a moment. 'A couple of times. Usually when I've overdone it on takeaway the night before.'

Gen nods slowly. I don't like the way she does that, I don't like the way she keeps looking at me.

'What?' I'm not attempting to hide my irritation.

'Umm, nothing.'

'What? What is it?'

Gen sighs. 'Is it possible you might be...' she stalls, 'you know...'

'What? What are you saying?'

'Pregnant,' she adds, wincing.

'What?' I sound like the record is stuck.

'When was your last period?'

'You know I'm irregular. Before Christmas, I think.' I suddenly have a sinking feeling.

'You've probably just got a low-level bug,' Gen says, her voice in reassuring mode. She does this, plants a seed then waits for it to grow while pretending she has nothing to do with it.

She's got me thinking now. And that was her plan. I'm running through my dates. The events of New Year's Eve are hazy. I know Zippy and I had sex. I know we used a condom. The first time. I remember that. Trouble is I know there were more times and I'm not sure what we did then.

'No,' I say, trying to convince myself.

Gen doesn't respond with words, just a little shrug.

'What makes you think that I might be?'

'Morning sickness. Enhanced sense of smell. Off

wine. I've had three myself, I recognise the signs.'

'No. I can't be. Can I?'

'When did you last have unprotected sex?'

I frown my annoyance at her.

The phone rings and Reception tells us our taxi is waiting.

The ride to the airport seems interminable. The alleyways out of the Medina seem narrower and darker than before. The donkeys seem scabbier, the shops seem noisier. We're hurtling around in the back of a rattly old Mercedes and I'm wracking my brain for memories of that night.

'I'm beginning to think you might be right,' I say to Gen once we've checked in.

'Only one way to find out. We'll stop off and pick up a test on the way home and you can come to mine and do it. We'll have the house to ourselves, they're all out, work or school.'

'Okay.'

On the flight home we're subdued initially, then Gen starts to joke about our spa experience. I laugh along with her because it *was* funny, especially in retrospect, but the idea that I might be pregnant is running through the back of my mind all the time.

Is it possible? Could I be? If I am, what will I do? Keep it? When will it be due? If I am I know exactly when it was conceived. I count the weeks and work out when it will be due. End of September, beginning of October.

'I can't be, can I?' I voice my thoughts out of the blue.

'We'll get that test on the way home.'

We get a taxi from Heathrow and Gen gets it to drop us on her local high street. It's a few minutes' walk to her house so we're not averse to dragging our suitcases that small distance.

In *Boots* Gen studies the pregnancy tests, picking them up, reading the info while I stand and look around us. It's unlikely but I hope no one I know sees me.

'They've changed since I last used one. I think they're probably better.'

'Good.' I really don't know what else to say.

My phone pings. I can't resist the urge to check it. Gen looks at me expectantly.

'My mum.' I force a laugh and show Gen the message. 'Her and my dad on their balcony with Honolulu behind them.

'They look well. I bet they're enjoying it.'

'They are. They look so happy.'

I try to imagine my mum's reaction to being a granny again.

'Let's get this one.' Gen heads for the tills with me trailing behind her. Though, of course, it's me who pays for it, and I use my *Boots Advantage* app to collect the points.

We're soon back at Gen's; there's just us in the house. Thank God. There are two tests in the box. Gen tells me that you probably only need the second one if you get a false negative the first time. When I ask what she means she explains how people often do tests when they are just two weeks pregnant.

'I don't think you'll get a false negative,' she says, smiling. 'If it's negative at this stage it's probably true. Here.' She thrusts a stick at me. 'Go pee on it.'

'Urgh.'

I feel like a naughty child as I lock myself in her downstairs loo.

Minutes later we're sitting side-by-side on Gen's sofa and staring at the stick. I can feel my heart beating in my chest, and my head, and my throat.

'I don't need to do another test, do I?'

'No. There's no mistaking that. You're pregnant.'

We both sit in silence to let the shock sink in.

I wish I could remember exactly when it happened. It was New Year's Eve. It wasn't the first time. Everything after that is a blur.

I wish I could remember Zippy's face properly. All I know is that his real name is Oliver and he was going back to Australia to visit his sick dad.

'Coffee?' Gen stands up.

'Please.'

She's back quickly and places the cups on the table in front of us.

'What do I do now?'

'Take some time to think about what you want to do.'

'You think I should keep it.' I know she does. She's a mother herself, she's often said I would make a great mum. But I don't think she meant for it to happen like this.

'I think you need to decide what you want to do. Keep it, or not. But, whatever you decide I will be there for you.

I want to cry. Not just because I'm in this bizarre situation but Gen will be going against her own principles to support me if I decide to get rid of it.

I look at Gen and force a smile. She picks up her coffee cup and takes a sip and that's when I notice silent tears running down her cheeks.

Eight

February slides into March and I oscillate between continuing my pregnancy or not, between pretending none of this is real and accepting my fate.

I receive messages from my parents; they've done Australia, now it's on to Manila, then Hong Kong and Singapore. I wonder what my mum's reaction will be if I decide to keep the baby. I imagine telling her; there are two versions playing out in my mind, horror or delight, but both come with shock.

I'm still in shock myself. I don't know what to do.

No one knows about the baby except Gen. She hasn't even told Ralph. She says she doesn't want him looking at me and judging me even if he doesn't mean to. Ralph is quite old school, he believes in marriage and children, in that order.

I haven't seen a doctor; I haven't had it officially confirmed. I *have* used the second test; the result is the same.

Gen warns me of the timescale. We think I'm nine weeks now. If I do want a termination I shouldn't leave it much longer, it may take a week or two to arrange.

It's so hard. I've never imagined my life with a child. I've never imagined myself pregnant. I've certainly never imagined myself as a single parent. I like my life as it is. I like my job. I'm happy as I am.

Except for CeCe and Yan, they're really getting on my nerves. Their relationship is getting more and more intense. I am the interloper in *their* home now. Here we go again. I hate this. If the past is anything to go by they'll soon be asking me to swap rooms. When that fails, which of course it will, then they will start making noises about moving out. They will see this as an ultimatum, a threat.

Eventually they will leave and I will have to go through the hunt for new tenants again.

How could I possibly do all this with a baby? Can I continue to live here with a baby? How will I pay the rent? I can take a year off, but there's no generous maternity pay where I work, no six months on full pay. It's statutory only and that means six weeks at 90% and eighteen weeks of maternity benefit. Could I survive on that until I went back to work? Then I'd need childcare. How much is childcare? Where is childcare? How does that work?

'Hi Charlie.' Bastard Bryan Smith plonks his backside on the corner of my desk. I resist the urge to poke a pen in his squashy buttock.

'Hi Bryan. What can I do for you?' Other than burst you with my ballpoint.

'Just wondered how your…' he looks around to ensure no one can hear, then drops his voice, 'appraisals are going.' He grins, showing all his teeth, like a smiling tiger just before it bites.

'Fine thanks. I passed them up to Merv for approval last week.'

'Ah. Good. Merv's off sick this week.'

'Yes. I know. I hope he's better soon.' The rumour is that Merv, my manager, is skiving. That's hardly news; Merv does a lot of that. To be honest I don't care, it keeps him out of my way and allows me to run my team as I please. Merv's been my manager for years and we have an unspoken agreement; he leaves me alone and I don't take any problems to him. It also means that Merv keeps away from my staff, which given his reputation – he's known as *Merv the Perv*, not that I've ever witnessed or experienced it – is just as well. Apparently, he likes the young, pretty ones. Or so I've been told. That says a lot about me; neither young nor pretty. A part of me wishes he would try it on because then I'd stamp all over him, report him to HR and never let it drop until justice was done. But, as I've never experienced or witnessed it, it's just rumour to me.

Gen and I have discussed it several times over the years.

'Surely someone has complained to HR?' I couldn't believe no one had.

'No, I've checked. There is no record of any complaints,' she'd said, sighing. 'He's a cunning little git.'

Merv the Perv or not, he's off sick now and Bryan Smith hasn't removed his lardy-arse from my desk.

'Do you think I could have a look through them?' Another smile. As though I have a choice.

'If you really need to.' I don't smile. I'm aware that I don't officially know about the quota. 'But Merv usually likes to go through them himself.'

'Merv's off sick,' he says, heaving himself off my desk. 'Can you email them to me today, please?' It isn't a request.

'Sure.' I don't smile, I don't look up, at least not until he is walking away. Even from the back he is a smug bastard.

Bev, his PA rings me later. 'Can you pop round to the office when you get a minute?' There's a fake smile on the end of the phone. When you get a minute means now.

Obediently, I trot round.

He tells me to shut his office door, beckons me into a seat. He's the spider; I'm the fly.

'Would you say your team is exceptional?' It's a trick question, I know it is.

'They're very good.'

'But not exceptional?'

'What do you mean?'

He flicks through the pages on his desk, just the corners. No doubt Bev has dutifully printed and sorted them for him, for *my Bryan*.

'What I mean is that you have marked everyone as good except for one, who, if memory serves me correctly, is still training.'

'Yes. Well, there's isn't a very good category now, is there? Otherwise I would have put them in that.'

'So, you do think your team is exceptional? Compared to other teams, I mean.'

'I don't know how other teams perform because I'm not privy to that information, but I know my team is very good. I know that because I've been working here for years and I've seen good, bad and awful. So, in answer to your question, I think they probably are exceptional, that is, exceptionally good.'

He looks at me with his gimlet eyes and I look away. I glance down at the photo of his wife and children. Picture perfect smiles.

'Mmm. Then we have a problem.'

'A problem? Surely an exceptional team isn't a problem.'

'Well,' he strokes his chin with his thumb and forefinger. It makes me focus on his face; he's trying to grow a beard, I can see the stubble, ginger and grey. 'It's all about ratios. We need comparisons. We can't have a team full of *goods*, can we?'

'Why not, if they are?'

'Where is the contrast?'

'Other teams?' I offer.

'It doesn't work like that. Some in the other teams are good. Not everyone can be good.'

I sit and stare at him. I suppress a tiny smile that could so easily be a sneer.

'Are you talking about quotas? Is that what you mean?'

'Not a word I would use.' He glares at me, attempting to stare me out. He wants me to say something, I don't know what. 'Thirty percent,' he says when I don't reply.

'Thirty percent what?'

'Only thirty percent can be good, everyone else will have to be below that.'

'But that means that seventy percent won't get pay rises. That means that those who had good last time have underperformed and that's not true.'

'Standards.' He looks elated as though the word has just popped into his head. 'You'll have to tell them that standards have risen.'

'I don't tell them anything, Merv does that.'

'Merv's off sick.'

'He'll do the appraisals when he comes back.'

'Merv's off on long term sick.'

'Oh. Is he okay?'

'He'll be fine, I'm sure.' Bryan's voice is carefully flat. 'But in the meantime, you will have to do the appraisal interviews. I suggest you go through your appraisal forms carefully and sort out the goods from the averages.'

'But I'm not a manager.'

'Maybe it's time to step up, Charlie. Maybe it's time for *your* standards to rise. Maybe, who knows, if Merv doesn't come back, you could apply. You've been a team leader a long time.' He smiles and stands up; the meeting is over. Ended with a veiled threat, or is it a promise? If I don't do this I'm a failure, I'll get no pay rise myself; if I do I *might* be promoted.

I let Bastard Bryan's door clunk shut behind me and now I'm in Bev's domain. She looks up; she's shredding documents, her favourite pastime. She loves to shred because it makes her feel powerful, as though only she is privy to company secrets and they must be protected. I watch a pile of magazines and brochures stacked on a chair quiver as though they are ready to topple.

'Having a clear-out, Bev?' I ask as I move past her desk.

'Yes, well. You know how things accumulate.'

I glide past her magazine pile, it starts to slide. We both grab at it to catch it before the magazines fall to the floor. I'm left with an *Ann Summers* catalogue in my hand, a black-rubber clad lovely smiling up at me. I glance at Bev, she blushes.

'It's not mine,' she says, a little too quickly. 'It's …' A silent B forms on her lips before she clamps them shut.

I smile and place the catalogue carefully on top of the pile.

'He's such a bastard,' Gen says when I tell her

about the appraisals at lunch the next day.

'I know. I feel as though I don't have any choice. I got the impression if I didn't do it then I wouldn't get a good appraisal either. I need every penny now, if I am keeping this baby.'

'Are you? Really?' Gen's face lights up.

'I think so. I don't know how I'm going to manage financially…' I leave the sentence unfinished. I'm as surprised by my announcement as Gen is.

'That's such good news. I'll help all I can. And there are benefits, I'm sure you'll be entitled to something until you get back to work. A baby won't be allowed to starve.'

'I hope you're right.' I'm not convinced.

'You're definitely keeping it?' She wants reassurance now.

I think for a moment, I wait for the doubt to creep in. It doesn't.

'Yes,' I say, decisively.

Gen jumps up and hugs me. The smile on her face is so wide it must be making her jaw ache.

'You are so doing the right thing. You won't regret it. It'll change your life. For the better,' she adds.

'Yes. Okay. Let's change the subject now.' I don't want to dwell on it too much just yet, least of all in public. 'I have a more immediate problem to deal with.'

'Yes. The bastard.' Gen sits back down and bites into her panini.

'I have an idea. A solution. Maybe.' I tell Gen all about it and when I've finished she sits back and stares at me, her eyes wide open in wonder.

'That's really brilliant. I don't know if Bastard will buy it, but it's worth a try.'

'I'm seeing him later. I managed to force Bev into giving me half an hour with him. Sometimes she behaves like his mother, protecting him from all the nasty employees.'

'She doesn't want to be his mother, she wants to be his lover,' Gen says nastily. We snigger together. Mean, I know.

'Oh, I almost forgot,' I start, then tell Gen about the *Ann Summers* catalogue.

'Sounds like it's Bastard's,' Gen spits. 'I think that's enough to convict him of dildo buying.'

I laugh then cringe. 'Yuk. Anyway, I don't think it would stand up in a court of law.'

'It stands up in the court of rumours and that's good enough for me.'

'Don't go repeating it.'

Gen laughs.

'No. Don't.'

'I'll try not to. Can't promise.'

Ten minutes before my appointment with Bastard Bryan and Bev rings to change the time. I have to wait until five pm.

I'm there early but he keeps me waiting, it's nearly quarter past by the time Bev ushers me into his office.

'Sorry about that, tricky call.' He nods towards the telephone on his desk.

'Right.' I nod back. I don't care about his tricky call.

I open my notebook and lay it out before me. Bryan leans over in an attempt to see what I have written, but it's just keywords, nothing to give away what I want to say.

'The floor's all yours,' he says unnecessarily.

Patronising arse.

'What is the pay rise likely to be?'

He raises his eyebrows. 'Come straight to the point, Charlie.'

'Percentage wise, I mean.' I ignore his snide comment.

'Three, but only for those attaining good in their appraisal.' He says it as though I am stupid, as though I could have forgotten our previous conversation.

'Well, I've been through my team again and again and I can't, in all good conscience, say that any are not good.'

'Then we have a problem. We...'

Before he can carry on I jump in. 'I may have a solution.'

He opens his hands, a gesture I assume means he's willing to listen.

'This is all about money, isn't it? There is only so much in the pot. I assume.'

'We're a business; everything is about money, Charlie. The bottom line.' He smirks the smile of the smug. Condescending arse.

'What about we just lower the percentage rise and give it to everyone who deserves it. That would be everyone in my team. I've worked out the figures, based on three percent.' I shuffle through my papers until I find the right one, because I have worked this through on everything from one percent to ten. I push the paper towards him. 'That would be fairer.' I wait for his answer as he scans the sheet of paper. 'And less divisive,' I add.

'Mmm.' He pushes the paper to one side.

'Well. Maybe. Can you write that up as a proposal and email it to me this evening? By seven, if possible.

I'm going out later.'

He's throwing out a challenge now. What I've given him is very detailed; it *is* the proposal. But he's playing the power game.

'Um. Yes. Of course.' I stand up. I'll send him exactly what I've just given him.

'Make sure it's on the right form, Charlie. The one we use to prove business cases.' He smiles. Cunning bastard.

I message Gen as soon as I get back to my desk. I have no idea what form he means but I wasn't going to admit that to him. Gen's on her way home but promises to send it to me when she gets home and logs back into her work email.

I'm still at my desk at half-past-six and working on the proposal, I've transferred all my figures into the correct boxes on the official form. I send a copy to Gen and hope that she has time to check it for me. If not, I'll just have to chance it.

I wait and I wait. I go through my figures again and again. Numbers are floating across my eyes and my stomach is rumbling.

Gen's email pops up. She's corrected a few figures. I accept her changes and send the proposal to Bastard Bryan Smith.

I've done all I can for now. I just hope it's enough.

On my way home, I pop into our Tesco Metro and buy one of their finest ready meals – Spag Bol. I should make this myself really. Especially now that I'm growing a baby; I need to ensure only good stuff goes in. But I don't have the patience tonight.

Ping. I get another message from Mum. She's asking me if I will be at their place over Easter, they're due back just before.

I reply that yes, I will be there for Easter. I'll have some news for them too, but I don't put that in my message.

I wait all day for Bastard Bryan's response. Realistically, I didn't expect an immediate reply. The call comes at five pm, just as I'm leaving.

'Bryan says can you spare some time now?' Bev's irritating voice sounds especially whiney over the phone.

'Okay.' What choice do I have?

'Charlie,' he says, smiling. 'Thanks for coming.' He waves at the chair meaning for me sit down.

'I've looked over your proposal. Well done. Well done.' He's patronising me again. 'I can see you've worked hard on these figures.'

I nod.

'I can also see the logic in it. Yes. I can.'

This isn't going well. I can tell from his tone that he's going to say no.

'I've given it a lot of thought. A lot of thought.'

Here it comes.

'But I'm afraid it won't work.' He smiles a *there, that's done, magnanimous of me* smile.

'Why?' I hear my voice ask before I've really considered whether it is wise to argue. 'The figures work, don't they?'

He smiles again, his mouth a straight line with a tiny curve on the left side. A forced smile.

'The figures work. Yes. For your team.'

'I'm only suggesting it for my team.'

'No. It doesn't work like that. If we do it for your team we'll have to do it for the other teams. And then it gets complicated.'

'I don't see how that is complicated.' I'm digging my own grave here. I can tell from the look on his face that he doesn't like me questioning his decision.

'Cause and effect, Charlie.' He stands up, waiting for me to do the same. 'But well done for taking the initiative. When Merv's jobs comes up you should definitely apply. In fact, I'll support your application.'

'Merv's leaving?'

'Left.' He shrugs. 'Taken early retirement.'

'Very early. He's only fifty, isn't he?'

'What can I say? Not for repeating, which I'm sure you understand, but Merv was a little handy, with his hands, so to speak.' He laughs at his own pun.

'He's not the first. I doubt he'll be the last.' It's a throwaway remark I instantly regret. I can't look at Bastard Bryan in case he thinks I'm referring to his pathetic attempt to fondle my leg under the table at the Christmas party.

He takes a deep breath. He's taking control of the conversation again.

'Well, not for discussion outside here. And I'm sorry we couldn't entertain your idea, but it wouldn't work. Cause and effect. You understand.'

I head for the door, my hand on the handle. I glance through the porthole onto Bev's empty desk, everything put away, filed or shredded.

I turn back to face Bastard Bryan, he's standing behind his desk, his arms hanging loosely in front of him.

'I do understand cause and effect.' I force a little smile. I wonder where my bravery is coming from. Is it the little person inside me? 'I understand it very well,' I continue. 'The office Secret Santa Christmas present killed my brother's dog?'

I watch Bryan's face, he looks down. I think I see his cheeks colour.

'Yes, my brother's dog got hold of my Secret Santa present and ate it.' Not strictly true, of course, but near enough. 'And because it had batteries in it he died a horrible death. On Christmas Day. The children were hysterical.' I open the office door. 'So, I do understand cause and effect and if I find out who gave me that vile present so will they.' I smile and walk away.

A week later Bryan stands up in front of a staff meeting and explains how times are hard, how money and resources are limited, how belts must be tightened. He's delighted that so many staff have been appraised as good. He says it's an honour to work with such a dedicated workforce. Then he announces the new pay rise. It is met with subdued relief; rumours have circulated that pay rises were not being given to everyone. I've been told I can say nothing about my idea. The rumours have not emanated from me. Bryan declares himself the hero of the hour.

He has also reiterated his support for my application for Merv's job when it comes up.

I feel as though I have sold my soul to the devil.

I go alone to my doctor's appointment. After that everything happens efficiently; a scan is booked, a due date agreed.

Gen comes with me to the scan and we stare at the grainy black and white blob as it wriggles around. I leave with photos. I give Gen one. She's delighted. I'll let Mum choose the ones she wants.

Happy Easter. Hope it goes well. I'm sure they'll be delighted. I get Gen's message when I'm on the train to Swindon. It's Thursday, the day before Good Friday, and the train is bursting with people and bags. I'm lucky; I have a seat.

I take a taxi to Aston Bassett and let myself in without knocking. I walk past Dad in the lounge, the door is open, he's sleeping in front of *Emmerdale*. He hates Emmerdale.

Mum is ironing in the kitchen. After we've exchanged greetings she moans about holiday washing before switching the iron off and putting the board down.

'We've got so many photos; your Dad has done a slide show. I think you'll be subjected to it later, on the TV.'

'Sounds like you had a great time. I've enjoyed reading your messages and I got six postcards.'

Mum frowns. 'We sent seven. That other one had better turn up.'

'I'm sure it will.' I don't really want to talk about the vagaries of foreign postal systems.

'Have you heard, your brother's got a new dog?' Reading my reluctance, Mum has changed the subject. 'Honestly, I don't know why; they found Herman a tie. A German Shepherd puppy. It'll be enormous like Herman was. Fritz, he's called. Fritz. Honestly. Fortunately, they're not bringing him with them, although Marlene says he's house trained.'

I nod my sympathy and smile. Then I take a deep breath and smile again. It's now or never. I remind myself that this is good news.

'I've got something to tell you, Mum. And Dad.'

'Your dad's asleep. Tell me.' She stops. 'You

haven't brought a boyfriend with you, have you?' She looks pleased, very pleased.

'No. No boyfriend.' I shake my head.

'Oh. Well?'

Another deep breath. 'The thing is, Mum, I'm having a baby.'

Nine

'They were shocked, then elated,' I tell Gen. It's Easter Monday and I'm sitting on Gen's sofa telling her all about my weekend. 'And to make it even better the trains were all running and I didn't have to sit on a skanky coach coming home like I did at Christmas.'

'I can imagine your mum being very pleased. I bet she's got the knitting needles out already.'

'She has. She has. We wandered round to the high street on Saturday and bought some wool. She really is excited.'

'I bet she'd given up on *you* ever being a mum.'

'I think she had.'

Mum had been delighted but also a bit concerned that there was no father on the scene. I hadn't told her the full story, not the part about me getting stuck in Zippy's head or how he disappeared after a night of drunken sex. I'd like her to think better of me, especially now.

'Of course, she wanted to know who the father is and when they would meet him.'

'Oh dear. What did you tell her?'

'A version of the truth. Said our relationship was short and he'd gone to Oz and wouldn't be coming back.'

'I don't suppose that went down well.'

'No. She called him all sorts, but I just kept quiet.' I roll my eyes and Gen laughs.

'But she's okay with the baby?'

'Oh yes. More than okay. In the end she sort of talked herself round and decided it would be better without a father to interfere. I don't know what that says about my dad. My brother was pleased too. But it was Marlene's reaction that was the best.'

'Really?'

'Yes, she goes all Germanic when she's stressed, like when Herman died, or shocked, as she was when she found out.'

'Oh. My. Gott. Charlie.' Marlene's eyes turned saucer like in my direction and her mouth dropped open before she composed herself. 'Is this right? Is it real?'

'Oh yes.' I couldn't help smiling, a part of me knew that she had allotted us both roles years ago, hers was *supermum* and mine was *ladette-girl*. She based my role entirely on my antics, which I often related to her, when I first went to London. It's been a long time since I've been that reckless.

Actually, on reflection the last time was New Year's Eve, I suppose.

'I hope it's easier for you than for me.' Her voice had gone up at the end. 'But, of course, I have your brother by my side.' She made a little sad face but decided to say nothing more.

'Anyway, once Marlene got used to the idea of not being the only mother in our generation of the family she was happy for me. And the kids are excited that they're going to have a cousin.'

'I'm so glad it went well. When are you going to go public?'

'Not yet. I want to wait and see how this Merv

thing pans out at work.'

'He's definitely gone.' Gen raises her eyebrows. 'Not that you heard it from me.'

'Not that you heard it from your friend in HR.'

'No. Definitely not.'

'I heard that he finally got caught. That someone complained and it was investigated and it stuck.'

'Yes.' Gen sighs. 'That's what I heard too, though not from the horse's mouth.' She nods knowingly. 'Apparently, he took the honourable way out and the person who complained is happy with that.'

'Who was it?'

'No idea. But it's not before time, apparently, though I never had any problems with him, did you?'

'No. Never.'

'Thank God, I thought I was the odd one out.' Gen laughs and I join in.

'What a sorry pair we are, thinking we're too old and ugly to be perved after.'

Gen's drinking wine and takes a sip, I'm on blackcurrant squash. Ralph has taken their youngest to the cinema and the other two are out with their friends, which according to Gen is a euphemism for playing computer games until their eyes pop.

'At least they're doing it in someone else's house today,' she says. 'Last time it was here I had six smelly, hormonal, teenage boys cluttering up the place while their giant trainers stunk out the hall. I had to feed them too. Six extra-large pizzas went nowhere.'

I nod in sympathy and Gen nudges me.

'This is what you've got to look forward to.'

'I might have a girl.'

'You might. Girls are the best. I would have liked another girl. It would have evened up the numbers in this house.' She gets up and goes to the kitchen, bringing back a large plastic jug she keeps in the fridge full of ready-made blackcurrant squash. She says she has to do that otherwise they make it too strong and go through a month's supply in a week.

I'm wondering what I've let myself in for.

'Do you want me to come with you for your twenty-week scan? You can find out the sex then.' Gen's voice rises with excitement.

'Yes. Please. Although, my mum was making noises about coming up to go with me.'

'Okay, well keep me in reserve if she can't make it.'

'Or you could both come.'

'We could?'

'My mum was asking how I would manage with work and a baby, when I'd be going back, how I'd pay the rent when I wasn't working. I felt quite depressed by the time she'd finished.'

'You'll manage. You're resourceful. And, we can explore what you're entitled to. I'm sure after all the years you've worked you must get something.' Gen leans over and pats my knee. 'We'll find out.'

'Good, because Mum wants me to go and live with them.'

'What?'

'Yes, she suggested that I move into the granny annex. It's self-contained and I can redecorate to my taste, or rather Dad will do it to my taste.' I shudder at the thought. 'Living with my parents again at my age. God forbid.'

'Lots do,' Gen says wistfully. 'Look at Phil at work; he had to move back to his parents after his marriage broke up. He's not the only one either.'

'No. Well, my marriage hasn't broken up and I'm

not moving into my parents' bloody granny annex.'

'It's a good fallback to have.'

'No, it isn't.'

The weeks pass and the day of my twenty-week scan looms. Mum has declared that she will travel up to London and she doesn't mind Gen joining us.

As we watch the little person inside me wriggle around we have a clear view of its face, its jaw, its tiny little head.

'Everything seems to be as it should.' There's a brief, polite smile from the scanner woman.

'Are you sure?' I ask, suddenly alarmed.

'Quite sure. I do this every day. Baby is the right size for your date. 1st October, isn't it.' She smiles. 'And there's the heart.'

We see a tiny black thing beating away like fury.

I don't know why she has to be so sour faced about it.

'Can you see what sex it is?' As I ask, I wonder if I even care. Boy or girl, I'm already in love with this baby. I have felt it moving and kicking around inside me for weeks now and I'm excited and enthralled and ashamed that I even, albeit briefly, considered getting rid of it.

'That's not the purpose of the scan,' the woman says.

'I know,' I say, realising that it hadn't occurred to me that this wasn't the purpose. 'But, can you see.'

She sighs, flicks the probe around my belly and speaks. 'Boy, I think. Not guaranteed. Obviously.' She switches the screen off and hands me some paper towel to wipe the gel away.

'She was having a bad day,' Gen says once we're

outside.

'Maybe she's had to give someone bad news. Be grateful it wasn't you, Charlie.' Mum always has to take the other person's side.

'She was a grumpy cow, Mum.'

'And that,' Mum says, laughing. 'Let me see those pictures again.'

We pour over the scan pictures, picking out the arms, the legs, the spine. There's a real, live, little person growing inside me. It's quite incredible.

'Still no sign of the father?' Mum knows how to put a dampener on a good occasion.

'I told you, he's not involved. At all. I've got no way of contacting him.'

Mum gives me a cockeyed look.

'Shall we go and have something in the café here before you get your train home,' Gen offers, trying to keep the peace.

Mum looks at her watch before agreeing. If I'm honest I'm glad she decided not to stay overnight even though I offered. She made excuses about feeding the cats – which Dad could easily have done – but the truth is she can't stand staying in London. All sirens, flashing lights and stale odours, she says.

Gen and I escort her to Paddington on the Tube then head back on the Bakerloo Line for home. My home. It's four pm, so not worth going back to work even though technically I probably should, but Gen is fine as she's taken the afternoon off as holiday.

We flop onto the sofa in the living room.

'This place doesn't change.' Gen smiles fondly as she looks around the room. 'How many times have we danced on this rug?'

'Too many.'

'You should get it cleaned before little man in there starts to crawl.'

'Crawl. Give me a chance; he hasn't even popped out yet.'

'Popped out. I hope it's that easy. Have you done your birth plan yet?'

'No, I haven't and don't you start. All I want is quick and easy and pain free.'

'That's all anyone wants.' Gen gives a brittle laugh, then forces brightness. 'You'll be fine. You're tall. That makes it easier.'

I don't know whether that is true or not but I'm taking it and believing it. Gen had a tough time with all hers and had caesareans every time, the first one an emergency.

'You kept going back for more,' I say, more to reassure myself than anything.

'That's true.' Gen is pensive for moment. 'You know what you said to your mum about not getting in touch with the father?'

'Yeah?'

'You could contact him. If you wanted to, I mean.'

'How?'

'Via that fancy dress shop.'

'What?'

'You said they'd been texting him when he didn't return the Zippy costume on time. They must have his number. You could ask them.'

I'm dumbfounded and can't say anything for a minute or more. It's Gen who breaks the silence.

'I'm not saying you should, or anything. Just, you know, if you wanted to.'

'Yes. No. I don't know. He never replied to them; they might have the wrong number. It's a UK phone, he probably doesn't even have it with him in Oz.'

Gen shrugs. 'You won't know unless you try. It's up to you. Obviously. Not for me to say.'

'But you have an opinion. You think I should.'

'No. It's not for me to say. I mean that. Just that you could try. If you wanted to. I'll say no more.'

After Gen has gone home and while I'm making myself something nice and tasty to eat, I give her suggestion some serious thought.

Do I want to contact Zippy? Do I want him to know I'm having his baby? Do I want to share *my* baby?

Thanks to Gen I have a disturbed night's sleep and wake up in a foul mood. I suppose I always knew that if I really wanted to I could contact Zippy. Even if getting hold of him via the costume hire shop wasn't possible, there's always Facebook, or even Twitter. I could even go next door and ask if they knew how to contact him, after all, he stayed there over New Year. I could contact him, if I really wanted to.

The truth is, and Gen is now forcing me to face it, I don't want him to know. I don't want a father for my baby. My baby. Our one-night stand was exactly that. It didn't come with any consequences, least of all for him. I've made my choice, I'm keeping my baby. He didn't have a say in that.

I'm going to tell Gen to keep quiet and keep her nose out. We can't all be Gen and Ralph.

At twenty-two weeks I have to come clean at work. People are starting to notice and there have been a few less than subtle comments about me putting on weight.

There is, also, no sign of Merv's job being advertised. In fact, the official announcement of his leaving only came this week, dripped out via email and with very little detail.

'I hear congratulations are in order.' Bryan Smith smarms in my ear when there are just the two of us in the lift.

'Thank you.'

'Who's the lucky man?'

'I'm not getting married,' I snap, a bit too quickly.

'I meant who's the lucky father?'

'No one you know.' I can't be bothered with sucking up to Bryan. Now he knows I'm pregnant, there's no way he'll support my application for Merv's job – if it ever comes up.

'When's it due?'

'Beginning of October.' I really don't want to tell him anything, but what can I say?

'Do you plan to come back afterwards?'

'Oh yes. I'll be back as soon as I can.' Now I am sucking up to him, just in case there is a chance of Merv's job.

'Cool,' he says, stepping out of the lift and almost jogging along to his office, his fat arse wobbling in his trousers.

More weeks pass and there is still no sign of Merv's job being advertised. As my bump increases I see my chances of promotion diminishing.

Every day I seem to grow bigger. Mum has already told me what big babies me and my brother were yet she didn't have a caesarean with either of us. She too, had trotted out Gen's adage about being tall and it being easier. I hope she's right.

I almost miss the email from Anand; it comes on a day when I receive an extra amount of junk email. I spot it just before I press the delete button.

It's the usual chatty start that he always gives; hope all is well, blah, blah, blah. I skip that part in my search for the point to his email, because he rarely contacts me between his annual visits and the latest one took place in November. During that visit we renegotiated – argued about – the rent and discussed any issues, not that we had any. So, I'm a bit alarmed when he says that he and Shilpa plan to make a visit in two weeks' time, late afternoon. He says – and this alarms me more – that I don't need to be there. Shilpa has never visited before, not since she moved out seventeen years ago.

Oh my God, I hope they are not planning on selling. I live with the constant fear that they will sell my home from under me to an owner-occupier and leave me homeless, or, and I suspect this would be just as bad, find me a new landlord.

I check the date of their proposed visit and see that it coincides with the date for my next antenatal appointment. In fact, with a bit of luck I should be back home in time to see them.

When the day arrives, I take the whole day off work, as holiday, even though I'm entitled to time off for maternity appointments. My appointment is 2.15pm and I fancy a lie-in in the morning. Anand and Shilpa are due around 3.30pm. In the end I don't stay in bed but spend so much time washing my hair and painting my nails that I'm running late. I'm on my way there when I realise that in my haste to leave I haven't locked my bedroom door. I just hope I'm back before Anand and Shilpa arrive because I don't want them poking about in my bedroom while I'm out.

I need not have worried about being late because, as per usual, there's the inevitable delay in the doctor's surgery. Finally, I see the midwife and am delighted when she pronounces that everything is progressing well and I'm the right size for my dates. I listen with a smile on my face as she runs the probe over my bump so I can hear the baby's heartbeat.

'Is the baby big? Only I was and so was my brother.'

She smiles a smile that suggests this is a common question.

'It's really hard to tell. A good size. The main thing to focus on is that everything is as it should be. Have you done your birth plan yet?'

'I'm working on it,' I lie.

Ten minutes later I'm in the back of a taxi hoping that I get back in time to see Anand and Shilpa. I've decided that I might as well tell them about the baby today. I'm six-and-a-half months and they'll need to know sooner or later. It makes no difference to them, but I owe them the courtesy. They'll probably guess anyway when they see the size of me.

Anand is just letting himself in as I approach my front door.

'Hey,' he says. 'How are you? You didn't need to be here.'

'Oh, I was going to be in anyway, half day,' I lie and follow this with a laugh which sounds false.

Anand bounds up the stairs in front of me and waits as I drag myself up behind him. I see him cast his eyes over me but he doesn't say anything, I don't think he suspects I'm pregnant, he probably just thinks I've put on a lot of weight. I've noticed how my face is puffed up a bit too, and my shoulders, so I could just be a fatso.

We go into the kitchen and, as is usual on his visits, I offer him coffee.

'I won't,' he says. 'We had a long, late lunch.' He rubs his slim line stomach and smiles.

'I thought Shilpa was coming with you.'

'She is. She's just popped into that Baglatari next door.' He rolls his eyes in a mock gesture of irritation. 'She saw some briefcase thing in the window. I don't know how much that will cost me.'

I smile and make myself a camomile tea, having already had my one-cup-of-coffee-a-day quota.

'You won't be wanting a biscuit either,' I laugh as I help myself to a chocolate digestive.

'No, thanks.' As he speaks to my back I can almost feel his disapproval and his silent suggestion that I shouldn't have one either. I hope his disapproval goes when I tell them the news, although now he's here, and Shilpa is due imminently, I'm getting nervous about it.

There's a loud knock on the door and Anand bounds off to let his wife in.

Ten

When Gen and I lived here with Anand and Shilpa it was fun and we were all good friends. After they moved out, despite Anand's annual visits, I've never seen Shilpa since. I'm astonished when she walks into the kitchen and greets me like the old friend I once was.

'Charlie. So good, so good. You've hardly changed.' She puts her hands up to my shoulders and air kisses me on both sides. That's weird and so unlike the Shilpa I knew.

'Older and fatter,' I joke.

'Yes. Tell me about it.' She pats her tiny, flat stomach.

Shilpa isn't any older and, despite having four children, definitely not fatter. She's miniscule, smaller than before. The last seventeen years have been very kind to Shilpa's face and figure. Anand and Shilpa are both the same age and, at three or four years older than me, that means they must be about forty-three.

Shilpa used to wear clothes she'd made herself out of her mum's old saris – she'd had a stint as a fashion student before deciding it wasn't for her – coupled with *Dr Martens* boots which she covered in hand painted flowers. The *Dr Martens* were so good that people used to ask her to paint theirs.

The Shilpa that stands before me screams extreme maintenance; loose raven-black curls fall onto her shoulders. Unlike Anand who has a few grey hairs around his temples, Shilpa has not one strand. She's dressed in a cream, designer silk shirt over elegant jeans and wearing cream stilettos which allow her dainty, painted toenails to peep through. Her face is an advert for every beauty technique and technical-facial going – she looks amazing, no lines, wrinkles or spots and she's beautifully made up too. I lean forward to get a closer look and I'm sure her dark, arched eyebrows are micro-bladed. She's swinging a Baglatari carrier bag which Anand pokes at.

'That does not look like a briefcase,' he jokes.

She pulls the carrier open and we all peer inside. It looks like a satchel to me.

'It is.' She tuts at Anand then addresses her next comment to me. 'Men, eh?'

'Yeah,' I say, mentally guessing that the satchel-briefcase probably cost at least a thousand pounds.

I once spotted a purse in the Baglatari's window and thought it would make a lovely Christmas present for my mum. I went inside and looked at it but when I asked the price the assistant replied, with a sneer, that it was a bargain at just one-hundred-and-ninety pounds. I made some excuse about it not being quite what I was looking for and left. Despite living next door to Baglatari's I've never been in since, even when they have a sale.

Shilpa looks around the kitchen, taking in the detail, her eyes flicking back and forth.

'It's just the same as I remember,' she says with a laugh.

'We had a new washing machine a few years ago. And the dishwasher wasn't here when you were.' I'm feeling rather defensive of my home even if they do own it.

'Oh yes.' Shilpa smiles.

I feel the need to get to the point of their visit and put myself out of my agony.

'So,' I start, 'what brings you here? You're not planning on selling, are you?' I let the alarm I'm feeling sound in my voice.

'Oh no,' Shilpa answers. 'Don't worry. Quite the opposite.'

'Oh. Okay.' I'm not sure exactly what that means but I don't have to wait long to find out.

'Ahem.' Anand clears his throat before he speaks; that doesn't bode well. 'Shilpa's going to be taking over managing our properties now.'

'Properties?' I echo, making it a question.

'We have four at the moment, but we're looking to expand the business. Now the kids are all at school I want to get back to work. I think property management plays to my strengths. We all know how me and offices don't really fit.' She laughs and I join in. I remember Shilpa's short-lived office career; she came to work with me and Gen. I had got her the application form and we had both given her a reference. She sailed through the interview but was a disaster in the office; she didn't seem to understand that her job was to sit at her desk and work. She didn't even make it through the six-week training period; she lasted less than two weeks before she was asked to leave. She laughed it off but it was embarrassing, especially for me, I hadn't been there long myself.

'Does that mean you'll be dealing direct with the tenants?' Given that I'm having a baby it might be good to let someone else have the hassle.

'What CeCe and Yan?' she asks.

'Yeah.' I don't like how she uses their names. I didn't think Anand even knew their names. She's obviously studied the paperwork well. 'Loo still through here?' Shilpa asks before stomping out of the kitchen and heading towards the bathroom. 'That has definitely seen better days,' she says on her return.

'Has it? I don't know. I never go in there.'

'No. Don't blame you. Shall we go up?'

Anand leads the way up to our living room, followed by Shilpa. I trail in their wake, my nose three inches from Shilpa's miniscule backside.

'This is cool. It's just the look I love.' Shilpa runs her hands over the Yan's plank table. 'This will look fantastic in the kitchen. So will this,' she adds, stroking my painted sideboard.

'They won't fit,' I say, trying not to add *idiot* to my statement of the obvious. Shilpa has just stood in the kitchen and seen exactly what it's like; she'd declared that it hadn't changed yet seems to have missed that it's too small for this table and sideboard.

She gives me a bland smile by way of an answer and I experience a horrible feeling in the pit of my stomach.

'This carpet is so shabby, isn't it?'

'Mmm,' I agree. I have imagined my little boy playing with his cars on that shabby carpet, though in my imagination it didn't look as worn as it does now that Shilpa has pointed it out. Maybe it would look better after a clean as Gen suggested.

'The windows are just great, aren't they? On both sides of this massive room, I mean.' She marches over to the windows on the street side and peers out.

'Double aspect,' I say, sounding like an estate

agent.

Shilpa smiles at me and Anand before heading out through the door and up the stairs to the bedrooms. She flings open the door to CeCe's room and stands in the square metre of floor that isn't covered by furniture. Then she does the same in Yan's room while Anand and I stand on the landing.

'Ah,' she says, seeing my bedroom door. 'May I?'

I shrug. I think she will anyway. She does and I follow her in.

'Wow. This is a lovely, big room. I'd forgotten quite how big.' She spins around then marches into the bathroom, and I follow. She scrutinises the room, and I see it through her eyes, the cream bathroom suite, the floral tiles, my matching cream towels with their floral edging. I'd chosen them to co-ordinate with the bathroom and always thought they looked retro and country. Now, seeing the whole bathroom through Shilpa's eyes it looks dated and naff.

Shilpa smiles and nudges me back into my bedroom.

'You've got this quite nice.'

I nod. 'New bed, new curtains, redecorated and new carpet. All my own work and at my own expense.' I hope she isn't going to increase my rent because I've made my own room nice.

A horrible thought suddenly occurs to me. Maybe CeCe and Yan have already been in contact with her and she's going to make me give them my big room.

'Harshad couldn't get in here, it was locked. But it'll work just great.'

'What will?' Here it comes, the demand to give my room to the lovers. Duplicitous little toads, they might have said something to me first. I tense myself and get ready for the fight. 'Who's Harshad?'

Shilpa ignores my questions but carries on talking.

'We're going to put a door from the landing through to the bathroom. There's plenty of room out there. That means the other two rooms can use the bathroom, which is going to be refitted, of course. Power shower and all that. It's just not acceptable in this day and age to expect people to go down two flights of stairs in the middle of the night.'

'What about my en-suite?'

'Don't worry,' she titters, 'I have that covered. We'll take an extra bit out here and give you a luxury en-suite shower room just for you.' She points to the exact corner I had envisioned putting the baby. You don't need a room this big, just for you.' She titters again and I want to slap her face.

'That's going to be messy.'

'We'll cover everything with dust sheets.' She says before marching back downstairs to the living room while Anand and I scurry along behind her. It's no wonder she's so slim, she moves with super speed.

'Who's Harshad?' I reiterate my question.

'Our architect.'

'Oh.'

'We're going to split this room to create another double en-suite room, and still keep a good size living room. Then knock the kitchen and bathroom together to create a dining-kitchen. That's what people want now, don't they?'

'Do they? I don't.'

Shilpa smiles, then tosses her head back. 'You'll love it. Trust me.' She lays her hand on my arm and I flinch but it doesn't deter her; she's on a roll. 'Then we'll do a complete refit, new kitchen, new bathrooms as I've already said, hardwood flooring, white paint job throughout, new furniture, except for that table and sideboard which are exactly the look we're going for. All clean and fresh and modern. Shabby chic meets techno geek, we'll get the TV mounted and install a good sound system. And a new front door, that one is a disgrace. Then we'll get you some nice new flatmates, young professionals, lawyers, bankers and the like.' She gives herself a congratulatory smile.

'Oh. Right.' I imagine the mess, the chaos, the disruption. I imagine the finished product; I remember the glossy white tiled hall floor next door, the folded bike statuette sitting elegantly in the corner.

'Don't worry. I know what you're thinking. The mess, eh?'

'Yes, a bit.'

'We'll put you in hotel for a month, somewhere handy for work. You still working in Holborn?'

'Yes.'

'What, same place I worked at?'

I nod. You hardly worked there, Shilpa.

'Really. Wow, you are super loyal. Has it got any better? I remember how awful it was.' She laughs again and I *really* want to slap her. 'Anyway, we'll pay for you to stay in the Travel Lodge at High Holborn for a month.'

'The Travel Lodge?' I try to keep the disgust from my voice.

'Or somewhere else. You choose.' Finally, Anand has found some space to speak.

'That Travel Lodge is near her work,' Shilpa snaps. 'And it's better value.'

Charming. She's spending a fortune refurbishing this place and she doesn't want to spend any more than she has to on accommodation for me.

'Yan and CeCe are fine with it?'

'Are they? So they know all about these plans? Already. Before me.'

'Ah, yes, well…' Anand stumbles over his words. 'They contacted us immediately after we sent the email. They wanted to know what was going on?'

I didn't even know they had been sent an email. It seems I've already been removed from my role as house-mother.

'They also want the new double room we're creating. They're super excited about it.' Shilpa grins.

'Good for them? When were you going to tell me all about this?'

Shilpa frowns at me. 'We just did.'

'Yes, but you said I didn't need to be here.'

'I was going to ring you,' Anand says, sounding decidedly unconvincing. 'Tonight.'

I sigh. I have no choice but to accept my fate or move out.

'When does this all start?'

'Don't worry, you've got a while. We're planning it for the end of September, beginning of October. Exact date to be confirmed when we've sorted out the builder.'

'Perfect,' I say, fighting back the tears that are stinging the back of my eyes and catching in my throat.

After they leave I climb into my bed and cry. This wasn't how it was supposed to be. The baby, my baby boy, starts to fidget inside me and I lay my hand over my bump, stroking and soothing him while frantically trying to work out how I am going to cope with all this.

I didn't tell Anand and Shilpa about my baby, somehow, I don't think a newborn baby fits into the new order with my proposed new flatmates: the young professionals. And it obviously didn't occur to either of them that I wasn't just fat, but pregnant.

'Don't worry,' I say patting my bump, 'I'll find us somewhere better, just the two of us.' The baby kicks against my hand.

I really don't know who the hell I am kidding.

I'm not very happy with Yan and CeCe either; how long have they known about this wonderful plan. At least, I should be grateful that they didn't tell Shilpa and Anand I was pregnant. I suppose.

'How did your antenatal appointment go?' Gen bounces up to me as I enter the office; she always asks, she's almost living every moment with me. I'm bleary eyed from crying and lack of sleep. 'Is everything okay. There's nothing wrong is there?'

I feel the tears form in my eyes and drip down my cheeks. What a clown I am; I'm blaming the hormones.

'Come on.' Gen ushers me into a meeting room and helps me into a chair. 'What's wrong? Tell me.'

'It's just awful,' I say, between sobs.

She grips my hand and squeezes.

'What did the midwife say? They're not always right.'

I shake my head.

'Is it really bad? They can work miracles now, they can.'

'It's not the baby,' I manage to say.

'Thank God.' A look of relief comes over her face. 'So, what is it?'

'It's the flat. Shilpa is taking over and modernising it.'

'Oh.'

I fill Gen in on the whole story, she sighs and rolls her eyes in all the right places.

'And CeCe and Yan knew about it all before me. They've known for over a week but, according to Yan, Anand told them not to tell me. How's that for loyalty. All these years count for nothing. Shilpa is a right bitch now.'

'What did she say about the baby?'

'Nothing. She doesn't know. Yet. I don't think it's going to go down well. She'll probably evict me or put my rent up so high I can't afford to stay. I'll have to find somewhere else.' I start crying again and Gen digs around in her suit pockets until she finds me a clean tissue.

There's a knock on the door and Bev, Bastard Bryan's PA, sticks her head around the door.

'Sorry, Gen. Meeting is starting now.'

'I'll be along in a minute.'

'No. Now. You're needed now.' She runs her eyes over me with a look of disgust on her face.

Gen stands up and Bev closes the door with a slight slam. I hate Bev, she's as smug and arrogant as Bastard Bryan.

'Sorry, I'll have to go.' Gen sighs.

'Sounds serious.'

Gen shakes her head, purses her lips, pats me on the shoulder and leaves.

I don't see Gen all day, she doesn't reply to emails and her phone goes straight to voicemail. In the end I check her diary; the whole day is blocked out and marked private.

She's still in the meeting when I leave.

I've been home an hour when my phone pings. A message from Gen.
Need to see you tonight. Can I pop round now?
Me: *Sure. Everything okay?*
Gen: *Will explain when I see you.*
I have that sinking feeling again.

I make Gen a coffee when she arrives and we head upstairs to the living room. CeCe and Yan aren't home from work yet but I think, after I called them sneaky last night when I confronted them, that they might be keeping out of my way.

Gen and I sit down on the sofa. Gen looks tired, exhausted actually. She sips her coffee and stares into the distance.

'Okay?' I ask, feeling like she must have done this morning.

She offers me a weak smile, takes a breath and speaks.

'There's no easy way to put this,' she begins. 'They're moving the business to India.'

'Oh.' I hadn't expected that. Given how much hassle Gen has had from Bastard Bryan Smith, I'd assumed she'd had some row with him about appraisals or bonuses again, suddenly that seems so trivial by comparison. Now I know why they haven't advertised Merv's job. No promotion for me, then.

'I suppose we always knew it would come to this. There have been rumours for years.' She takes a large gulp of her coffee.

'Yeah. I suppose. But we never believed it, did we? When?'

'The date's yet to be finalised but probably October or November.'

'I'll be on maternity leave then.'

'I know.'

'What will happen to everyone?'

'We'll be made redundant.'

'Including Bastard Bryan, I hope.'

Gen lets out a bitter little laugh and shakes her head. 'You must be joking; he will come out of this smelling of roses. Bastard.'

'What?'

'Not only, as I sort of suspected, was it his job to oversee such a move, it was actually his idea. He was the driver. If not for him everything would have carried on as before.'

'Bastard.' My baby boy kicks me as if he agrees. I pat my bump to soothe him.

'Yes, he's done similar in other parts of the group. Apparently, it's his speciality, he's the company expert. Once we're all cleared out, like rubbish, he'll just move onto another company in the group.' She shakes her head.

'Bastard,' I repeat, because I really can't think of anything else to say.

'Yes, it's all right for him. You should have seen the smug, arrogant bastard telling us all about it. And that damn Bev sat next to him making notes and smiling the whole time. They were a proper double act, but then they've had plenty of practice.'

'Why did it take all day?'

Gen looks at me and offers a weak smile. 'Because we were arguing.'

'Sounds like that was pointless. You couldn't save us.'

'You're right, closure and moving to India was a foregone conclusion from the day he arrived. No, before he arrived, whenever it was that he hatched his evil plan.'

I find myself snorting when Gen says evil plan.

'We weren't arguing about that, we were arguing about you.'

'Me? What, just me?'

'Yes.'

'Why?'

'Because you're special.'

I snort again. 'Certainly am, pregnant by Zippy, single, possibly soon to be homeless and now jobless. I am definitely special.'

'Did you know that you are longest serving member of staff?'

I think for moment. 'I hadn't thought about it before, but I suppose I am, except for you.'

'Yes, but I've had breaks, as have others, but your service has been continuous.'

'I still don't see why you were arguing about me.'

Gen sighs. She rubs her left temple with her forefinger. 'What I'm about to tell you is confidential. You cannot, and I mean cannot, tell anyone else. They'll know where it has come from and I'll get the sack.'

I laugh. 'How can they sack you, we're all getting the boot anyway.'

'No, I'm serious. They'll sack me on the spot, no redundancy, nothing.'

'Okay. I won't tell anyone. Whatever it is.'

'Right. First, no one is being told about the move

to India until just a month before it happens. They don't want a mass exodus; they want the work to continue as usual; we're committed to our current contracts.'

'Right.'

'Secondly, they are only paying staff on your level and below the basic minimum.'

'Charming. What about your level and above?'

'We're all getting an enhanced package.'

'No disrespect to you Gen, but how unfair. Some of them have only there a year.'

'I know. I agree with you.'

I nod. I don't know whether I'm waiting to hear good news or bad. In my head I'm frantically working out how much money I will get. Over the years, every time there's been a new rumour about closure I've looked up the latest rules on redundancy, so I'm fairly familiar with them. Eighteen years equals eighteen weeks, plus my notice, paid in lieu. My contract is only for one month's notice although I think they'll have to pay me for a longer notice period because I've been there so long. If it's only bare minimum I'm not going to get much though, and certainly not enough to fund the deposit for a new flat and pay the rent.

'Did you know,' Gen cuts across my thoughts, 'that your team is consistently the highest performing?'

'No.' I frown. 'I mean I do know that we do well, but I don't know how it compares with other teams, other team leaders.'

'Well, you are the best. Repeatedly.'

'That's nice. Why didn't you tell me before?' A part of me is annoyed with Gen, I know she's senior management, but she is also my best friend.

'I didn't tell you because I didn't know. Today, we were given a raft of information, reams of paper. While Bastard Bryan was wittering on about business opportunities and how the company can get bigger contracts when it moves to India, and all that bullshit, I started sifting through the pages. And, there it was in black and white, a league table comparing all the teams and their leaders.'

'Oh.'

'And not just recently, it went back years. So, even if they didn't originally produce a league table, they had the data.'

'No one ever told me. I've never had so much as a pat on the back.'

'No. But your manager did.'

'Merv the Perv?'

'The very same. He got the pats and he got the bonuses.'

'The what?'

'Bonuses. In the paperwork I read today it detailed that too.'

'Don't tell me how much it was, I'll just cry.'

'I felt like crying on your behalf. I was so incensed that I could hardly pay attention to Bastard and his wittering. In fact, at one point he asked me a question and I didn't know how to answer.'

I feel sick. Merv was a creepy little pervert but he was always nice to me. Now I know why.

'Yep, he was getting bonuses off your back for years.'

I retch, I think I might actually be sick. Gen jumps up, pats my back then runs down to the kitchen for a glass of water.

'Sip slowly,' she says when she comes back.

I start to cry and between sobs I manage to speak. 'It's just been one bit of shit news after another these last two days. I'm beginning to think I should never have kept this baby. How will I ever get another job? I like my job. I'm good at it. Even better than I thought.'

'You are good at it. Very good. I always wondered why you didn't get promoted like I did. I never asked you but I did wonder if they'd offered you promotion and you'd turned it down.'

'No. Never.' I sob.

'No. And I know why now. Merv blocked it at every turn. He didn't want to lose his cash cow.'

I let out a wail.

'Stop crying it's not good for the baby and don't ever let me hear you say you're sorry you're keeping him.'

'I didn't mean it. I really didn't, but everything seems so helpless,' I manage between sobs before blowing my nose.

'And unfair. Hence the fight. We had forty-five minutes for lunch, it was brought into the adjoining meeting room, and there was even a glass of champagne each to celebrate. How crass and insensitive. I didn't want to be part of that. We weren't allowed to take the papers out of the room, and that includes at the end of the day. Bev collected them up and shredded them. She even had the shredder in the room. For God's sake.'

'Yes, Bev loves her shredder.'

Gen reaches for her coffee, which must be cold by now, and takes a sip.

'So, I stayed in there through lunch so I could go through the papers and extract the details and check that what I thought I was reading was correct. And it was.'

I nod, I'm not sure what she's going to tell me, I just hope it's good news.

'To cut a long story short I argued and fought your case. I brought up the Merv bonus situation, and several of those duplicitous bastards looked ashamed, so they obviously knew. The good news is that you're going to get the same package as the senior management. And you bloody well deserve it.'

Gen tells me the deal, it's equivalent to a year's salary.

'Oh.'

'But you have to leave at the end of this month and they won't pay you maternity pay.'

'Bastards.'

'Yes. I agree. I tried to fight that one too but there was no way they would concede. I've worked it out and you're much better off taking the deal, much better off. As you know they only pay the bare minimum for maternity. And, I think you'll still be able to get maternity benefit, because that's based on your national insurance contributions.'

I sit for while trying to take in everything Gen has told me.

'Bastard Bryan is having the papers drawn up first thing tomorrow and he will call you in to tell you in the afternoon.'

'Does he know you're telling me all this?'

'No, he doesn't. Which is why you can't tell anyone else, and you have to act shocked.'

'Huh, I am shocked.'

'We all are.'

I look at Gen, see how sad she is, how drawn her

face is, how tired she looks.

'I appreciate you fighting for me.' I lean towards her and give her a hug. She's losing her job too, a job she loves as much as I do.

'What are friends for?' She gives me a little half laugh. 'I wanted to tell you because I thought it would be better coming from me. I thought you should know the truth. But, please, don't let slip that I told you.'

'I won't.'

'I thought if it didn't come as a shock tomorrow, then you wouldn't have to cry in front of that bastard.'

'Yes. You're right.' I'm feeling a bit numb now. 'But why do I have to leave so soon.'

Gen shrugs and looks away.

'Gen?'

'I feel it might be spite. I think Bastard Bryan has never quite forgiven you for refusing his advances at the Christmas party. But, of course, that's only what I feel, there's no evidence. He's way too clever for that.'

'Bastard,' I hiss.

'Yep. No doubt about that. Psych yourself up. When you meet with him give him hell. Remember that he's the architect of all our sorry futures. But don't let on you already know.'

Eleven

At work I sit and seethe all morning. I've hardly slept for going through the situation over and over in my head. I can say nothing to anyone about the impending doom, not even Gen, or at least, not in the office or anywhere where we could be overheard. I have to sit here and pretend everything is normal and I have to wait for my call to see Bastard Bryan Smith.

If anyone speaks to me I am smiley and bubbly, which is not necessarily my normal demeanour. I've painted on a happy face, covering the dark circles under my eyes with makeup and wearing lashings of waterproof mascara, even though I am determined that I will not cry in front of Bastard Bryan.

'Hey Charlie, what do you want to do for your leaving do?' one of my team shouts over at me during a lull in incoming calls.

I blink. Do they already know? Before it's even settled? Before I've been officially told. Of course not.

'Yeah, we want to start planning it,' someone adds, 'but we realise it has to be appropriate, what with you being pregnant. Not much point in going out-out.'

Several of my team snigger. I force a smile in return.

'I'll have a think,' I call back. 'And I'll let you know.' Whatever it is, it will have to be soon.

The chatting ends abruptly as the incoming calls

start up again and I continue to wait to be summoned.

The call comes at 2.30pm. I see Bev's name on the caller ID display and brace myself.

'Bryan wonders if you've got time to pop along and see him,' Bev chirps when I answer after the tenth ring.

'Um, when?'

'Well, as soon as.' Bev doesn't sound so chirpy now.

'Oh, right. Only we're a bit busy here, you know, answering calls. Can it wait? What about tomorrow?' I admire my own bravado, but then there's no need to hasten my own doom.

I hear Bev sigh down the phone; she makes no attempt to hide her exasperation. 'He wants to see you now. Please come now.' She puts the phone down before I can even answer. Rude bitch.

I go to the toilet, get myself a glass of water and pick up my notebook and pen. Finally, ten minutes after Bev's phone call I saunter towards Bryan's office.

'Where have you been?' Bev hisses as I stand in front of her desk waiting for her to let me pass.

'Had to go to the loo, you know how it is when you're pregnant.'

She doesn't answer, just glares at me.

'Oh no,' I continue. 'You don't, do you? It's Bryan's wife who has his children, isn't it? Not you.' Two can be bitchy and I'm playing the super-bitch today.

'You can go in,' she says, snatching a piece of paper and heading for her shredder.

'Still shredding evidence, eh Bev?' Laughing, I walk past her desk as she glares at me.

'Charlie, how are you? Blooming, I see.' Bastard Bryan waves me into a cranky office chair and watches me sit down, he doesn't get up from his own sumptuous leather throne.

'Will this take long?' I make a show of looking at the clock on the wall. 'Only we're very busy today.'

'Don't worry about that.' He grins. I want to punch that stupid grin down his throat.

'But I do worry. I pride myself on having a high performing team, in fact I think we're probably one of the best, and I'd like to keep it that way.' I give him the briefest of smiles that really isn't a smile at all.

'That's, err, very good. Yes. Very good. Um, would you like a coffee? I can get Bev to get you one.'

'No thanks. I brought my own drink.' I nod at my glass of water sitting on his polished desk and enjoy the irritation I know he is feeling because condensation is running down the sides and pooling on the wooden surface. He keeps a clean desk, does Bryan and he doesn't like it spoiled.

'I'll get you a coaster,' he says.

'As you please.' I shrug. I'm astonished at my own boldness, but I no longer care about Bastard Bryan, his opinion or his favour and least of all his precious furniture.

He stands, shakes himself and totters out to see Bev, returning seconds later with a folded piece of paper.

'No coasters,' he says as he lifts my glass and pushes the paper under it. The paper is a folded leaflet, one that hasn't yet made it into the bin or shredder.

He clears his throat. 'I won't beat about the bush…'

'Good,' I cut in, 'because, as I've said, we're rather busy.' I can tell how irritated he is now by the furrow on his brow. I think he's nervous too; beads of sweat are forming along his hairline, glistening in the stark office light.

'Charlie,' he smiles, as if using my name is his privilege and his alone. 'No doubt you've heard numerous relocation rumours over the years.'

I shake my head; I'm not going to make this easy for him. 'No.'

'Right. Okay.' I've thrown him off script already; he has prepared his patter but I am not responding as he had planned. Nevertheless, he carries on. 'This time the rumours are true. I'm sorry.'

That's it? That's it? Oh no, I'm not playing along with this.

'Sorry, you're going to have to elaborate on that. I'm not sure what you're talking about.'

A look of barely suppressed annoyance flashes across his face.

'We're relocating the company.' There, he's said it. He sits back, relieved and smug.

'Where to? I'm looking for a move out of London what with having a baby, so…'

'No,' he cuts in. 'I'm not making myself clear. We're relocating to India.'

I blink several times, simulating shock.

'No.' I shake my head for the second time. 'That's a bit too far for me. My family are all in the UK.' I lean towards him and wait.

Now it's his turn to blink. What I'm saying does not match with the dialogue he has allotted me in his head. He stares back at me for a moment longer than he should before pulling himself back together.

'What I mean, Charlie.' He leans towards me as he says my name and I automatically reel back. 'We'll be closing down the operation here and relocating to India. Everyone will be made redundant.'

'Oh. I see. What about the Indians?'

I see his brow furrow again as his face moves into a heavy frown. 'What do you mean?'

'Our Indian employees. Some of them might want to move with the company.'

I watch him blink now, but, unlike me, he's not pretending.

'Of course,' I continue. 'I don't know their preference; you'd have to ask them. But, definitely some are only here short term and do plan to go home.' I smile at him. There you go, work that into your plan. 'It could be they don't want to go where you're relocating to. India's a big country, isn't it?' I wait expectantly for an answer.

'Um. Yes. Yes. I suppose. We're going off the point here though.' A quick smile to unnerve me.

I flash back a big smile to unnerve him and raise my eyebrows in question.

'Yes, right. The point is that everyone will be made redundant. It's not happening for a few months, but, Charlie, you, being pregnant, can leave at the end of the month.'

'Okay, thanks. I'll think about it.' I push my chair back and start to stand up.

'Please sit down.' There's no accompanying smile, no obsequious use of my name. 'You'll be made redundant at the end of the month. We've drawn up a very generous package.' He pulls a folder out of his drawer and opens it out before him. I see a large white envelope addressed to me, he puts it aside and flicks through the pages which I assume are his copy of the envelope contents.

He outlines the deal Gen has told me about, including telling no one else, and during his diatribe I say nothing. I rest back in my chair and I watch his face intently, I stare at his mouth as he forms the words and trots them out; this part of his speech is exactly on script, and well-rehearsed. When he's finished he leans back, pleased with himself.

I say nothing. I pick up my glass of water and drink, peeling off the makeshift coaster which has stuck to the bottom. He watches me as I gulp back half a glass. I put the leaflet-coaster back down and glance at it as I put my wet glass straight onto the desk with a clonk. I feel him bristle as it hits the polished wood.

'Why?' I say.

'It's about economics, we need to relocate…'

'No, not that.' I put my hand up. 'Why must I leave at the end of the month? I go on maternity leave in early September, so why must I leave now?'

'It'll be better all round.'

'Not for me.'

'It's a very generous offer.' He shuffles the pages in front of him. 'Yes, very generous.'

'Maternity pay. You haven't mentioned maternity pay.'

'No. But we're giving you a very generous payoff, much higher than your colleagues on the same grade. Much higher.' There's a brief show of teeth to emphasise the point.

'Yes. Good. Though I think I deserve it. I think

I'm the longest serving member of staff, aren't I? I'm loyal. I'm an excellent team leader.'

'Yes. Hence the offer.' He folds his arms. 'We're not prepared to pay any more on top of that. It's far more than we're obliged to pay and far more than you'd be entitled to via our maternity policy. We want to be fair; we could have let you go on maternity leave and made you redundant during it and given you the same as everyone else. We didn't want to do that to you, Charlie.'

Liar.

I fold my arms, two can play at that.

'I want more.' I take a deep breath. Oh my God, what am I saying? Have I gone too far?

'More? More?' He leans in, he's almost laughing. 'Take the offer, Charlie, and you can get out of here with a good amount of money and plenty of time to plan for your baby.' He pushes the envelope towards me.

He's right. Leaving sooner, rather than my planned date *is* actually better for me. It means I can spend those extra weeks finding somewhere new to live.

I pick up my glass and take a sip. I watch him wince again as I plonk it back down on his desk. I pick up the leaflet-coaster and unfold it, it's damp but glossy, so still intact. I spread it out on the desk and smooth it flat with my hands. I smile at him.

'I want more. You're depriving me of a few months' pay and it will be harder for me to get another job when I'm ready to go back to work. At least here I was guaranteed a job on the same grade and pay. And I think the company is probably legally bound to pay me maternity pay.'

'But we're making you a very generous offer…'

I hold up the leaflet and flap it about. Other than a suppressed look of irritation, he doesn't react, so I place it back on the desk and turn it around to face him, and then push it in his direction.

And I wait as his eyes scan the leaflet.

He doesn't move for a while, long enough for me to pick up the photo of his wife and sons.

'I'm having a boy,' I say, putting the photo down in front of him. 'Do your boys still believe in Santa?'

I see him blush; pink blotches creep along his fat neck.

I stand up. I pick up my glass and my notebook. I snatch the envelope addressed to me from his folder and tuck it under my arm.

'I'll read this, but I'm expecting a revised offer.' I head for the door but turn back to him with my hand on the handle. 'Thanks, Bryan.'

'He rang me later and offered me two months' extra pay. In the end we agreed on six months extra. And, the company is paying for my leaving party at the end of the month.' I lean back and smile to myself. 'I'll get it in writing tomorrow.'

'Oh my God, do you think Bev did that deliberately?' Gen asks. We're sitting in her lounge while Ralph whips up one of his culinary delights in the kitchen and supervises the kids' homework at the same time. He's a catch, Gen's husband. I just never realised it before.

'I don't know. She wasn't there when I left; otherwise I would have thanked her. Anyway, it was Bryan who gave me the leaflet.' I laugh. 'To save his precious desk. He should have looked at it first.'

'*Ann Summers* special offers leaflet. Two for one on

dildos. It couldn't get any better.' Gen is giggling like a kid herself. 'Handed to you just like that. The irony.' She laughs again then turns serious. 'But what would you have done if that hadn't happened?'

'I would have mentioned the leg fondle at the Christmas party. I would have accused him outright of sending me the Secret Santa dildo. I know I didn't have any proof, but that was my plan. As it was, I didn't have to say anything. Not, one thing. Guilt was written all over his fat face.'

'It's just fabulous. What a result. How do you feel about leaving earlier than you planned?'

'It's probably for the better. I need to find somewhere new to live, and I've got a bit of spare cash now too. Quite a bit.'

'Cool. I'm so glad it's worked out so well.'

'I know. And, to make it even better, if that is possible, HR are organising my party. It's going to be in the early evening in a restaurant of my choosing in Covent Garden.'

'Wow. Bastard Bryan must be very afraid.'

'He is. And he's already told me he can't come because he goes home early on Fridays to travel back to his family.'

'Shame,' Gen says, feigning sorrow.

'I know.'

'Apart from me, and your team of course, who else are you inviting?'

'Everyone. Whole company. The email will go out just as soon as I sign the paperwork.' I received the email yesterday and sent it straight to my personal email so that I could forward it to Gen's personal email address. I didn't want anyone being able to track any traffic between us. 'Have you read it yet?'

'No, but I will as soon as we've had dinner. I couldn't really read it at work, much as I wanted to. But you think it's okay?'

'I do.'

'When have you got to sign it?'

'I have an appointment tomorrow afternoon with Bastard.

'Will you say anything to Bev?'

I shrug. 'I'll see how the wind blows, how my mood takes me.'

Gen and I giggle together.

CeCe and Yan are cuddled together on the sofa in their dressing gowns when I get home. There's a smell of warm chocolate in the air. It's really rather lovely, and the aroma hangs in the air, pricking my taste buds, which given how much of Ralph's lovely meal I've just eaten, is ridiculous.

'Hi,' they both chorus.

'Hey,' I say, feeling like the spare part again. I hate this, the sooner I get another place the better. But, on the other hand I will not be made to feel like an interloper in my own home. I flop down on the armchair to prove the point.

CeCe starts to speak; I'm fascinated by CeCe's voice, so soft and sweet when she speaks English. But, I have heard her speaking Chinese on the phone to her family and her voice takes on a much lower tone, almost guttural.

'Shilpa called round.'

My heart sinks.

'What did she want?'

'She left a card for you.' CeCe points at the sideboard.

I heave myself up and retrieve it. I must be getting enormous now as I'm starting to notice how some things are an effort, especially at the end of the day.

I rip the card open and read it. Shilpa has booked a hotel for me from 1st September, she's included the booking reference. I know she's done this way ahead of time to get a cheap rate. It riles me when I think of how much she is spending on this renovation and she begrudges me a better hotel room.

'You in the Travel Lodge too?' Yan asks.

'Yes. Bloody cheek. I said I didn't want to stay there.'

'It's okay, we'll be near you. We'll look after you, Charlie.'

'Thanks, CeCe.' I try to keep the sarcasm from my voice. I don't want anyone looking after me in the Travel Lodge. I am not staying there.

'It's good that she's paying for it. And we don't have to pay rent then either.' CeCe's eyes shine brightly.

'I should think not.' I can't pretend to be happy about it.

I mentally work out how many weeks I have to find a new place to live. Ten if I start now. Eight if I wait until I finish work. I flop back down into the armchair.

'She said she's booked us in for six weeks. We might have to stay a bit longer if the work isn't finished,' Yan tells me.

'Great. I'll be having my baby in a Travel Lodge.'

'We'll look after you,' CeCe says again.

'Have either of you told Shilpa or Anand I'm pregnant?'

'No,' they chorus.

'Good, please don't.'

'Don't she know?' Yan screws up his face in disbelief. 'Didn't she see you?'

'Yes, she saw me. I don't think she guessed.'

Yan frowns, unconvinced.

I sit for a few more minutes just to make the point that this is currently my home too, and then haul myself back up again. It's only as I do that I notice the empty pot of chocolate body paint on the coffee table. Then I spot the body paint brush on the floor, resting on a brown-smeared cream towel with floral edging.

I blink several times, screwing up my eyes to ensure I'm seeing correctly.

'Is that my towel?' We all know it is.

Yan doesn't answer but CeCe looks suitably embarrassed and ashamed.

'Sorry, Charlie. I'll wash it for you.'

'That had better come off.' I stomp up to my room annoyed and disgusted. To think that I was savouring the chocolatey air when I came in. Yuk.

I sign my redundancy papers the next day in Bastard Bryan's office. I don't get a chance to check whether Bev sent the leaflet in deliberately or not as she's not there.

'Where was she?' Gen asks when I tell her.

'On holiday, apparently.'

'What, when he's not? But she always takes her holiday when *my Bryan* takes his.'

'I don't know and I don't care anymore. I have other things to worry about, like my home situation.'

'You could stay with your parents instead,' Gen offers, trying to be helpful.

'I know. I know.' I let out a great big sigh. 'Mum has sent me some paint charts in the post. Perfect timing, they arrived today, and she doesn't even know about the flat being tarted up or the Travel Lodge situation. But no, it's a real step back, isn't it, living with my parents. I'm pushing forty, for God's sake.'

'It doesn't have to be permanent, just until you have the baby.'

'No, I've got to get myself somewhere else to live. I've contacted a few agencies.'

'I'll come viewing with you.'

'Thanks Gen, I hoped you would.'

We've viewed five flats in my price range now and none of them are suitable. I originally had a list of twelve but seven of those didn't accept children so that soon whittled the list down.

I cannot tell my parents about the looming Travel Lodge situation because Mum will never give up her pleas for me to come and live in the granny annex. She's fairly insistent as it is and that's without knowing what's going on.

'You'll find somewhere great,' Gen says when she arrives to escort me to my party. 'There's the perfect place out there for you and your little one. You just haven't found it yet.'

'I think I might have to up my price range.' I blink as I apply my mascara, waterproof, of course, just in case. 'I can't really afford another two hundred a month but the agent says that should take me into a different bracket quality and suitability wise. And, I've agreed to broaden my areas; after all I don't need to live close to work, do I?'

'None of us will soon.' Gen sighs.

'I'm sorry. I know I'm not the only one in this shit.'

'You're the only one, or two,' she laughs lightly, 'who matters to you. That's all you need to think about. You'll find somewhere lovely.'

'Course I will.'

I hope Gen's right, because so far, every place I've seen has either been dirty and dingy or up a lot of stairs with nowhere to put a buggy. They've all been very small too; I'd forgotten quite how privileged I am to have lived in this lovely flat for so long.

'Maybe I could stay in the flat,' I say to Gen as we take the short walk to the restaurant in Covent Garden. We have a private room for my party and over seventy are coming.

'You could. You should consider that. You could stay with your parents when you have the baby then come back when all the building work is finished.'

'Yes,' I say, but I'm not convinced. The sitting room will be half the size and there will be two more people living here – so called young professionals. I so want a place of my own. 'I'm not going to think about it anymore tonight, it's my leaving party. Let's celebrate.'

'Yeah, bring on the champagne,' Gen shouts, a little too loudly and heads turn. 'Or the fizzy water in your case.'

'Great party,' Gen slurs several hours later. She's stuck to her word and kept on champagne.

'Yeah,' I smile. 'It is. But I think I've had enough. I'm tired.'

'No, we haven't done the pressies yet. You just stay here.' She totters away and disappears into the crowd.

I glance at my phone to check the time, it's barely ten pm. We've had a lovely meal courtesy of the company and numerous bottles of wine and champagne, then the room was cleared away for a bit of dancing. Gen wanted me to join in with her, do our old favourite like we do every year at my New Year's Eve party, but I feel too whale-like and lack the energy to bob about, so Gen has performed her one-woman show. I did warn her to be discrete – she's the one who will have to face everyone at work on Monday.

Suddenly the music stops and there's a hush around the room. A clearing is made and a table is brought into the middle of the dance floor, swiftly followed by presents wrapped in blue baby paper.

'My God, there are so many,' I hear myself say.

'Testing, testing,' Gen's voice slurs again, but this time into a microphone. Where the hell did she get that? 'Can Charlie come forward please?'

I stumble forward and stand in the middle of the room next to the table. I'm both excited and horrified. This is a bit cringe.

'As Charlie's bestest best friend and long-time colleague,' Gen begins, 'it has fallen to me to present the presents.' Gen titters while a few others, also suitably oiled by alcohol, join in. 'Charlie has been with the company for eighteen years, she's the longest continuous serving member of staff ever in the history of the company.'

A round of applause goes up and I want to crawl away. Gen, who is enjoying every minute in the limelight, beams a broad smile around the room before continuing.

'And now, both sadly and happily, Charlie is taking a much-earned break. Although, it won't be much of a break once her little baby makes an appearance.'

Everyone laughs and I smile graciously while at the same time willing Gen to just get on with it.

'Charlie was a youngster when she joined the company, as was I, and together we made many discoveries and mistakes.' She laughs at her own memories but doesn't bother sharing them, which is just as well. All I can remember from those early days is that we worked hard and we partied hard.

'Now Charlie is leaving to start her family, a day she, and many of us I might add, never thought would come.' Gen giggles again and I want to clamp my hand around her mouth. She sees it in my eyes but just grins back at me before continuing. 'So, Charlie, we, your lovely colleagues, not the nasty ones mind you, had a bit of whip round and bought you a few things to help with that little baby inside you.' More sniggering from Gen before she waves her open arms at the present table and starts the final round of applause.

I step forward and take the microphone from her before she says something she might regret and thank everyone for their good wishes and presents. Then I start to open them.

There are clothes and blankets and a bath and all sorts of things I never even knew existed. It's as I open these presents that I realise I have done very little research into just what is required to bring a baby into this world. Other than scans and antenatal appointments I haven't explored much further. I know I need a cot and have seen one online I quite like, but that's about all.

When I've finished opening all the presents and cards and thanking everyone I am both overwhelmed and exhausted. Gen, who is now slumped on a chair in the corner and slowly swigging from a bottle of water waves over at me.

'Time to go?' she calls.

I nod my reply and smile then look at the pile of presents and wonder how the hell I am going to get them all home and what I am going to do with them when I do.

'Don't worry, I've got it covered.' Gen is suddenly beside me. 'You say your goodbyes and I'll get it sorted out.

Ten minutes later I am outside the restaurant with Gen who is pushing a shopping trolley laden with my baby presents.

'Perfect, isn't it?' she says when she sees my frown.

'Where did you get it?'

'Where do you think? Your favourite shop just around the corner.

That's when I notice the M&S logo on the trolley handle.

'Oh no.'

'Don't worry,' she says. 'I'll drop it off on my way back to the Tube station once we've unpacked it.'

Twelve

'Why is there a shopping trolley blocking the hallway?' Yan asks, his tone irritable. 'We could hardly get through the front door last night.'

'Sorry about that.' I take a mouthful of cereal so I don't have to offer further explanation.

Yan stands in the kitchen watching me for a few seconds.

'Okay. Want me to take that stuff up to your room?' I wander to the top of the stairs and look down on the pile.

'That would be great, but don't feel you have to. I can manage.'

But Yan has already run down the stairs and is lifting the heavy items up as though they weigh nothing and grasping them in his immense arms. By the time I've finished my breakfast the trolley is empty.

'I'll take the trolley back,' CeCe says in her sing-song voice.

'It's M&S,' I tell her, waiting for her to shriek.

'No problem.' She waits while Yan lifts the trolley over the threshold with no effort at all – unlike Gen and I last night – and they leave together.

Back in the kitchen I lean across the window and watch them going up the street, tiny CeCe pushing the trolley, giant Yan's arm around her. From the back they could be pushing a baby in a buggy. For one silly moment I find myself tearing up. I sniff, shake myself and start tidying the kitchen.

Hey hun, what was I on last night? Gen's message pings through at noon.

I start to type *a lot of champagne*, then wipe it off and write, *lol xx* instead.

I can't even remember getting home. Are you okay?

Lol, I write although I'm really pissed off with Gen.

On our journey home she had climbed on top of a builder's skip and shouted out that she was queen of the world. After I had coaxed her down she sang *My Heart Will Go On* at the top of her voice all the way home while I pushed the laden trolley. I really don't know where *The Titanic* film fits with me having a baby.

When we got to my place we were like the *Chuckle Brothers* getting the trolley through the door. *To me, to you*, over and over, it was the sideboard all over again. We were too exhausted to take my presents upstairs, that's why the trolley was dumped in the hallway. Gen never made it back to the Tube station, she fell asleep at the kitchen table while I was making her a sobering coffee. I had to ring Ralph to get some help. In the end I put her in a taxi and he dealt with her at the other end.

Ralph's hardly speaking to me and the kids have been super noisy all morning.

I send a sad face emoji back.

Hope I didn't spoil your party.

You're okay, I message back. She hadn't spoiled my party, fortunately we left before she could, but she was a pain in the arse afterwards.

Still on for flat viewing this afternoon?
Absolutely, xx.
Meet me here at two pm.
She sends back a thumbs-up emoji.

We're seeing two flats this afternoon. I don't hold out much hope for either because they are in my original price bracket.

The first one lives down to my expectations; it's up two flights of rickety stairs with nowhere in the hall to leave a buggy. It's been described as a one bed flat but the reality is somewhat different. It's a large room that has been split in two to form a bedroom and a living room, but there's no door between them, just a wide gap.

'It's a bit of a bedsit,' I say to the agent.

'No, it's got a separate kitchen.' She waves her arm at the kitchen which is, indeed, separate and a reasonable size but it only contains a sink, one unit, a battered old fridge and two-ring cooker sitting on the worktop. 'You could easily get a table in here.'

We go through to the bathroom which is old and cold. 'Original Victorian bath,' she says.

'Original Victorian lime scale,' Gen counters, turning away. 'Grim,' she mouths at me.

The next flat doesn't look any better from the outside; it's in a purpose-built block, all slabs of grey concrete and primary colour panels. Gen and I exchange looks of horror.

'Ex-local authority,' the agent beams at us, suggesting this is a selling point. 'Private landlord now.'

We go through the communal door and head for the lift.

'Better than expected,' Gen whispers to me as we stand in the tiled hallway waiting. The walls are clean and painted cream, the tiles are shiny and clean. The lift doors open quietly in front of us.

'Only eight flats in the block. Six are privately owned.' The agent beams at us as we ascend to the fourth floor. 'Only two flats per floor.'

The landing at the top is light and airy, the floor covered in a good quality brown corded carpet.

'Are there stairs?' Gen asks. 'For when the lift breaks down?'

'Of course, though I'm assured it never does.'

I imagine dragging a buggy up three flights of stairs on my own.

'You could always leave it in the entrance hallway,' Gen says, reading my mind.

'Then lug a crying baby up the stairs.'

'It's three flights of stairs up to your bedroom where you are now.'

'But I can leave the buggy in the hall.' Is that true? The shopping trolley had made opening the front door difficult. Would Yan, CeCe and the young professionals tolerate that indefinitely?

Gen shrugs. 'Let's see what it's like.'

The agent opens the door to the flat and we step inside. There's a tidy bathroom off the left-hand side of a small, neat hallway, and a large bedroom off the right. The door immediately in front of us leads to a long and spacious room which the agent informs us is a lounge-diner, off which is a small kitchen.

'This is more like it.' Gen marches through the rooms alone then hauls me around after her. I have to admit I could see myself living here but the stairs put me off. What if the lift did break down? 'Look at this.'

Gen is standing at the window and pointing out the large green and leafy space below. 'A park. Perfect.'

'It's miles from Covent Garden,' I hear myself say even though I know it's irrelevant.

'Yeah, it is. But look, there's a kiddies' play park down there.'

I look down to see swings and slides and know that she is right and this is what I should be wanting now.

'School and preschool just over there,' the agent joins in, pointing out the attractions. 'Big new supermarket just a short walk away.'

'Perfect,' says Gen. 'What's the deposit and rent. How soon could Charlie move in?'

Before I know what is happening Gen has all the information and is making another appointment to look through the papers and legalities.

'You'll need to make a quick decision,' the agent pressures. 'I've got three more viewings on Monday evening.'

Gen comes back to my place when we've finished the viewing and we flop down on the sofa with drinks. Coffee for Gen, orange juice for me.

'My head's in a whirl.'

'It's just perfect for you and the baby. Nice area, nice flat.'

'I suppose. And it is in my original price bracket.'

'Even better.'

'Yeah, that's a bonus. It's just so far from…'

'From what?'

'From here, I suppose.'

'Yes, it is. But you'll have to get used to that because your whole life is going to be far away from here, far away from everything it's been so far.'

'Yeah. I know, you're right.' I yawn as I finish speaking and Gen takes this as her cue to leave.

'I'll see you on Monday, at the agent's office.

'Thanks Gen, for coming with me today and Monday, and for talking sense.'

'My pleasure.' She laughs. 'I had to get out of Ralph's way anyway, he wasn't very happy with me and my hangover. And, I've got a *doctor's appointment* on Monday.' She gives me a complicit smirk.

I spend the rest of my weekend sorting out my baby presents; there are so many. I make a neat stack in the corner and imagine these things in my new flat. Gen is right; I do need to leave my old life behind. I chose to have this baby so I need to make him my priority. This is the part I never thought seriously about. Despite being very obviously pregnant and feeling his kicks daily, I really hadn't thought very much about the reality of life with a baby. Or, a child.

A wistful little part of me wonders if I should try to contact Zippy. I remember his kind face, his wavy hair, his taut, toned body, his soft Australian accent. A little voice in my head tells me he has a right to know he is going to be a father. What was it he said? In other circumstances he'd have asked me out on a date.

I wonder how that would have panned out?

I meet Gen at the agent's office and we sit down to go through the paperwork. Within an hour I have signed the lease and parted with a lot of pounds in deposit and first month's rent.

'I need to get organised if I am moving in a week.' I feel excited and enthusiastic; I'm starting to come to terms with the fact that my life will be changing no matter what. My new flat is a much more suitable environment for bringing home a baby.

Now the deal is done I ring my parents and give them the good news. Mum puts the phone on speaker so that they can both shout into it.

'Oh, that means you definitely won't be living with us?'

'That's right, Mum.'

There's silence for a moment or two then Dad, who worries about logistics more than Mum, asks if I have chosen a removals company yet. I know what he's thinking; he's worrying that it will be him humping stuff across London on one-way streets he's unfamiliar with.

'Don't worry, Dad. I've got it organised. Anyway, I haven't got much furniture to move.'

I hear Dad sigh his relief before offering to come up and decorate if needs be once I've moved in. There's a conspicuous silence from Mum and I can almost hear my dad nudging her to speak.

'Oh yes,' she says, 'just let us know when.' She doesn't sound very enthusiastic.

I've hired a *man-with-a-van* for a day and he's given me a good price. He has also agreed to dismantle my bed and reassemble it. Although I don't have much I actually have more than I realised. And, I am definitely taking my sideboard with me.

I send Shilpa and Anand an email asking them to pop round at their convenience. I feel I owe them my notice face-to-face. I'm moving at the end of the month, that gives me a day or so overlap which means I can come back and make sure my room is clean.

I pay my rent via direct debit at the beginning of every month, so I cancel next month's. I've never actually paid a deposit to Shilpa and Anand, so there won't be any arguing about that, either. The way I see it, Shilpa is a winner in this, she can cancel my Travel Lodge room and relet my bedroom for more than I pay.

Ten minutes after the email is sent, Shilpa replies to say that they are in the area and will pop round in the afternoon.

I start to pack up my belongings, the *man-with-the-van* has left me some strong boxes and tape. I start with the clothes that no longer fit me. As I hold them up I wonder if they ever will again. Perhaps I can use them to stuff the Moroccan pouffe which I've found languishing in the bottom of my wardrobe. It'll be perfect in my new place.

Shilpa arrives alone and uses her key to come into the flat without knocking. I am knee deep in clothes – I'm using the opportunity to have a good clear out – when she appears in the doorway.

'Whoa,' I shout. 'I didn't know you were here.'

She frowns at me then pastes on a professional smile.

'If this is about the Travel Lodge, okay, you can stay somewhere else.'

'It's not, although I did tell you I didn't want to stay there.' I start scrabbling around picking up my clothes, mostly underwear at this stage and stuffing them into bags. I don't need Shilpa scrutinising my big knickers.

'We're not going to increase the rent too much,' she says sighing. 'I'm sure you can afford it, you've got a good job. And look what you'll be getting, a state of the art, modern, fantastic place. Not shabby like it is now.'

'I wasn't expecting any kind of rent increase,' I snap.

'Well, okay, we'll defer yours. Six months until you have to pay the new rate. How's that?' She folds her arms across her chest as I begin to think about getting up off the floor.

'Too late, really. Look, Shilpa, I've decided to move out.'

'What? Why? You love it here.'

I haul myself up and stand tall, next to Shilpa I feel like a giantess.

'Oh no. When did that happen?' She points at my obvious bump.

'Thanks for the congratulations.'

'Oh sure. Yes, of course. Congrats, darling.' She steps forward and attempts a couple of air kisses. Then she steps back and surveys me. 'Probably just as well,' she says. 'Babies won't really fit in with what I have in mind. I know what babies are like. Messy.' She laughs. 'And noisy.'

'Good, then we're all happy.'

'Where are you going?'

I tell her about my new flat, the park, the handy preschool, but as I'm speaking I watch her eyes glaze over so I stop speaking mid-sentence and she doesn't even notice.

'Cool,' she says, realising I'm no longer talking.

'Yes, so I'll be moving out next week. End of the month.'

'Oh.' That's surprised her. 'Okay. That's not much notice.'

'I've stopped my direct debit, so that works out

well with the rent.'

'Oh. Okay,' she repeats when it clearly isn't okay at all. 'We'll try to give you the balance of your deposit as soon as we can.'

'What do you mean?'

'Well, you know, after we've inspected and stuff. And probably had the curtains and carpet cleaned.' She glances around my bedroom.

'I'm taking the curtains with me and the carpet is mine too, although I'm not taking that, obviously. You can have it, with my compliments. The gas, electric, water, council tax and internet are all paid up to the end of the month too. But I'll be cancelling all those direct debits once I leave as well.'

'Oh but…' she starts but doesn't know what else to say.

'Don't worry, I'll send you all the details so you can pick all those up yourself.'

She stares at me for a moment or two. 'Okay, well we'll take any balance out of your deposit.'

'Not really,' I smile. If I'm honest I'm enjoying this because ever since Shilpa stomped around my home and condemned it as old fashioned and in need of updating, I've not felt much love for her. 'You don't hold any deposit from me.'

'We must do.'

'No. You don't. And there won't be any balance, I told you, it's all paid to the end of the month.'

Shilpa's mouth gets tighter and tighter as her eyes flit around the room. 'Those wardrobes are ours,' she says.

'Yes, they are. But the bed is mine, and the chaise and various other bits and pieces. Oh, and the sideboard in the living room.'

'You can't take that. It fits in with my new scheme.'

'I can, because it's mine.'

'But it's been here forever. It was here when me and Anand lived here.'

'Yes, but it's still mine. I got it from a skip, I painted it up. It's mine. And I'm taking it.'

'Okay.' Her tone does not match her agreeable word. 'Well if that's all, I'll be off.'

'Okay. Bye.' I turn back to my room clearing. She let herself in so she can see herself out.

'Probably just as well.' She smiles before delivering her parting shot. 'We'd have had to ask you to leave anyway.' Another smile, then she turns tail and trots down two flights of stairs, slamming the front door behind her.

At least we're in agreement.

The phone call comes the afternoon before I'm due to move. I've been living with cardboard boxes and bin bags all week and I can't wait to move into my new place.

'Hello.'

'Oh, hi Charlie.' It's the letting agent and I don't like the way she has just said my name. Maybe I'm paranoid but her silence following my name makes me more so.

'Everything okay?' I cross my fingers.

'Um, no. We've run into a bit of a problem.'

'Don't tell me they won't accept children now, we went through all that at the start.'

'No. No. It's not that. Look, I'm going to get straight to the point. You can't move there.'

'What tomorrow?' I'm running scenarios through

my mind, furniture in storage; bunk up with Gen for a few nights. It's doable.

'Not ever. It would appear that the landlord isn't the landlord at all. The flat is owned by a housing authority, he was a tenant and he was planning to sublet. It's a scam and he's been caught.'

I sit on the end of the phone in silence letting the horrible truth sink in.

'Are you all right, Charlie?' And, when I don't answer. 'Are you still there?'

'Yes,' I offer. I'm dumbfounded.

'Don't worry about the money, fortunately we found out before it was transferred to him, so you'll get that back. I'm really sorry. We'll keep looking and find you somewhere just as good.'

'Right.'

'Okay, well I'll call you as soon as I find something suitable.' With that she says goodbye and ends the call, happy to have done her duty, glad to have got it over. I sit staring at my phone, at my room, at my boxes and bags.

I ring Gen but it's the middle of the afternoon and she's at work, probably having another tedious meeting with Bastard Bryan, so doesn't answer. I leave an urgent message.

Twenty minutes later she rings me back.

'What's wrong?'

I tell her the sorry subletting tale. Gen is silent as I speak.

'The thing is, I was really arsy with Shilpa and I think I've burnt my bridges there.' I can feel the tears coming.

'Will you get all your money back?'

'Oh yes.'

'That at least is something.'

'I was wondering, could I bunk up with you for a few nights? I could put my furniture in storage.'

Gen is silent for a moment. 'Absolutely. Yes.'

'Okay. I need to sort out the storage now. I'll talk to you later.'

I don't tell CeCe and Yan about my disaster, they won't be about when I move out so they don't need to know. Despite living together for over a year we're not best friends, just flatmates. I carry on as though everything is fine.

I feel guilty when they present me with a new home card and a little present for the baby. Yan, not for the first time, offers to help lug stuff around for my move, but I tell him I've got it covered. I don't tell him *Big Yellow Storage* will easily take the lot.

After an exhausting day I arrive outside Gen's with my wheelie-case and a pulling backache. She isn't home from work yet but her fourteen-year-old son, Tom, answers the door and lets me in.

'You're having my room,' he says, trying not to sound surly. No doubt Gen has warned him, warned them all.

'Thank you, I do appreciate it.'

'Do you think you'll be here long?'

'I hope not.'

'Yeah,' he says, picking up my wheelie-case and hefting it up the stairs as though it weighs nothing.

I follow him into a typical, teenage boy's bedroom. The single bed has been changed and the surfaces cleared; I can imagine the cleaning frenzy that went on here last night. I can also feel Tom's antipathy towards me no matter how polite he is.

'See you later,' he says, closing the door on me. Tom's the oldest so has the biggest room but even so it's half the size of my old room.

I haven't cried all day, I've been too busy, but now I cannot stop myself.

Me and my big mouth; if I hadn't been rude to Shilpa I could have stayed a bit longer. As it is, I couldn't even bring myself to ask her.

'She'd have kicked you out anyway,' Gen's says as we sit down to a coffee around their kitchen table. It's big and old and made of scrubbed pine. Everything happens around this table; meals, the kids' homework, Gen's late-night work emails, and every major discussion or decision this family makes. 'You said as soon as she realised you were pregnant she was horrified.'

'Yes, she was. But she might have been more forgiving and let me stay longer if I hadn't been so arrogant.'

'Well, you were. It's done. You are where you are. So, make the most of it.' As Gen delivers this instruction, out of the corner of my eye I see Tom roll his eyes at his brother. They're sitting on the sofa at the far end of the room playing something on their phones.

We hear the front door open and Ralph comes in with Emily, their nine-year-old daughter. Emily proceeds to tap dance all the way down the hall and into the kitchen. She's still wearing her tap shoes.

'Good lesson?' Gen asks, hugging both her daughter and her husband.

'Yes. Look. I can do this now.' Emily starts

tapping ferociously. She looks good to me but the sound of her shoes on the tiled floor is ear-piercing.

There's an audible groan from the boys' end of the room and they get up to leave.

'I used to do tap when I was your age.' I say this in support of Emily against her brothers. My brother used to mock me too. I remember all the hours Mum must have spent ferrying me to lessons and putting up with *me* dancing in the kitchen when I got back.

'Did you? Were you as good as me?'

'Probably not.'

'What size shoes do you take?'

'Seven.'

'Ooo. Same as Mummy's tap shoes.'

'You've got tap shoes?' I turn to Gen.

'Don't ask. Needless to say, I rarely wear them.'

Emily starts to tap her new steps again, really fast, galloping around the kitchen like a newly shod pony.

'That's wonderful darling, but take your shoes off now. You know what we've said about tapping in the kitchen.' Gen smiles as Emily taps out of the kitchen, along the hall and clomps up the stairs, still wearing the tap shoes.

I lean back in my chair and breathe in the smell of a lasagne cooking in the oven. I'm looking forward to it, I'm starving. What would go really well with that would be a lovely glass of chilled pinot. Oh well, I'll just have to make do with fizzy water, I probably wouldn't like the pinot anyway.

Minutes later, Emily appears in the doorway again, she's still wearing her tap shoes and she's holding another pair in front of her.

'Try these, Charlie.' She drops down onto the floor in front of me and deftly removes my flip flops before stuffing my feet into what are obviously Gen's tap shoes.

'Where did you find those?' Gen's voice comes out in a squeak.

'In your wardrobe, Mummy.'

'I've told you not to go in there, haven't I?'

'It was just this once, Mummy.'

I am finding it hard not to snigger until Emily, evidently incapable of being told off, turns her attention back to me.

'Come on, Charlie. Up you get and do your steps.'

'I don't think I can. It's been a long time.'

'Oh Charlie,' Emily whines. 'Don't be such a pooper.'

'Pooper?' I mouth at Gen over Emily's head.

'Charlie can't do tap dancing; she's heavily pregnant. She needs her rest.'

'Oh, like Mrs Baron's cat? Are you having lots of babies, Charlie?'

'No. Just one.'

'Mrs Baron's cat had six, but one of them died. It was the punt.'

'Runt,' Gen and I chorus.

'Oh yes. I always get that wrong, don't I Mummy?'

'Yes, sometimes very wrong.' Gen raises her eyebrows at me. 'Out of the mouths of babes.' I can just imagine what she means.

'Okay, Charlie, you can stay sitting down while you do the steps. You just have to copy me. Okay?'

'Okay,' I say, a little gingerly.

Five minutes later, I'm sitting on my kitchen chair, my leggings neatly pulled up to my knees by Emily and I'm giving it all I've got as instructed by her. It's only as we finish our routine that I look up to see

Tom, Harry and a group of their friends watching me from the doorway.

'Give me that phone, Aaron Collins,' Gen says, snatching an iPhone from one of the boys. She flicks through it and deletes the video the boy has just made of me then hands it back.

The boys turn as one and exit the kitchen.

'Too late, Mum, it's already on YouTube,' Tom says as they hurry out of the front door.

'It had better not be,' she calls, but he's gone. 'Ignore them,' Gen says to me. 'They're not that quick.'

'We could have a look, Mummy,' Emily says.

'No. He was joking. Take your shoes off and take mine off Charlie and go and put them all away.'

'Oooh,' Emily starts.

'Do it now.'

I let Emily remove the shoes and attempt to put my flip flops back on myself as she stomps up the stairs.

'Any more viewings lined up?'

'Two next week, Monday and Tuesday. They're in my higher price bracket so they should be better.'

But they are not. Although better in style and décor they are not suitable at all. Both top floor flats, no lifts and no decent hallway to fit a baby buggy. When the agent tells me that she has no other suitable properties in my increased price bracket, which her tone suggests is pathetic anyway, she hints that I might want to try other agents.

Back at Gen's empty house I trawl through the internet on my phone and give a few more agents a ring. By the end of the day I have six more viewings lined up.

I dutifully trot along to every one, nothing is suitable and by the end of the week I am exhausted, especially as Tom's bed is so narrow and uncomfortable. It creaks when I turn over and wakes me up then I can't get back to sleep and start churning stupid thoughts around in my head.

Not helped by my Mum's frequent messages. I've had to confess the truth about the sublet flat.

Have you found anywhere yet?

No. Still looking. I always follow this with a smiley face, even though I don't feel like smiling at all.

After two weeks and ten viewings I am starting to feel despondent. It's Saturday morning and the whole house is quiet, no doubt everyone is having a much-deserved lie-in. It's just before eight and I snuggle down to do the same, turning over, which is becoming increasingly difficult as I swear I am getting bigger every day. After several wriggles and turns I finally get myself in the right position and settle down, the bed makes its normal creaking sound and then there's silence.

Then a crunching sound.

Followed by a cracking.

Followed by a yelp, from me.

I have fallen into a hole in the middle of the bed. The mattress is being forced by my bulk down into a pit. I don't have the strength to pull myself out.

The door bursts open and Gen and Ralph's sleepy faces stare at me, blinking in confusion. Gen has her dressing gown wrapped tightly around her and her hair is dishevelled from sleep. Ralph is wearing only short pyjama bottoms and despite my distress I can't help noticing his muscular torso. Who knew that was beneath his sensible clothes? Gen, obviously.

'What's wrong?'

'I'm stuck. I'm so sorry; I think I've broken the bed.'

Gen and Ralph haul me out. Ralph yanks the mattress from the bed and we survey the damage; three shattered slats.

'I'm so sorry,' I say again.

Ralph squats down and examines the bed. He pulls several towers of Lego and small pieces of wood from beneath it.

'Little bugger,' he says, waving the wood at Gen.

'Tom,' Gen shouts, 'get in here.'

'But it's my fault. I'm so sorry,' I mumble.

Gen puts her hand on my arm, silencing me as a sleepy Tom stumbles onto the landing, followed by his smirking younger brother, Harry.

'When did this happen?'

Tom peers over at the broken bed.

'Dunno.'

'Okay, then, let's try another tack,' Ralph says, standing up. 'When did you repair it?'

Tom shrugs. I have some sympathy for him; I remember similar situations with my brother.

'Well?'

'Christmas,' Harry pipes up from behind.

'Oh really?' Ralph says. 'Tell me more.'

Gen takes my arm and leads me downstairs to the kitchen where she puts the kettle on.

'I'm sorry I spoiled your lie in.'

'We weren't asleep,' Gen quips back.

'Then I'm more sorry. And I'm so sorry to cause all this upset. If I hadn't been in the bed with my giant baby bump it probably wouldn't have happened.

And you'd be none the wiser.

'It would have come out eventually. Don't worry about it. It's what passes for normal here. Last summer Tom and Harry burnt the bottom corner of the shed door. They just wedged the wheelie bin up against it and we didn't notice for nearly two weeks. Until bin day. They'd been playing with a magnifying glass – you know, and the sun.' She laughs. 'Bless 'em, little sods.'

'Me and my brother did that, but we only burnt a patch of grass. Pocket money stopped for a week though. Fond memories.'

'Yes, this will be one of those family stories we tell.' Gen puts a cup of camomile tea in front of me.

Ralph and Tom appear in the kitchen, they're dressed. Tom is the same height as his dad and strikingly like him.

'Coffee?' Gen asks Ralph.

'Yes, thank you. Tom's on his way to the garage to find a suitable piece of wood to affect a proper repair, aren't you Tom?'

Tom, keeping his head down, nods.

'But before that he's got something to say, haven't you?'

'Sorry, Charlie.'

I want to cry. For him. For me. For all of us.

'No harm done,' I manage.

'Off you go,' Ralph says to Tom. 'And remember what I said about suitability and size.'

'Yeah. Okay.' Tom shuffles out of the kitchen door and disappears into the garden, heading for the garage.

'I'm so sorry, this is all my fault.'

'Trampoline practice apparently, on Boxing Day.'

Ralph raises an eyebrow and sips his coffee.

'You know, I vaguely remember a bit of commotion. We were watching a film. I called up and asked if everything was all right. I think.'

'I've told him he's a bit big for bouncing on a bed like a five-year-old.'

'What's going on?' Emily, suddenly appears in the kitchen door. Standing next to him she too is the double of Ralph, only a feminine version.

'Tom's bed broke.'

'Again.' She shrugs and grabs the orange juice that Gen has just poured for herself.

Despite the *effective repair*, or maybe because of it, the bed is more uncomfortable than before. At least it no longer creaks. After two almost sleepless nights I am beyond despair.

Everyone is at work or school; Gen's house is empty and I have no more viewings. Even though I've signed on with six agents now, there are no suitable flats in the areas I want and in my price bracket. I've been urged to increase it, but I cannot. I want to sit and wait for the right place, but time is running out.

My phone rings and the caller ID tells me it's Mum. She never rings.

'Is everything all right?' I ask when I answer the call.

'Oh fine. We're fine. I was just wondering how you were. Your messages sound so despondent.'

Do they? Even with the smiley face?

'Oh Mum,' I start.

Thirteen

The *man-with-the-van* picks me up from Gen's with my belongings from the storage unit already packed in the back. He picks up my wheelie-case and stows it away for me then helps me into the passenger seat.

I said my goodbyes to Gen and her family last night. It was Tom who hugged me the hardest; I think he's just so pleased to be getting his bedroom back.

I should have just gone to Mum and Dad's in the first place and saved us all the trouble and aggravation.

The *man-with-the-van's* name is Lyle. He's younger than me, has a young daughter and his wife is expecting their second.

'Not as far on as you,' Lyle says, smiling. 'Are you comfortable there?'

'I'm fine.' I am struggling with the seat belt but only because I am so tired and clumsy now. I wonder if it is like this for everyone or just me because I am older than most first time mothers.

He punches Mum and Dad's postcode into his satnav and we're off. We chat initially, exchanging life stories, not that I tell him about Zippy or how I became pregnant. I just leave that bit out and let him make his own assumptions. From the things he says, and the things he doesn't, he thinks I'm having a baby via sperm donation, just to make sure I have one before I'm too old.

Maybe he's right.

After a while he puts the music on, turns the air-con on, for which I am very grateful because the sun is now streaming in through the windscreen, and I find myself dozing off.

'Hello,' Dad says as he opens the van door to let me out. I'm barely awake and am surprised to find that we are already parked on Mum and Dad's drive.

'Hi, Dad.' I haul myself out of the van and bend backwards. My backache from sleeping on Tom's bed seems to have been alleviated by dozing in Lyle's van.

'Don't worry about your things. You go on in and have a cup of tea with Mum.'

I don't argue. I haven't got the energy.

I find Mum in the kitchen pouring tea into four mugs from her big old brown teapot. She doesn't use it for just her and Dad so relishes any opportunity to make a *good old pot*.

'Sit down, Charlie.' She gives me a quick hug before pushing me into a chair at the table. 'You looked so peaceful we didn't want to wake you.'

'I think that's it.' Dad comes into the kitchen with Lyle behind him. 'Good job, well done.'

'Would you like tuna-mayonnaise or cheese and pickle in your roll?' Mum asks Lyle.

'Tuna, please.' Lyle sits down at the table and smiles at me. I can smell soap on his hands, evidently freshly washed and the smell makes me sneeze. 'You okay?'

'Yes. I'm fine. I must have dozed off.'

'Don't worry, you didn't snore.' He laughs as Mum puts a big bread roll down in front of him and another in front of me.

I wasn't hungry until I saw that roll, now I can't

get it down fast enough. I also eat most of the crisps from the bowl Mum puts in the centre of the table.

Soon Lyle is standing up, shaking hands and getting ready to go. I start flustering around for my handbag but Lyle waves me away when I do find my purse.

'Your dad has already paid me, and tipped me generously,' he says, heading for the door. He gives me a backward glance, opens his mouth to say something, thinks better of it, closes it, then opens it again.

I'm cued up now and ready for whatever he was going to say. 'Go ahead.' I give him a smile of encouragement.

'There's a video on YouTube of a woman who looks just like you, she's tap dancing sitting down. It's so funny. She's fat, rather than pregnant, but she's your double otherwise.' He laughs.

'Is she?' I smile and look down.

'Yeah. Uncanny.' He shakes his head, smiles and leaves.

'What was that about?' Dad asks.

'Nothing.' I must tell Gen, maybe she can get it taken down. 'How much do I owe you, Dad?'

'Sort it out later.' Which means he'll never mention it again, but I certainly will. I can't be sponging off my parents at my age.

After helping Mum clear up lunch I finally steel myself for my entrée into the granny annex. This is what I've been dreading ever since I let Mum convince me that it was my best option. I feel such a failure. Even more so now that I can feel tears welling up. I sniff hard in an attempt to stop them.

'You okay?' Mum asks, concern emanating from

her.

'Yes.' I feel a sob trying to escape. 'No.'

'What's wrong. Baby all right? Are you ill?'

'Mum, I've lost my job and now I'm homeless.' I wait for Mum to rush over and comfort me, but she doesn't.

'You're not homeless. I saw homeless in Manila when we were on the cruise. Homeless.' She shakes her head. 'I saw a young mother dressing her daughter for school while her toddler looked on. They all looked clean and well cared for, so that was good. But, this all took place in the park, under the trees. That was where they lived. Lots of families lived there. So, don't consider yourself homeless, you're not.'

'Right.' That's me told and now she's put it like that I can see her point. I grab a tissue and wipe my nose before eyeing the annex door which leads off the kitchen. I feel anxious. Mum catches my stare and smiles at me.

'Want me to come and help?' She looks eager so I agree.

I open the door and we step into the little kitchenette where Herman puked and shat and gasped his last. It's freshly painted in a pale cream and there's a brand-new tumble dryer next to the washing machine.

'Thought you might need it,' Mum offers. 'A baby makes a lot of washing.'

'Thank you.' I bite my tongue even though I want to remind her that this is a very temporary arrangement. I'm only here to have the baby and until I sort out a new place in London.

'And these.' She points to two new machines on

the worktop. 'This one makes milk at the right temperature and this one sterilises the bottles.'

'Wow. I didn't know these even existed.' My home situation has overshadowed my baby preparations completely and I have still done very little homework on the practicalities.

'Yes, I thought they'd be useful whenever you came to stay, you know for Christmas and stuff.' She's trying to make it sound as though she doesn't think we'll end up being here for longer than a few weeks either.

I turn to the living room. And I gasp. It's been completely transformed. Gone are the floral high-backed, winged chairs that Granny Suze favoured to be replaced with a modern corner sofa. If I were going to furnish this room it is exactly what I would have chosen. The floral wallpaper has been replaced and the walls are now a soft, cool putty colour, the new carpet is a perfect match.

'We thought it was long overdue.' Mum offers me a nervous smile.

I spin around the room and notice my sideboard against the wall. It fits right in as does my TV sitting comfortably on top of it.

'This is just amazing.' I can feel tears pricking the back of my eyes again so I furiously blink them back. I am not crying over a bit of paint and some new furniture.

We go through to the bedroom, the one I have slept in on every visit since Gran died. I have become so used to sleeping in her wide single bed with yet more floral embellishments that I'm shocked to see my own bed fully erected and made up and standing proudly in yet another redecorated and re-carpeted room. It's almost the double of my room at home – correction, my ex-home. They have even hung my curtains at the window and my chaise is lined up beneath them.

'I've hung your clothes up in the wardrobes but not unpacked your personal things,' she points to the bags and suitcases on the floor. 'Let me know if you want me to help you.'

I nod slowly. I don't know what to say.

'Come and see the bathroom.' She takes my hand and pulls me along.

I prepare myself to show how impressed I am even though I doubt it can match these two rooms, because Gran's bathroom was a big old institution-type wet room with a high toilet and pull-up handles all over the tiled walls. Apart from adding some new towels there's not much can be done to change it, there are no walls to paint a nice colour.

'Oh. My. God.' I stand in the bathroom. There's a new walk in shower, a new bath and a normal toilet, as well as a sink in a vanity unit. 'This is stunning.'

'Long overdue,' Mum says, trying to play it down. 'Been meaning to do it for a while now. In fact, we're so pleased with it we've started doing the upstairs one now. It's not quite finished, the bath is a special order and the plumber is just waiting for it to come in.' She grabs my hand again. 'Come on, one final room.

The baby's room; pale blue and perfect.

'I hope you like the wallpaper, but it you don't we can change it easily, it's just the one wall.' Mum sounds nervous.

I turn and see tiny trains and cars and planes travelling across a soft blue sky complete with clouds made of fluff, and rainbows. I can't stop the tears now.

'It's. Just. Perfect,' I manage between tears. 'Thank you.'

Mum is cuddling and hugging me now and telling me that the cot and the changing unit should arrive later this week.

'I suppose we'll need a crib to start with,' she says. 'We could go and choose it together. Unless you've already got one sorted.'

I shake my head. 'I haven't,' I sob. 'I'm useless.'

'Not to worry.'

She leaves me alone to unpack and to luxuriate in all this space just for me. And my baby. It's so perfect.

If only it were in London and not a granny annex.

A week later and the nursery furniture has arrived and been assembled, including a swinging crib which is by the side of my bed. I'm registered at Mum and Dad's doctors' surgery, had a midwife appointment and am due a health visitor visit. I've slept better than I have for months and I've let Mum persuade me to attend some antenatal classes held locally that she's found on the internet. She's insisting on coming with me and we attend the first one this evening. We're joining halfway through, having missed the beginning.

It's the start of September and we're having a late summer heat wave. The roses are blooming and their heady scent fills Mum and Dad's garden. I'm sitting under a parasol messaging Gen, who's at work.

You'll enjoy it. I did,' she messages, referring to the antenatal classes.

Yes, but you had Ralph. I've got Mum.

Others took their mums. Especially after the first one when a couple of the husbands dipped out. Lol.

Why?

You'll see. She follows this with several laughing emojis.

Oh no.

It's a good way to meet other new mums at the same stage as you. Really useful network afterwards too.

Network. I don't like the sound of that. I hadn't thought of myself being in a network of mums, never. Network has always meant work to me, proper work. I change the subject before Gen says something that I might use as a good reason not to attend the class tonight.

How's work? Got a date yet?

Big staff meeting next week. Rumours are rife. I've not been privy to any info. Bastard Bryan is a super controlling arse. Message you later.

I put my phone down as the tinkling of ice against glass heralds Mum's return from the kitchen. She puts the tray down on the table and hands me a fizzy water. I put the straw to my mouth and suck.

'This is lovely.' I lean back on my chair and put the foot rest up. The sun is warm on my skin, the air is sweet and it's so perfectly peaceful apart from the hum of an occasional lazy insect or the odd trill of a bird. 'I wish it could always be like this.'

'Yes. It's lovely, isn't it. So peaceful,' Mum says. 'Make the most of it while you can. Do you fancy a slice of Victoria sponge?'

I swear Mum's been baking for England since I moved into the granny annex, and I'm sure I've put more weight on, and not just baby weight. Too lazy and weak-willed to resist I hold out my hand and take the plate Mum proffers.

'Gorgeous,' I say, because it absolutely is.

'Will you be in tomorrow morning, about ten?'

'Yes. Why?'

'The plumber is due, the bath's in and they're picking it up on their way here. They should get it fitted and the tiling completed tomorrow. Then the upstairs bathroom will be finished.'

'Won't you and Dad be in?' I'm faintly alarmed, which is ridiculous, but since moving here I've been in a bubble, a cocoon almost, where I haven't had to think too much or put up with any hassle from anyone.

'You Dad is doing his stint at the Citizen's Advice tomorrow and I'm going to my card making group. We only meet once a month, in each others' houses. It'll be my turn next month, but tomorrow it's at Elaine's. I'll only be a couple of hours but it starts at ten. You just have to let them in and make them a cup of tea. They'll just get on with it.'

'Okay, no problem.' I really can't be bothered but Mum's done so much for me, I can hardly refuse.

I'm up and dressed when Mum leaves at quarter-to-ten; Elaine's is just around the corner, apparently.

The plumber arrives promptly at ten and rings the doorbell. I let him in and introduce myself. He's my age and really rather attractive.

'Hello, Charlie,' he says, offering his hand. 'I'm Paul. I've heard a lot about you from Penny.' He smiles; he has a lovely smile that lights up his face; small white teeth and his blue eyes seem to sparkle just for me.

He's not wearing a wedding ring. Why did I have to notice that? Oh God, I hope this isn't one of

Mum's clumsy attempts at matchmaking. She wouldn't, would she? Not with me giving birth imminently, she just wouldn't.

'I hear you're new in town. If you ever want someone to show you around, just give me a call.' Oh God, she has.

'Thanks,' I say, trying to sound grateful. 'Do you want a cup of tea?'

'Milk and two sugars for me and my assistant out there,' he nods towards his van, 'will have milk and no sugar. He thinks he's sweet enough already.' He laughs at his own ancient, corny joke.

'Okay.' I trot off to the kitchen to make tea while they manhandle the bath up the stairs. It sounds a tricky job and reminds me of when me and Gen found the sideboard ...*to me, to you.*

Once the commotion has died down I take the tea upstairs and hover on the landing with the two mugs in my hands. Paul appears and takes both cups from me.

'Tea's up,' he calls and his assistant appears behind him.

I'm grateful I'm not holding the mugs as I start to slide down the landing wall, my head buzzing with a host of mixed emotions as I blink my horror at the man standing before me.

Iain.

The reason I went to London in the first place. And, he's hardly changed.

Then the world goes blank.

I wake to find myself lying on Mum and Dad's bed, staring at their rather showy chandelier.

'You okay?' Paul's concerned face is in mine. 'Do you want us to call you a doctor?'

'No. No. I'm fine. Really.' I sit up slowly. I do feel fine. Just shocked. 'Where's Iain?'

'Who?'

'Iain. Your assistant?'

'You mean Josh. He's gone down to get you a glass of water.'

Josh appears in the doorway, glass in hand.

I gulp down a few mouthfuls and try to work out what's happening.

'You okay? Shall I call Penny?' Paul's concern isn't diminishing.

'No. Really. I'm fine. I just had a shock. Josh reminds me someone I used to know. That's all.'

'Not my dad, is it?' Josh speaks for the first time.

'I don't know.' I hope it's not.

'You're nothing like your dad.' Paul frowns his disagreement.

'Not now. He's a big, fat baldy now. When he was young and fit. Like me.' Josh flexes his arm muscles in jest.

'Is his name Iain?'

'Yes. Do you know him? Shall I tell him?'

'No. Don't. It was a long time ago. I doubt he'd remember me.'

Josh pulls his phone out of his pocket, swipes the screen then thrusts the phone at me. 'That's him,' he says, showing me a picture of a man who is indeed, big, fat and bald and quite unrecognisable from the Iain I knew.

'Maybe it's not him.' I push the phone back at Josh and get off the bed, albeit carefully. Trouble is, I know it is.

'You might have warned me that was Iain's son,' I

stage whisper at Mum as soon as she comes home.

'Who?'

'Josh, upstairs.'

'Who?'

'Plumber Paul's assistant, Josh.'

'Oh. I've never met him. Your Dad dealt with all that. I've only met Paul.'

'Well, he's Iain's son. He's his absolute double.'

'Iain who?'

'My old boyfriend, Iain.'

Mum frowns for a second or two then stares at me.

'That's a very long time ago, Charlie. Just forget about it.'

I feel foolish. She's right; it was a long, long time ago. He's moved on. I've moved on. I need to let it go. Only, I realise that I have never let it go, not really. It's always been there, lurking. Not him, or not him specifically. But what he did. What happened. The baby I never had.

But everything's different now.

Paul knocks on the kitchen door and treats us both to a lovely smile when Mum answers it.

'All finished now, Penny. Ready for inspection.' He laughs and Mum joins in.

She goes upstairs with him to check out the bathroom and I follow them up. The last thing I want is Paul walking up behind my voluminous rear, which I'm sure is as large as my front.

'Lovely. A lovely job,' Mum declares. 'Thank you so much.' We're all standing in the bathroom, four of us; it's a bit of a tight squeeze, so I step out and so does Paul who smiles at me. He really is rather dishy.

'Now for the nasty bit,' Paul says as we trundle

back downstairs. 'Shall I email the invoice to your husband?'

'Yes, please. He'll handle that.'

Josh picks up the last few tools and heads for the van, Mum goes back to the kitchen and suddenly it's just me and Paul together in the hallway.

'I meant what I said about showing you around,' he says, flashing me another of his smiles. 'You might even enjoy it.'

'Um, thank you. I'm not much of a party animal at the moment.' I pat my bump to make the point.

'Me neither,' he laughs. 'I'm more play park and McDonalds than pubs and clubs.'

'Has Aston Bassett got any night clubs?' I cock my head and realise I'm flirting.

'I don't know,' he laughs. 'But if you ever fancy a walk around a park, let me know.'

I smile and nod and say thanks. He's lovely, but I can't imagine myself with anyone at the moment. I feel like a beached whale.

'What's the story with Paul?' I ask Mum after he and Josh have left.

'What do you mean?'

'Did you tell him I was free and available?'

'I most certainly did not. Why?'

'He sort of asked me out. I think. A walk around a park, or something.'

'Ah. He's divorced. Has a little boy of four.'

'Okay.'

'I haven't said anything to him about you.'

'I believe you.'

'Good, because I haven't. Your life is going to be busy enough.'

'Yes, I know.' I turn to go back into my own little

domain, the granny annex which we've renamed the baby annex.

'You're right,' Mum says to my retreating back.

'About what?'

'That Josh lad. He is the double of Iain.'

I stop and turn to face Mum. 'You remember what he looked like?'

'I'm afraid I do. I know what he looks like now too. That was a lucky escape.'

'You've seen him?'

'Only from a distance, I saw him in the Designer Outlet in Swindon. Apparently, he has five children by five different women and he's not stayed with any of them.'

I smile. I can't help it. After seeing Josh, I assumed Iain was a happily married father, now I find his life is a great big mess. Serves him right, I just feel sorry for the children. And the mothers.

'Then it *was* a lucky escape for me, wasn't it?'

Just didn't feel like it at the time.

We're ready for the antenatal class. I'm wearing leggings and a giant loose top in case there's any crawling around on the floor. Gen has suggested that there will be.

The class is being held in the local primary school.

'Ready?' Mum asks, hunting for her car keys while balancing her handbag and a large holdall.

'Yep.' I really don't want to do this.

At Mum's insistence we arrive early, she wants to get the *lay of the land*. We go to what we assume is the correct place and wait, we're on our own and I'm starting to think we've got the wrong place. I'm also starting to be grateful for the reprieve.

'Maybe it's been cancelled,' I offer when Mum starts tutting about timekeeping. 'Or we've got the wrong week, or the wrong place.'

Mum pulls up an email on her phone and checks the details. 'No, we're correct. I only got this yesterday.'

Five minutes after the official start time a woman comes bustling down the corridor; she's carrying several large bags and her hair needs combing.

'Hello,' she beams, her face so cheery and welcoming even Mum initially finds it difficult to be annoyed, although she soon gets over that.

'Are we in the right place for the antenatal class?' Mum cannot keep the tone of irritation from her voice.

I want to go home, this isn't a good start.

'Oh yes. You must be Penelope and Charlene. I'm Philly.' She offers her hand for quick handshakes then bustles into the room ahead of us.

'Charlie,' I correct just before Mum asks if we are early.

'No, you're on time. It's everyone else who is late. But that's okay.' She smiles as though this is perfectly normal. 'Come in, come in.'

We enter the room, I half expect to see little chairs and desks but there are none, just a grubby carpet and a few soft chairs around the edges of the room.

Suddenly four people burst in giggling and chatting. Two couples who introduce themselves as Holly and Glen, and Jess and Sam. I look at them and then at me and Mum and I feel uncomfortable, left out and odd. Not for the first time during this *pregnancy journey* I wish Zippy was with me.

Two more couples come rushing in and names are

hastily exchanged. The final pair to arrive save the day; a mother and daughter couple – Lucy and her mum Sharon.

Lucy is the complete opposite to me, so small, so tiny that from the back she looks like a ten-year-old. From the front she looks as though she is about to explode. It's probably just because she's come with her mum but I feel an immediate connection with Lucy, who sits down next to me.

'Everyone brought their mats?' Philly asks and smiles when everyone says they have, including Mum. 'Good, because we'll be doing some more floor work this week.'

I try my best to suppress a groan as everyone else smiles their approval. I've told Mum I'm not keen on this sort of thing; I've told her I just want to go into hospital, take all the drugs available and leave with my baby.

Philly is talking away about partums and postpartums, about episiotomies and C-sections and other words I try my best to block out. This is why the fathers drop out after a few weeks. She's also suggesting that pain relief isn't always necessary and that we can do just as well on our own endorphins.

When she says endorphins, I think of dolphins and use this image to try to block out the rest of her monologue.

She also advocates the use of a doula. I have no idea what that is and I'm happy to keep it that way.

I'm miles away thinking about the large slice of Mum's cake I'm going to devour when we get home, when zips start sliding and mats are being pulled out of bags and unrolled onto the floor. I have to lie down with Mum supporting my shoulders. No mean feat given that I am twice the size of Mum.

'Breathe through the pain,' Philly is saying in her well-meaning, though bossy, voice.

I feel tense and uncomfortable and am willing the time to pass quickly so I can get out of here – that cake is calling. I'm so grateful that we're joining this fiasco with only two more weeks to go. The full course was six weeks and that would have been horrendous. If Mum hadn't already paid for it, I wouldn't be coming back again.

Eventually it's over. I haul myself off the floor, which smells of old shoes and chewed biscuits and whip the mat up and roll it up so quickly that Mum watches me with her mouth open.

'Everyone down the pub?' Lucy yells as we all head for the door.

'Yay,' comes a collective chorus.

I glance at Mum who smiles back at me. I just want to run to the car and get home, but when I see Mum chatting to Sharon, Lucy's mum, I know I'm going to have to endure this too.

'Philly's funny, isn't she,' Lucy says in a conspiratorial tone as she sits next to me in the pub.

'Hilarious.'

'You didn't enjoy that, did you?'

'Not a lot.'

'Me neither. Mum booked it for me.'

'Ditto.' I laugh, because the connection I felt when I saw Lucy is getting stronger. We seem to have a few things in common.

'Yes, she meant well. And, I think it has helped.'

'Oh?'

'This little one is my second baby; the first time was so awful I thought I'd never have another. But.'

She pats her bump. 'Here we are.'

So, Lucy isn't the same as me.

'Does your husband usually come with you then?'

'God no. Liam won't do any of this *knit-your-own-yogurt* stuff. He hates it. He's as shit scared as I am.' She laughs to mask her fear.

'Did you have a normal birth before?' I don't know why I'm asking, I'm positively afraid of the answer.

'Yes. In the end. But it went on for days.' She sees the look of horror on my face. 'Don't worry, you'll be fine, you're tall.'

'Everyone says that.'

'Cos it's mostly true,' Jess cuts in, smiling. 'My sister is tall and has popped two out in the last two years, and I'm taller, so I'm relying on it. She lifts her glass of fizzy water and invites me to clink glasses with her.

'And I'm even taller than you,' I say, raising my own glass of fizzy water to hers.

Soon we're all chatting like old friends. The mums sit together, the men gather at the bar and the mums-to-be huddle around the table. I suddenly realise I'm enjoying myself, especially when they add me to their messaging group.

'It's mostly about stretch marks and the best travel system to buy at the moment, we're yet to progress onto nipple cream and incontinence pads,' Lucy laughs.

'What? No.' I can't hide my disgust.

'Don't worry. You'll be fine. What travel system have you got?'

'We're looking tomorrow,' Mum cuts in, saving me from the embarrassment of admitting that I don't even know what a travel system is.

Back in Mum's car I ask her.
'Pushchair, car seat, all that.'
'Oh. I hadn't even thought about it. I suppose I'll need all that.'
'Yes. I thought we could go tomorrow.'
'Yes. That would be nice.'
'I also thought you might want to drive. I've put you on my insurance now.'
'But I never drive. The last time I drove your car was a year ago.'
'I know. But this isn't London. There are no tubes, and the buses aren't that frequent and don't always go where you want them to. So, you can borrow my car.' She gives me a sideways glance as she starts the engine. 'When I'm not using it,' she adds with a smile.

I drive into Swindon the next day with Mum twitching nervously beside me. We head over to Mothercare where I'm overwhelmed by the choice of travel systems and the cost. Thank God I got such a big redundancy payout. After spending nearly a thousand pounds on a buggy thing with attachments Mum has to put the rear seats of her car down so that the sales assistant can fit it all in.

'It had better be good after spending all that,' I say to Mum as I start her car. 'I'm quite getting into the swing of driving now.'
'Good, let's go and have some lunch.'

We arrive back home mid-afternoon and we're both exhausted. Mum makes a pot of tea and we flop on the sofa without getting the travel system out of the car, although we've left the boot wide open so that Dad can do it when he's finished mowing the lawns.

A knock on the door wakes us both with a start, especially as neither of us intended to doze off.

I answer the door to a smiling Paul carrying one of the travel system boxes.

'I assume you want this brought in,' he says.

'Um, yes.'

'Hello Paul,' Mum says from behind me.

'Just got your invoice, Penny.' He puts the box down in the hall and hands over an envelope.

'Oh, I thought you were going to email it.'

'Yeah, I was passing, so thought I'd drop it in.'

'Thank you. I'll give it to George.' Mum turns and heads for the kitchen leaving me alone with Paul.

'Shall I get the rest?'

'If you don't mind.'

Paul makes short work of bringing the rest in and soon the boxes are stacked on the floor.

'Getting ready for the new arrival? You must be excited.'

'Yeah, I am.' And scared witless after last night's antenatal class, I don't add.

'What about the dad?'

'Not on the scene,' I say, pursing my lips and annoyed at having him mentioned at all.

'Yeah, that's what your dad said.'

'My dad? Did he indeed?'

'Oh, no, he didn't mean it in a nasty way. I'm sorry, I shouldn't be prying. But my offer to show you around still stands. If you're interested.' He twinkles his smile at me and for one, mad moment, I'm tempted. 'Okay,' I hear myself say. 'You can take me for a fizzy water tonight.'

'Fizzy water,' he repeats with a smile.

'Yes, it's my new favourite as opposed to Pinot Grigio which was my old favourite before…' I pat my bump.

'Okay, it's a date.'

I frown, he smiles, but he doesn't retract his date comment.

Fourteen

'Well, it might be my last chance,' I tell Gen on the phone later.

'It won't be,' Gen laughs. 'But go for it anyway.'

'I'm not going for anything other than a drink,' I counter. 'But he's nice and smiley, and attractive and kept offering, so why not? It's not like we're getting married or anything. And I probably won't have the time or the inclination in a few weeks' times, so…'

Gen laughs again, then gets serious. 'How's it going now? Are you settling in down there?'

'Yes, I am.' I can hear the sigh in my voice. 'We went travel system shopping today.'

'Oh God, I remember that. So expensive.'

'I know. But, apparently, so necessary. I've been driving Mum's car too.'

'Wow. That must be weird; it must be years since you drove a car regularly.'

'I've slipped back into it surprisingly easily. I might even buy myself a car, I can afford it now.'

'But…' Gen starts then stops herself.

'What?'

'Nothing. You go for it.'

'You're thinking I'll be spending my flat deposit and future rent on a car, aren't you?'

'Maybe.'

'Maybe you're right. I'm starting to think it's quite nice here. My biggest ghost has been laid to rest.' I tell

Gen about Iain and how he's doing now and how I hadn't realised that I had carried the *Iain incident* around for so long.

Gen is silent on the other end of the phone.

'You still there?'

'Yes. Yes. Just thinking.'

'Thinking about what?'

'I think you might be settling back where you came from.'

'I didn't come from here,' I remind her. 'And I still plan to come back to London once things get back to normal.'

'You're splitting hairs; you were born a couple of miles from where your parents now live. And there is no getting back to normal; you'll have a new normal once the baby's born.'

'Ten miles,' I correct, but I can't argue with her last remark, because I fear she might be right. Which sets me thinking; would it be so bad if I stayed with my parents for a few years, just until I get back on my own two feet? My parents want me to stay; they are so excited about the baby. They've made it easy for me too, my own self-contained annex but with all the convenience of their love and support on the other side of the door.

It's too easy.

Paul arrives bearing flowers, pink roses to be exact.

'I saw them and thought of you.' This should sound cheesy, it *is* cheesy and yet from him it sounds nice, sincere.

He helps me climb into his plumbing van then starts to apologise.

'I'm sorry, but I don't have a car anymore.'

'Not to worry,' I assure him, settling myself down in his passenger seat. 'I came all the way down from London in a van like this and had the best sleep I'd had in weeks.'

The look of relief on his face is enhanced by his smile. He does have the most attractive smile.

'My wife got the car,' he says before staring the engine.

We drive a short distance into the town centre and pull up outside The Angel on the high street. I've been in this bar before, it's rather nice with soft wooden floors and a gourmet menu, not that we're eating.

Paul orders himself an orange juice and gets me a fizzy water with plenty of ice and a slice of lemon.

I take an immense gulp and immediately get hiccups.

'That's not me,' I joke, 'it's the baby.'

Paul humours me by laughing.

'So,' he says, leaning in, 'are you planning to stay here long term?'

'You're the second person today to ask me that.'

'Who was the other?'

'My friend in London.'

'So, what's your answer?'

'I don't know about long term, but probably for the time being.'

'Cool, cos I'd like to see more of you.'

I spread my arms wide. 'More than this. Oh, I hope not.'

We both laugh again, polite and a little nervous.

'My mum says you've got a little boy.'

'Yes, Jonah is four. He's as cute as a button, not that I'm biased.'

'I bet he is. But you're not with his mum?' I try not to make this sound like a judgement; after all, I'm hardly in a position to judge anyone and I have no desire to either.

'No. Thanks to her.'

I can see I've touched a nerve so decide to change the subject.

'Are you from around here? Have you lived here all your life?' I think I'm on safe ground with this.

'No. I moved here with my wife, her family live in Swindon. Now I'm pretty much stuck here until my son grows up. I'm from Essex originally.'

'But you've got your own business here,' I offer, trying to be positive.

'Yeah, that and my son.' Paul now looks quite morose and I wonder what happened to the nice smiley plumber who refitted my parents' bathroom.

'Did you do the bathroom in my part of the house too?' I know he did but I'm trying to jolly him along.

'Yes, I did.'

'It's a great job. So much better than the old granny shower that was there.'

'I fitted that too,' he laughs, watching my face.

'That was great too, of course, for my gran…..you liar.'

He laughs and so do I, this is better.

'You're not with the father then?' He nods at my bump. It's a very direct question but I asked about his wife, so it's fair enough.

'No. It wasn't serious, it wasn't really anything. I made the decision to keep the baby on my own. He's not aware of it.'

I see Paul bristle as I speak.

'Don't you think he has any rights?'

Do I? Maybe, maybe not. But I don't think Paul is going to like me saying that. I don't really want to discuss Zippy and the drunken all-night stand that resulted in me having a baby, but I'm going to have to say something to redeem myself with Paul. This date, if that's what it is, really isn't going too well.

'Look, I'd rather you didn't broadcast this but I can't get in touch with him. We were ships that passed in the night, and we didn't exchange contact details. He's on the other side of the world now. So…'

'I'm sure he'd want to know.' Paul is taking Zippy's side when Zippy doesn't even know he has a side.

'You're right. And if I ever get the chance to tell him, I will. But, frankly, it's unlikely.'

'Good. Cos a man has a right to know about his own child.'

'Yes, he does.' This evening is getting heavier and heavier. 'Anyway,' I start again, brightly, trying desperately to think of something to say. Then I realise it doesn't matter what I say because Paul's attention is elsewhere; he is glaring across the bar and is no longer taking any notice of me.

'Bitch,' he hisses to himself.

I don't think I've said enough to warrant that so turn to follow his gaze. The object of his cussing is standing at the bar with a male companion, ordering drinks.

'That bitch,' he says again as he gets up and strides towards them. 'Where's Jonah tonight?' His face is straight in front of the woman's. I'm guessing this is his ex-wife.

'With my mum,' the woman spits with matching

vitriol. 'Not that it's anything to do with you cos it's not your night.'

The man with Paul's ex-wife backs away then glances over at me as if for moral support. I look away. I do not want to be involved in this.

'I told you I'd have him tonight, I told you I wasn't doing anything special.'

Well, thanks for that, Paul.

'I didn't know I was going out until about an hour ago.' His ex reaches for the drinks which the barman has tactfully placed in front of her before retreating to the far end of the bar. 'Anyway, what about her?' She nods in my direction.

'She's nothing to do with this.'

'Yeah, well…' his ex-wife says, marching towards a table and plonking the two glasses down. 'It's a free country.'

'I'll talk to you tomorrow,' Paul says, backing away and slowly turning towards me. He slumps down in his chair and glowers across at his ex-wife and her male companion.

I pick up my drink and sip it slowly. I really don't know what to say and drinking is giving me an excuse not to speak.

Paul knocks his drink back and stands up. He glares at his ex again.

'Shall we go somewhere else?'

'Sure,' I say, slurping back my water and making the most horrible sound as I suppress a burp which then escapes through my nose. I sound as though I am tuning a trumpet. Paul's ex-wife and her friend squint across at me as does the barman and the few other customers.

Paul strides outside and I trot behind him. I decide

to take the initiative before this evening gets any worse.

'Actually, Paul, I'm feeling really tired, could you just drop me home please?'

'Okay,' he says, without a hint of a smile. 'Sorry about all that in there.'

We clamber back into his van and I can't stop myself from asking the question that is making my lips itch.

'How long have you and your wife been divorced?'

'We're not. Not yet.'

Well, that makes sense.

'Good evening?' Mum asks as I let myself in through the front door.

'Mum, I don't know where to start.'

Half an hour later we have dissected and examined my *date* from all angles.

'Seems to me,' Mum says, 'that he needs to conclude his relationship with his wife before he tries to start another one.'

'Yep, and it won't be with me.'

I'm putting tonight's date, or rather non-date, in my box of crap dates. It's actually quite a big box.

We're outside the antenatal class again and we're waiting for Philly and the others. Mum's given up complaining about people's bad timekeeping but has still made us arrive a little early – just in case.

I don't care if they never get here, I'd rather stay at home.

Eventually everyone does arrive and we're soon unrolling our mats and getting comfortable on the floor. Not that lying on a thin yoga mat on the floor is comfortable when you're nine months pregnant. I've discovered that I'm a month or more ahead of everyone else and I should have joined the previous class. I'm just glad I couldn't.

We're soon huffing and puffing and pretending we're in labour and we're learning how to breathe and how to pant while making a face like an owl. I feel stupid and self-conscious as everyone else seems to accept this rigmarole as normal. It turns out that Philly is actually a doula herself and she is offering her services to anyone who wants them. For a price.

'I'd rather take the drugs,' Jess whispers to me as we lie side-by-side inhaling stinky carpet fibres.

'I came because my mum booked it, but why are you here if you feel like that?'

'To be honest I didn't think it would be quite so *natural.*' She giggles and I join in.

In the pub afterwards, we all agree that drugs are the order of the day and an epidural is a perfectly acceptable alternative to suffering. After all, it's not the dark ages anymore and it's also not a suffering contest.

I'm really starting to like these women and I'm grudgingly glad that Mum has booked us onto this course, even if the only benefit for me is meeting other mums-to-be.

Before I know what is happening I'm agreeing to meeting up for a mums-to-be coffee morning and before she knows what is happening Mum is offering to host it at her place.

'Plenty of room in our conservatory,' she says later when I question her about it.

'Are you sure you don't mind?'

'Course not. I won't be there and neither will your father. We're meeting up with the Farrells.'

'Who?'

'Our friends, Liz and John. We met them on the cruise. Remember?'

'Oh yeah.' I hadn't remembered, in fact I'm not even sure Mum did tell me. Maybe I've got baby-brain or pregnancy-brain or whatever it is that everyone talks about.

Mum and Dad leave early the next morning and it's just me alone in the house waiting until ten-thirty when everyone will arrive. We've got plenty of milk, coffee and tea but also plenty of soft drinks. The sun is out and already spreading across the garden and warming up the conservatory.

First to arrive is Lucy and she's brought her little girl, Florence, who's two-and-a-half. She's an angelic little thing with a halo of white curls and green eyes that follow you around.

'Don't be fooled,' Lucy says when she sees me staring at her daughter. 'She's little Miss Mischief; I can't take my eyes off her for a second.'

Then Jess arrives with Holly. We're soon giggling like old friends, it's quite strange really. I feel such a connection with these women yet I barely know them.

'It's the fear factor,' Jess says. 'We're all scared shitless.'

We're soon exchanging our full life stories and I'm relieved to discover that I am not the oldest, Lucy is. Tiny little Lucy who looks like a ten-year-old from the back is actually six months older than me. Holly and Jess are both thirty-one.

'Teenage mums don't go to this stuff,' laughs Holly. 'They just pop 'em out.' We're all giggling as though we've been drinking when all any of us has actually drunk is orange juice – purely for the vitamin C, we agree.

'I've actually got lemonade in mine,' I laugh. 'I'm addicted to fizz.' Then another burp, which can't quite match the one I performed in the pub with Paul, escapes from my mouth. But, this time instead of horror I laugh and so do my new friends.

'Your mum makes the best cake,' Jess says, helping herself to a second piece.

'Tell me about it. I'm sure I've put on weight since I moved here and it isn't just related to me being pregnant.'

'Haven't we all,' Lucy says. 'I'll soon be back in the gym. I look like a beach ball on a stick.'

Everyone is talking about nurseries and decorating and the inevitable travel systems and sterilising bottles. I show them the nursery and they're suitable impressed. They're also fascinated by my life in London, which when I lived it I loved, but now it seems a lifetime away.

'Big change for you then,' Holly says to me. We're sitting in Mum and Dad's conservatory enjoying the sunshine while Florence plays with the fridge magnets, she's taken them off the fridge and is trying to make them stick to the conservatory's glass doors.

'Yes, I suppose. But I'm realising how lucky I am. I don't realistically think it would be so good to have stayed in London, which was my original plan.' I think of the lovely flat I nearly had and imagine how isolated I would have felt even now, never mind when I'm alone with a baby to look after.

'Yep, we all need our mums,' Lucy laughs, rolling her eyes.

'We do,' the others agree.

'You're so lucky, it's beautiful here. Perfect place to have a baby. Look at this garden.' Jess waves her arm towards Mum's roses, still beautiful even though they are fading now. 'We live in a one-bed flat. Though we are hoping to move later this year.'

I know I'm lucky. Mum and Dad have come to my rescue, I'm just a bit sad that I needed rescuing at my age.

Soon my new friends are gone and after I've retrieved all the fridge magnets and realigned them up on the fridge door, I open the conservatory doors and let the smell of the garden roses waft in.

I make myself my one allowed coffee and put my feet up; I soon give up the urge to fight sleep and doze off.

'All right for some.' Mum's voice wakes me from a deep sleep.

'What?'

'You were snoring,' Dad says.

'Sorry.' I rouse myself and sit up properly.

'Where's Sydney?' Mum asks.

'Who?'

'Not who, where. Sydney, Australia. It's missing off the fridge.'

'Oh. Right. It must be in here somewhere. Lucy's little girl was playing with it.' I watch Mum's face for a sign of annoyance. She has collected fridge magnets from every port they stopped in on their around-the-world cruise. If Sydney is missing it spoils her collection and she's hardly likely to pop over there and pick up another one.

Mum shrugs. 'It'll turn up,' she says, sitting down

next to me.

The week soon passes and we're at antenatal classes again, lying on the floor and pretending we're giving birth.

Then Philly shows us a compilation video of her helping women give birth. Scented candles and soft music seem to be the common theme. We all wince as the babies' giant heads burst out into the world.

'I was blessed enough to be able to help these new mums, and, as you can see, none of them had any drugs or intervention.' Philly beams at us.

'She's always pushing her doula stuff,' Jess whispers as Holly grimaces behind Philly's back.

'It wasn't like that when I had Flossie; I shat myself. It was disgusting.'

'Nooo. Too much information,' Jess yells as we all laugh.

When we leave the class for the last time I feel quite sad, then I remember that I'll still be seeing my friends again.

In the pub afterwards we're all giggly and silly, as though it's the last day of school.

'My turn to host our get-together this week,' Lucy says before turning to me as she's fishing around in her handbag. 'This is yours.' She hands me a fridge magnet.

'Sydney,' Mum shouts, looking over my shoulder. 'Yes.'

'Sorry, I found it in Flossie's pocket. I meant to message you.'

'No harm done.' Mum retrieves the magnet from my hand. 'No doubt when my grandson is that age he'll be wrecking the place anyway.'

I don't remember her being so tolerant when me and Joe were little.

Lucy, Flossie and Liam live in a lovely new house on the edge of town. It has three bedrooms, two bathrooms and a pocket-sized garden.

'Not as lovely as yours,' Lucy says into my ear as I stand looking out from her kitchen window. I've arrived early as Mum wanted the car so she dropped me off.

'Not mine, my parents',' I remind her. 'I was just thinking how lovely this all is, you, your husband, your little girl and a new baby on the way. I don't have any of that, so don't envy me.' I laugh but inside I don't feel like laughing.

'What about the father? Is there no chance of you making a go of it?'

'No,' I say, feeling quite sorry for myself, and I find myself telling her the story of my baby boy's conception, of Zippy and Bungle.

'Ooh,' is all she can say. 'I assumed you'd split up.'

'We never had a chance to split up because we were never even together. Who knows, maybe if he hadn't disappeared to the other side of the world we might have made a go of it.' I shrug and force a smile just as the doorbell rings. 'Saved by the bell.'

He had said he'd like to see me again if things were different.

Or would he have ended up in the box of crap dates like so many others?

Soon the whole group is here and I forget about my wistfulness as we talk about Braxton Hicks contractions and lactation. I don't much like the sound of any of it. I'm not sure I'm cut out of be a mother, but it's too late now.

'You haven't forgotten it's my turn to host the craft session this month, have you?' Mum asks as I'm floating about in my pyjamas eating toast at five-to-ten the next morning.

'When? Today?'

'In a minute. They'll start arriving soon.'

'I'll just stay in the annex,' I say.

'Oh, don't do that. Do come and say hello. They all want to meet you.'

'What have you said about me?'

'Nothing.' Mum looks hurt. 'Just that you're my daughter and you're having a baby.'

'Right. Okay. Well, maybe later.'

'How late? We usually have a cake break about eleven. That would be a good time.'

'But I want to wash my hair this morning.' My voice sounds whiny.

'Well off you go then.' Mum pushes me towards the annex door just as the doorbell rings.

An hour later I appear from the annex with freshly done hair, decent clothes and even a bit of makeup on my face. Mum is at the kitchen worktop serving up cake and the dining table is covered in bits of craft paper and scissors.

'You must be Charlene,' a woman says, jumping up with glee.

'Charlie,' I correct. 'Hello.'

'I'm Elaine,' the woman extends an elegant hand towards me and we shake.

Then Mum introduces me to the other *ladies*; there are ten of them and their names wash over me.

'When did you say you were due?' Elaine eyes my

immense bump.

'Imminently.' I wish they wouldn't all stare at me as though I were a prize sow.

Mum pushes me towards the sofa and hands me a piece of cake and a napkin. Inwardly, I promise myself that once the baby is born this cake eating will stop. I look at Mum, still tiny after all these years and wonder how she does it with so much cake flying about.

'Will you be breastfeeding?' asks one of the ladies.

I want to say *mind your own business*, I want to say *what's it to you*, but instead I smile sweetly.

'Not sure yet.'

'See how it goes,' another adds. 'I fed mine for a year a piece and I wouldn't recommend it.' She rolls her eyes.

'Except at night,' another adds. 'No getting up to warm bottles.'

'There is that,' admits the first. 'But such a tie. I wouldn't do it again if I had my time over.'

Several nod and laugh with her, while one frowns.

'That's what they're there for,' declares the frowner. 'Natural. Mother's milk.'

Several look away. Several nod.

'You do what suits you best,' Elaine says, patting my arm.

I eat the cake as quickly as I can then stand up to make my escape back to the annex, but I'm prevented from reaching the door by pats and looks and smiles.

'Oh dear, I think someone's slopped their tea. We have a spillage, Penny.'

'Much?' she shouts back. 'Do I need kitchen roll or a mop?'

'Mop,' several call out at once and even I notice

the floor is wet, I am stamping in it.

'Oh dear,' says Mum as she mops around our feet. 'You sure one of you ladies hasn't peed herself.'

Everyone starts to laugh.

'Not guilty of incontinence yet, Pen,' shouts one.

'Yes, no *Tena Lady* for me, thank you.'

They're sniggering between themselves when I feel it, a warm trickle running down my leg.

Oh my God, it's me. I'm the incontinent one.

'I've wet myself,' I whisper into Mum's ear as she mops the floor around my feet.

'No dear,' Elaine says, 'you haven't.'

Fifteen

'You deal with Charlie, Pen, and I'll get rid of all these old bags.' Elaine ushers me and Mum away.

There's a chorus of 'charming,' 'thanks for that,' 'speak for yourself,' as I leave the room and step into the sanctity of the annex.

'You put your feet up,' Mum says, throwing a folded bath towel onto the sofa for me to sit on. 'I'll ring the hospital.'

'Have you got the right number?' I'm not even sure I do.

'Oh yes.' Mum smiles at me and I feel reassured.

'Tell them I'm not having contractions,' I call after her.

I lean back, feet up, backside on the towel and, closing my eyes, I pat my bump. A little kick from my baby excites and scares me.

'We're going to meet soon,' I whisper.

A tentative knock on the door precedes Elaine's entry.

'Everything okay?'

'Yes, thank you. Mum's just ringing the hospital. She's going to tell them I'm not having contractions yet.'

Elaine watches me for a moment or two and then frowns.

'I think you are,' she says.

'No.' I shake my head. 'I think I'd know.'

'When's baby due?'

'A few days ago.'

'They'll make you go in if your water's broken,' she says, with a knowing look in her eyes. 'Even if you don't have the baby straight away.'

'Really? Oh, I don't want to sit there waiting. I'd rather be at home.'

Elaine offers me a sympathetic nod but doesn't take her eyes from my bump.

'Are you sure you aren't having contractions?'

'Yes. Why?'

'It's just that I think I can see them from here.'

'What?'

'There.' She points and I look down at my bump and watch it squeeze then relax.

'Oh that, no, that's just a little squeeze. I've been having those on and off for days. Braxton Hicks, aren't they?'

'I think that's a proper contraction,' Elaine says. 'Is your bag packed?'

'Of course it is.'

'And there's another.'

We both watch my bump move again.

'They're quite close together.'

Mum appears in the doorway.

'What did they say?'

'Come up when you're ready this afternoon. Between two and three, they suggested, unless you start having contractions.' She glances at Elaine, then smiles at me. 'I could murder a cup of tea, anyone else.'

But Elaine doesn't answer Mum's question; she is too busy staring at my bump.

'And there's another. I don't think you should

wait.'

'Another what?'

'Contraction.'

'No.' Mum turns away.

'Penny, watch her bump.' Elaine puts her hand on Mum's arm.

Mum stares at me with a patient, though exasperated look on her face. Our eyes meet and I realise she's humouring Elaine, which makes me feel a lot better. It's only as the expression on Mum's face changes that I start to worry.

'I think you might be right,' she says to Elaine. 'Charlie?'

'It just feels a bit squeezy.' Now I'm starting to worry.

'Maybe I'll ring them again.'

'No. It's fine.' I start to get up to prove the point, then drop back down wishing I hadn't moved. 'Argh.'

'What is it?' Mum rushes to me.

'It feels like I want to push.'

Two worried faces stare back at me.

'I'll ring the hospital again.' Mum rushes back into the kitchen and comes back with the phone.

I don't hear much of what she says because I'm now in the throes of fighting off the urge to push. How can this have happened?

'You must have been in labour for quite a while,' Elaine says.

I wish she would just shut up.

'They're sending an ambulance,' Mum announces, putting the phone down. 'I've wedged the front door ajar.'

'I don't think there's much time,' Elaine says, dropping down onto the floor and putting her hands on my stomach.

'I need to push,' I shout. 'It's coming.'

'Don't worry, I'll help you. We used to farm pigs; I've helped dozens of sows. Penny, get some more towels, unless you want this lovely new sofa ruined. I don't suppose you've got any plastic sheeting?'

'No. Yes, I've got a new Christmas tablecloth, we never used it.'

Mum's back in seconds with a pile of towels to find that Elaine has whipped off my leggings and is peering up my nether regions. This is so undignified but I just couldn't care less.

I hear the rustle of the plastic tablecloth and feel myself being lifted up onto it. Soft towels are being stuffed all around me.

'Don't want him hurtling onto the floor, do we?' Elaine says, trying to lighten the mood while I am feeling more and more panicked.

'Here's another one,' I hear myself screech. 'Ow, ouch, it hurts.'

'I can see the head.' Elaine's voice sounds calm. 'You're doing really well. Any sign of that ambulance, Pen?'

I glance up at Mum's face which is ashen and her mouth is open but nothing is coming out of it.

'Ow, ooo, get it out.' I push again, but it doesn't come out.

As the pain subsides I look between Mum and Elaine's faces.

'What? Is it okay?'

'Of course it is. You just concentrate on…' But Elaine's voice is drowned out by my shouting again.

'Oh shit. Oh shiiiitttt. Get him out. Get him out.'

'Head's born,' Elaine shouts, triumphant.

'Just pant now, Charlie. Like in the classes.' Mum is patting my hand but I pull it away.

'Fuck the stupid classes. I wanted drugs and everything.'

Another contraction comes and I push with all my might, I cannot help it.

Then I feel his hot little body slither out before Elaine rests him on my stomach. I'm looking down on him and his eyes open and meet mine, then his mouth opens and he yells.

Elaine covers us both with towels. Mum starts crying tears of joy.

'He's beautiful,' she says, between sobs.

'He is.' Elaine stops and stares at my baby boy's adorable little face. 'He reminds me of my son. Even the hair is the same. Bless him.'

We all look at my baby's gunk-covered head, underneath are light coloured curls, I think.

'Got any string and scissors, Pen?' There's a sudden sound of panic in Elaine's voice. 'I think the placenta's coming.'

'Don't worry, we have clamps,' a male voice says.

We all turn in the direction of the voice. Two paramedics stand in the room with their kit on their backs.

'Oh, thank God.' Elaine scurries out of the way to let them gain access. 'The pigs used to just nibble off the cords.' She flumps onto the far corner of the sofa while Mum continues to kneel next to me.

In hospital, safe and sound and baby George declared as healthy, I lie back and breathe a sigh of relief, and joy. I'm incredibly lucky apparently, I don't need any stitches which, given George's weight, is quite incredible, and all my *obs* are as they should be.

If it weren't for the little gaggle of midwives and a junior doctor having a conference at the end of the ward whilst constantly glancing at me I wouldn't have a care in the world.

'Charlie,' the junior doctor approaches, trying to mask his concern with a smile.

'Yes. Everything okay?' I'm alarmed, despite his smile, further exacerbated by a midwife pulling the curtains around me.

'Could we just have a look at your skin again?'

'Skin?'

He doesn't answer but takes my hands and turns them over, then checks my arms and face, then my feet, ankles and finally, and without much dignity, the back of my thighs and my buttocks. I close my eyes and cringe.

'I've never seen this before; I think I need to refer.' He's talking to the midwife, not me. Then he's gone.

'What's wrong?'

'Your skin is a bit mottled. I'm sure it's fine but best to get it checked out.' She pulls the covers over me and opens the curtains. All the while George has slept through his mother's indignity. I'm mesmerised by his tiny little face. His eyes, though puffy have long, curly eyelashes, his mouth is a beautiful pink rosebud.

Two hours later I'm still waiting for the verdict on my mottled skin. I've fed George his first bottle, he refused to breastfeed and I don't think I want to force that even though the midwife had given me a pitying look. I've been to the bathroom and tried to get a look at this mottled skin but the mirrors are too high and I don't want to chance twisting too far round just yet.

'There you are,' a midwife says a little too sharply as I return to my bed. 'Mr Chandra is here to have a look at you.'

I see a tiny little Indian doctor smiling at me, he's accompanied by the junior doctor who saw me earlier. I feel like a giant whale and now they are going to stare at my immense backside. The curtains are pulled around as I haul myself onto the bed.

I lie on my side and focus on George asleep in his Perspex crib. The midwife offers to pull my knickers down so that Dr Chandra can get a better look.

'No, no. Wipe,' he says.

I cringe. What is he going to wipe?

I feel the cool sensation of an alcohol wipe on my leg.

Dr Chandra doesn't speak.

'Oh,' says the junior doctor.

'Everything is fine, Mrs Copeland,' says Dr Chandra as he walks away muttering to the junior doctor. I don't bother to tell him that I'm not a Mrs.

'So, what is it?' I ask the midwife.

'Oh, it's nothing. Nothing at all.' Then she scurries off too, ripping the curtains open a lot faster than she closed them.

'So, that's how I came to have my baby delivered onto a Christmas tablecloth by an ex pig-farmer,' I tell Gen on the phone that night.

'It could only happen to you. He looks adorable. Is he like you as a baby?'

'Mum says not. Not like Joe either. But he is a good weight like we were. 8lbs 12oz.'

'That is good. And everything's okay? You're

okay?'

'Yes. Just staying in overnight, just to be on the safe side because he's my first baby, then home tomorrow.' I'm not telling Gen about the mottled-skin drama over the phone.

'Got a name yet?'

'George. George Oliver Copeland. George, after my dad.'

'And Oliver, after his dad?'

'Sort of. I like the name. Anyway, I could hardly call him Zippy, could I?'

Gen laughs. 'It would have been okay, there are so many silly names out there.'

'Not for my boy. I keep looking at him, Gen. I can't believe he's mine. He's so gorgeous. I can't believe I can keep him and take him home. He's all mine.'

'Yeah, it's a lovely feeling isn't it?'

'I never realised it would be like this. I just looked at his little face and I fell in love with him. I never thought I'd have children, I'd got used to the idea I wouldn't. But now, everything has changed. I love it. I love him; it was instant, as soon as I saw him.'

'Yeah, love changes everything.' Gen's voice sounds wistful.

'Is it always like this? Every time?'

'Yes. Every time. Make sure you send me new photos tomorrow, because he'll change overnight.'

'Will he?'

'Yes, his face will be less puffy, his nose might be less flat.'

I don't sleep well that night, I'm too happy, too elated, too high on my own endorphins – and I didn't even have to visualise dolphins while I gave birth.

'Here Mum, take a picture of me with him.' I thrust my phone at Mum and grab George. 'I want to send it to Gen, and the antenatal girls.' We've dressed George in a soft blue all-in-one suit with a dark blue cardigan that Mum has knitted, he's wearing the matching hat too.

'He's changed,' Mum says, taking him from me while I start collecting up my stuff from my hospital locker.

'Gen said he would.'

'His little face isn't so swollen.'

'Gen said that would happen.'

'He still doesn't look like you or Joe.' Her voice is quiet.

'No.' I don't want to say anything to Mum but he looks like his dad, or what I remember his dad looking like. I wonder if I'd recognise Zippy if I ever saw him again? Surely, I would.

'He's beautiful.' Mum hands him back to me as we both stare at the car seat he has to go in.

'Looks tricky,' I say, holding him over it as though I'm measuring it for size.

'Need help with that?' A midwife appears and shows us the best way to fit George into the straps, padding and head supports.

As we wheel him through the hospital and outside towards Dad's waiting car, I feel like the cleverest woman in the world with the most beautiful baby.

Back home, after Dad has emptied the car and we've all marvelled over this incredibly wonderful blue bundle and he's taken a significant amount of milk from a bottle, Mum suggests I have a shower.

'Do I smell?' I joke.

'Course not. I just thought you might want one. I'm not suggesting anything.' She looks hurt.

'I know you're not, I was joking. And, yes, I will.' I didn't have a shower in the hospital because I knew I'd soon be home.

In my bathroom I discard most of my clothes and marvel at how light I feel. It's only as I catch sight of myself in the mirror that I see the saggy skin hanging around my stomach. I gasp. How horrible is that? While I've never been a skinny-minnie I've always had a smooth stomach. I hope it returns to normal although I can't imagine that it will. Then I think about my gorgeous baby and decide that he's worth it and I don't care.

As I turn to switch the shower on something else catches my eye in the mirror. The back of my legs, mottled red and green.

'What?' I screech, grateful that the sound of the shower drowns out my yell. I don't want Mum and Dad to come running in. This is what all the fuss was about in hospital, and no wonder. Yet they said it would be okay.

I get closer to the mirror and pull the back of my thighs about to examine the mottling. It's not just on my thighs, it's all over my buttocks too and I think I can see a bit on my heels. Is this permanent? Will it go away? No one mentioned red and green mottling in the antenatal class. *This* is the sort of thing they should be telling you about.

Then I notice that the mottling has a pattern to it.

Christmas trees and Santas. It's the print off the tablecloth. I've been examined by countless midwives and male doctors and they've all seen this and thought it was something awful. If only they'd asked me.

It takes quite a bit of scrubbing to get it off.

'You might have told me I had that print all over me,' I admonish Mum after I've told her about it.

'Didn't think it was important.' She's holding George in her arms and rocking him gently.

'It caused quite a commotion at the hospital.' I take my son from my mum and look into his little sleeping face. Everything is there, two eyes, a nose, a mouth. It's just incredible. I am the luckiest woman in the world with the most beautiful baby. He's just perfect.

Fatherless, but perfect.

'Elaine rang, she wanted to come and see him today, but I've put her off. I said maybe tomorrow.'

'Okay. Gen's coming tomorrow.'

'I'll put Elaine off for another day. Does Gen want to stay overnight?'

'No. She says she has to get back; she can only have one day off at work. The shit has hit the fan, they've announced the company move to India and everyone is up in arms.'

'Oh dear. Poor Gen. It's so good you're not there now.'

'Yeah, it is,' I agree with Mum, and it's mostly down to Gen that I received such a good payout. And Bastard Bryan Smith. And Bev, whether she intended to help or not.

'What's so funny?' Mum says, catching me grinning to myself.

'Just something that happened at work. Not

important.'

Gen arrives at eleven the next morning with a big card signed by everyone at work, except Bev and Bryan Smith.

'I didn't even ask them,' she says.

She's sitting down with George in her arms when the doorbell goes.

'I hope that's not Elaine, I told her I'd let her know when it was convenient.' Mum stomps off to answer the door.

When she comes back Elaine isn't with her but Mum holds a giant bouquet of flowers in her hand.

'For you, obviously,' Mum says, handing them to me.

'Ahh, they're from everyone at work.' I glance at Gen.

'Couldn't carry them on the train, supposing I had to stand up all the way here?' She laughs as do I, even though the card is from everyone, we all know that Gen arranged it. 'Bastard Bryan chipped in too, even though his name isn't on the card.' She sniggers, before adding. 'And he put in on behalf of Bev.'

We sit with George on our laps until it's lunchtime, passing him between Gen, Mum and me and when he's about, Dad.

Gen wants to know if I'm going to breastfeed; I tell her I'm not.

'Probably better to save yourself the angst. I tried with the first two and just bought myself a whole load of misery, and a grumpy hungry baby. Didn't bother the third time.'

'I don't fancy it. I think the antenatal class might have put me off. There was a lot of talk about mastitis and sore nipples. Feel a bit guilty though.'

'Don't,' Gen says, emphatically. 'He's adorable.' And when Mum goes off to make some lunch she says, 'He's so placid. Was his dad like that?'

'Hard to say,' I shrug and smile. 'On such short acquaintance. I've been thinking…,' I start, then stop.

Gen waits, her face a picture of patience betrayed only by her inquisitive eyes.

'Maybe I should try to contact Zippy. What do you think?'

'It's not about what I think.'

'I'm sure you have an opinion.'

Gen forces a shrug.

'Come on, share it. I know you want to.'

'I think you should try. He has a right to know.'

'Yes, I'm coming to realise that.' I think of what Paul said, even though I don't think he had any right to say it.

I get up and grab Mum's iPad from the sideboard and start flicking through it. I Google the costume hire.

'That's it.' I thrust the iPad in front of Gen's face. 'What do you think? Should I ring them?'

'What have you got to lose?'

I punch the number into my mobile and wait to be connected.

'What's wrong?' Gen asks.

'Number unobtainable.'

'I'll click on their website, see if there's a different number.' Gen stabs at Mum's iPad. 'Site's gone too.'

'Oh God. Serves me right, I should have done it when I was there. I'm sure I could have persuaded that old man to give me the number. Not that I ever thought I'd need to contact him.'

'I'll go. Do you think I can get there in my lunch break?'

'Maybe.'

'Huh, what does it matter. I can take an extended lunch break, what are they going to do, sack me?' She gives me a bitter little laugh. 'I'll do it tomorrow.'

'Are you sure?'

'Absolutely.'

'I'm so grateful. I'm also annoyed with myself for not doing it sooner.'

'You weren't to know you'd feel like this. You didn't even know you were pregnant then.'

Gen doesn't ring me the next day but I don't miss her call because I'm too busy crying.

'Baby blues,' Mum says and the health visitor agrees with her while at the same time telling me that I only have to ring if I find it's all too much. In the end, Mum is right, because the next day I feel a lot happier, how could I not with the most beautiful baby in the world by my side.

'Hi,' Gen's voice says when she rings the next day. 'Sorry I didn't ring yesterday, it got a bit manic in here in the afternoon.'

'Really. What happened?'

'Well, I didn't see it myself, but apparently Bev slapped Bastard Bryan's face in the middle of a big meeting.'

'No. Why?'

'No one really knows. But there's no sign of either of them today. Lots of rumours flying about and I'm enjoying myself listening to them.'

'Do tell.'

'They were having an affair, he dumped her, she caught him with someone else, stuff like that.'

'Having an affair, I don't think so. Well, only in Bev's mind.' I think of Bev's simpering over *my Bryan*.

'Yeah, that's what I think. More likely she caught him with someone else.'

We giggle together before Gen gets down to the point of her call.

'I went to the costume shop yesterday.'

'And…' I wait, my heart beating in my chest.

'It's closed down. In fact, I had to walk back and forth a few times to find it. There are builders in there converting it into luxury apartments.'

I hear myself groan.

'I know. I even went into that dodgy lingerie shop below and asked if they knew where the owner had gone.'

'Any luck?'

'Yes, I'm afraid so. He died; he was ancient according to them. He had no family but he did have a lifetime lease on the place with a peppercorn rent.'

'You got a lot of information from them, Gen.'

'Yeah, turns out they own the lease. I think secretly they were pleased he'd died. Anyway, all the stuff was either sold or chucked in a skip and the builders moved in.'

'Oh. I don't know what else to do.'

'If he's not using that phone it might have been pointless anyway.' Gen is trying to make me feel better. 'And, I gave it some thought and popped round to your old next-door neighbours on the way home last night.'

'What?'

'Well, wasn't that where Zippy was staying on New

Year's Eve?'

'Yes. Of course. Any luck?'

'No. They had no idea who he was. They were aware a friend of a friend had stayed there, but they didn't know him.'

'Urgh.'

'They did say that he left the place immaculate though and they would try to find out who he was, so I've left them your number. If they find anything, they'll text.'

'Thank you. I do appreciate you going to so much trouble.'

'No problem. Nothing much else to do now.'

'Are you at work?' I suddenly realise that it's only eleven in the morning.

'Yes. I'm in a meeting room. There's not much to do, well not much I want to do. A lot of the staff are on gardening leave – ha ha – not that many actually have gardens. It all shuts down completely in less than two weeks. The Indian call centre has already started taking a lot of the calls.'

'That Bastard Bryan. What an arse.'

'He is. We can only wish him good things though, can't we? I hope his wife doesn't find out about his *affair* with Bev.'

'You wouldn't, Gen, would you?'

'No. Not that I haven't considered it. But I don't have her contact details and I'm trying not to be bitter; I'm trying to move on.'

'Best way,' I say, staring at George.

'Yeah, Charlie. Your timing was perfect. Clever you. How is the little munchkin?'

'He's just lovely. Me and Mum are taking him out for his first walk after lunch. I can't wait to push that

pram. But Elaine's coming for lunch before that.'
'Elaine?'
'Yes, the ex-pig farmer who delivered him.'

Sixteen

'Oh, look at him,' Elaine says, striding into the room and grabbing George from my arms. 'Aren't you just beautiful?' she coos at him. 'Is he always this good?'

'So far,' I say.

'And, how are you?'

'Yeah, okay. I think.' She doesn't need to hear about my crying day yesterday.

'Course you are, who wouldn't be with this little bundle.' She hands him back to me. 'He reminds me so much of my son, it's quite shocking.'

'Doesn't remind me of mine,' Mum chips in as she comes through from the kitchen. '*He* squawked morning, noon and night. Lunch is ready.'

We follow Mum into the kitchen and I place George in his pram which is now secured to the wheels.

'Lovely travel system,' Elaine says. I wait for her to say she had one just like it, but she doesn't.

After lunch Elaine reaches into her handbag and produces a little wrapped package which she hands to me. She watches as I unwrap it. It's a tiny hand-knitted cardigan in a most beautiful turquoise blue.

'It's lovely, thank you so much. Did you knit it?'

'Yes, I finished it last night. And I've washed it in the right stuff so he can wear it as soon as you like.'

'You've knitted this since he's been born? But that's only a few days.'

Mum and Elaine exchange glances.

'You young girls, eh.' Elaine reaches over and pats my knee. 'I assume you can't knit.'

'No, but I'm hardly a young girl,' I laugh. But her comment does make me think; I will be forty soon. 'Poor George is going to have an old mum when he's a teenager.'

'You won't be that old,' Elaine offers, smiling. 'I was older than you when I had our Alistair, quite a bit older actually. Forty-seven. Can you believe it?' She laughs and that does make me feel a bit better.

Elaine has another cuddle with George, who's woken up for a feed, before she leaves.

'Hope to see you again soon,' she coos at him. 'You're such a lucky girl,' she says to me, then to Mum, 'and you, Granny or is it Nanny?'

'That's a point,' I say to Mum after Elaine has gone. 'What do you want to be called?'

'I don't know. I haven't even thought about it. Benji and Kiki call me Nanny.'

'Well, we'd better decide soon.'

'He's hardly going to start speaking yet.' Mum laughs.

'Yes, but I need to refer to you and Dad as something, otherwise he'll hear me calling you Mum and Dad and think that's who you are.'

Mum frowns.

'Well, you know what I mean.'

'Let's stick with Nanny,' she says, handing me George's bottle.

An hour later and we're finally ready to leave. After his feed George was sick on his clothes so had to be changed and is now wearing the new turquoise cardigan that Elaine has just given him.

Mum's keen that we're not out too long as it will be getting cold later. At the moment a weak October sun is warming the air but once it starts to fade it will be chilly.

We set off down the street and towards Aston Bassett high street. We're going to pop into Sainsbury's and pick up a few bits and pieces for George and something nice for tea – Mum has suggested a cake as she hasn't had time to bake one. I think about my wobbly belly and counter her suggestion with fruit.

'You're not fat,' she says, immediately getting what I mean.

'Mum, I'm all wobbly.'

'Course you are, you've just had a baby. It's normal.'

'I bet you weren't like it.' I glance at Mum's enviably flat stomach.

'What. Of course I was. I'm much shorter and smaller than you and Joe weighed 9lbs and you were 9lb 3oz. I could hardly stand up by the time you were born.'

I take another look at Mum's tiny frame, her slim waist, and I shake my head. How can that have been possible?

'Cake it is,' Mum says, countering no argument. 'Celebration cake.'

And that's exactly what she buys – a big sponge cake covered in blue icing to celebrate George's arrival.

'We'll never eat that between us.'

'Not in one sitting,' she says, laughing.

I've bought a thank you card which I hastily write

to Gen and my ex-colleagues and we head for the post office so that I can post it.

'This needs weighing,' I tell Mum, 'I'm not sure if it's standard or not.'

'I'll take it in.' Mum grabs it from me and goes inside while I roll George's pram to and fro so that he doesn't wake up. I hope Mum is quick although judging by the length of the queue I can see through the window, I worry that she won't be.

I spot Elaine heading away from me but, as though she can feel my eyes on her back, she suddenly spins around and looks in my direction. She waves, then turns and walks towards me. She's poking around in George's pram before she even manages to say hello.

'He's wearing it,' she almost shrieks with joy which makes George stir.

'Yes, it's a lovely fit.' I speed up my pram rolling to stop my baby from waking up.

'On your own?'

'No, Mum's in the post office.'

'I'd better catch up with them,' Elaine says, half-heartedly pointing at a man and a teenager who are waiting just ahead of us. 'Family dentist trip,' she says, grimacing before sticking her head back into George's pram. 'I can't get over how much he reminds me of my son.'

I glance over at her son standing with her husband; I nod and smile. He's a typical gawky teenager and nothing like my beautiful baby. He has ginger hair which seems to have a mind of its own which he obviously gets from his father, who, despite being bald on top has long ginger-grey hair hanging over his shoulders. I'm insulted and annoyed.

'Oh hi, Elaine.' Mum reappears from the post

office.

'Hi Pen, must dash. Dentist.' Elaine races to catch up with her family.

'Have you seen her son?' I ask Mum once Elaine is out of earshot. 'I wish she wouldn't keep saying George is like him. I don't want to be rude but…' I can't really say anymore without being rude so I shut up.

'Take no notice. All newborns remind mums of their own babies.'

'I hope you're right,' I say.

'I'm always right,' Mum says, as we pick up our pace to get home before it gets too cold.

'Is that Joe's car?' I ask as we turn into our street.

'Oh, he made it. He said he would if he could.'

'You didn't say.'

'Didn't want you to be disappointed if he couldn't make it. And, you'll be pleased to know that Marlene isn't with him.'

'I'm not pleased about that,' I say in my best indignant voice, but secretly I am. I don't need her telling me how many sit-ups a day I need to do to have a six-pack-stomach by the end of the week.

'I am,' Mum says, grinning at me.

Joe is drinking tea with Dad in the kitchen when we wheel George in.

'Hey Charlie,' Joe says, wrapping his arms around me. 'Long time no see.'

'Yes. Hello you.' I stop to think and realise that the last time I saw Joe was Easter.

'And is this my nephew?' Joe moves towards the pram and starts poking at George.

'Hey, don't wake him.'

Joe gives me a sideways look, laughs and whips

back the covers before lifting George out. George opens his eyes, stares, then settles back down in Joe's arms.

'Good looking boy,' he says. 'Does he take after me, Mum?'

'No,' Mum says flatly. 'He doesn't. And, he's better behaved.'

'That's true,' Dad says, eyeing the celebration cake Mum is now unpacking. 'You were a right squawker.'

'Charming.'

'Are you staying overnight?' Mum's voice sounds hopeful.

'I can't. I was over this way for work so thought I'd make a detour, but I need to get back for a meeting tomorrow morning. I just wanted to see this little man.'

'Better get tea ready, then,' Mum says. 'Good job I filled the slow cooker this morning.'

'I thought I could smell something fishy in the air.' Joe winks at me.

'It's beef,' Mum corrects before laughing.

'Though it might taste like fish,' Dad adds, before ducking a tea towel flick from Mum.

It's so good to have my brother here teasing our mum and holding my son. It's such a lovely surprise.

After tea it's just me and Joe in the living room where I'm giving George his bottle. Joe looks pensive.

'I never thought I'd see this day.'

'Me neither.' I sit George up for a burp.

'Mum says his father still isn't involved.' Joe's voice is questioning, no doubt Mum, or Marlene, has primed him to get more information from me.

'No, he's not.'

'Ever likely to be?'

'Did Mum put you up to this?'

'No.' He laughs. 'No.'

'Liar.'

'Well, maybe a little bit.'

'If she wants to know she can ask herself. But she hasn't.'

'Do you want me to tell her that?' Joe asks, his voice serious.

'No.' I sigh. 'Joe, there's nothing to tell. His dad isn't about, that's it.'

'Mum thinks he's married, that you were some kind of kept mistress.'

'What? She doesn't really think that, does she?'

He smirks and I throw a soggy muslin at him, which he expertly dodges.

'Well missed.'

'I've had practice.'

'Don't tell me Marlene used to throw soggy muslins at you.'

He laughs but doesn't deny or confirm. 'My days of stinking of baby sick are long gone.'

'Good for you.'

'So, you're not saying any more about George's dad?'

'No. But I wasn't a mistress or anything like that.'

'I'll tell Mum, she'll be relieved.'

'Tell Mum what?' Mum says from the door.

'Nothing,' I say. 'I'll tell you later.' I really don't want to discuss this now. I'm conflicted about how I feel about Zippy already.

'Joe, do you want to take some celebration cake back for Benjy and Kiki?'

Joe thinks for a moment. 'Thanks, Mum, but just

the two small slices. Marlene is trying to cut everyone's sugar intake down.'

'I thought you'd lost weight,' I rib my brother.

'Not willingly,' he mutters.

'How's your puppy?'

'Getting enormous and almost house-trained.' Joe rolls his eyes.

'Still not house-trained? I thought Marlene said he was.' Mum's eyes roll too. 'Don't bring him here until that's sorted out. I'm not having a repeat of last Christmas.'

'Me neither.' I shudder at the memory of Herman's puke and poo performance not to mention his demise. 'And he's not sleeping in the annex with me, just so we're clear.'

'Don't worry, he's going to stay with Marlene's friend. Don't say I told you this but Marlene's a bit sick of him at the moment. He's very demanding, he needs a lot of walking. She didn't realise what an easy-going dog old Herman was. Young dogs are another matter.'

Mum and I offer sympathetic looks while I can tell from Mum's face that she's pleased Fritz won't be coming for Christmas.

'I'd better get off,' Joe says, standing up as Mum hurries off to fetch the cake for the children.

Joe kisses George on the forehead and hugs me goodbye.

'Tell Mum. She might not have asked because she knows how prickly you are, but she's really concerned.'

'Okay.' I nudge him in the ribs as Mum comes back with the cake.

'See you all at Christmas. The kids just can't wait

to meet their new cousin.'

'Tell them he can't wait to meet them too.'

To be fair to Mum she doesn't say a word while I tell her the full, unabridged story of New Year's Eve, and me and Zippy, and his departure to Australia. She smiles when I tell her about returning the Zippy costume and frowns when I tell her how I mistakenly thought I'd slept with CeCe's cousin.'

We both sit in silence as she absorbs all the detail. Finally, she speaks.

'Is his name really Zippy?'

'No.' In my haste to spit everything out, I haven't told her his real name. 'It's Oliver.'

'Ah,' Mum says. 'Now I understand why you used that as George's second name.'

'I've told my mum everything,' I tell Gen on the phone a few days later.

'I think that's good. How do you feel?'

'Relieved. Although obviously I'm not telling everyone, just my nearest and dearest. Although I'm sure Marlene will judge me.'

'Do you care?'

'No,' I say a bit too quickly, but it's not entirely true. I like Marlene, she's been my sister-in-law for a long time. I don't want her thinking I'm *a person of loose morals* – her phrase, not mine. I've heard her use it when we've watched films on TV over many Christmases. I try to reassure myself that she's saying it for the benefit of the kids – even if they aren't always there.

'Well then. You're your own woman.'

'Yay,' I say in a way that makes the word sound

like a chant.

'Have you heard anything from your old neighbours about Zippy?'

'No.'

'I've been thinking,' Gen starts, then waits for me to bite.

'Yes?'

'There is another way you could try to trace Zippy.' She waits for me to ask for more.

'Yes?'

'Facebook.'

'What? No.' I've already considered and rejected that option.

'Wait. Hear me out. You could post on one of those Facebook groups where people are looking for people. I've had a look and there are Australian ones.'

I'm silent.

'Charlie?'

'I don't think so.'

'Why not? It's worth a try. You do still want to find him, don't you?'

'Yes, but not like that.'

'Then how?'

'I don't know. But I don't want to broadcast to the world that my beautiful baby is the result of a drunken one-night stand and that I'd never met the father before or seen him since. No. I can't do that.'

'So, I ask again, how? If you're serious about finding him.'

Am I serious? Am I really *that* serious? When I don't answer Gen pushes again.

'Private detective?' she offers.

I hadn't thought of that but, now I do, I suppose it's possible.

'Maybe. I have the money, well, up to a limit.'

'Do you want me to look into it?' Gen is eager, more eager than I am, I think.

'Not at the moment. For now, I just want to enjoy my baby. He's barely a week old.'

Gen backs off. 'Course you do. He's gorgeous.'

'What's happening at work?' I change the subject.

'We finish next Friday lunchtime, then it's a big farewell party all afternoon, not that many have the stomach for it.'

'Where are you going?'

'Ha,' Gen groans. 'Nowhere. The party is in the office. But they have been persuaded to supply food and beverages.'

'Not alcohol?' I feign shock.

'A limited amount. They don't want drunk and disorderly on their hands.'

'I bet they don't. Any sign of Bryan and Bev.'

'Bryan's back acting very subdued but there's no sign of Bev. He's even answering his own phone when he's not letting it go to voicemail. The rumour going around now is that there is no Mrs Smith and that photo he kept on his desk was his sister and her children.'

'What? No.' I can't help laughing.

'Well, it's a rumour. Obviously, he's not confirming or denying anything, not that anyone is asking him to his face. To be honest the rumours are probably more interesting than the truth. But he certainly looks miserable.'

'Good, good and good. I hope he's very miserable.'

'I think we all do. He certainly isn't popular here, as you can imagine. He's giving a farewell and good luck speech at the party though.'

'He'll be heckled. I wish I could be there; I'd certainly heckle him. Although I suppose everyone will be too worried about jeopardising their payoff if they cause trouble.'

'All the paperwork has been signed so I don't think the company can go back on that. I think he's brave to even be in the office.'

'That sounds like admiration. Gen, I'm surprised at you.'

'Oh. Did I say brave? I meant stupid.'

'Will you heckle him?'

Gen is silent for a moment or two.

'Gen?'

'Sorry, I was just thinking about that. Call me a chicken, but no, I don't think I will. He's my direct manager; I'm going to need references from him for any jobs I apply for. So, sadly, no, I won't heckle him. Anyway, he looks seriously bloody miserable at the moment, so I'll have to content myself with that.'

I give work little thought over the next few days I'm too busy looking after George. Mum and I take him out every day and so far, October has been lovely, sunny and dry, and, if not exactly warm, not as cold as it could be. The leaves have turned golden, red and brown and are dropping to the ground. When we walk through the park I see toddlers kicking through the piles of leaves and I marvel that this time next year George could be doing that.

I've given a lot of thought to Gen's suggestion about posting on Facebook and I am definitely not going to do that; it's too demeaning. But the private detective idea is a possibility. A vague one. I've looked on the internet and tried to get an idea of costs. I even rang one and gave a false name, explained my situation and asked what they think the cost would be. While the receptionist didn't actually laugh down the phone, she did explain that it would depend entirely on how long it took them to find him. She also suggested trying Facebook first.

I've decided to leave it for now. George's first Christmas is just around the corner and I want to enjoy it with him before worrying about the future.

Gen rings me on Friday night, I can tell when she starts to speak that she's had a few wines.

'How was the work party?' I ask as soon as she's stopped saying hello and giggling.

'Yeah, great. Some of us took some extra wine in.'

'I can tell.'

'I'm not drunk.'

'Course not.'

'No. I've had a couple but I'm not drunk. I'm a responsible mother of teenagers so I can't be drunk and disorderly around them.'

'Course not.'

'Good job they're out.' She giggles again. 'Anyway, to business. Bastard Bryan has also got the boot. Yay!' Gen cackles down the phone.

'What? But wasn't moving the business to India his master plan? Wasn't he the golden boy?'

'Not any more, apparently. Rumour has it that Bev complained about his inappropriate behaviour towards her and to make it all go away they've paid her off and given him the boot.'

'That can't be true. Can it?'

'Well, he stood up and wished everyone good luck

which elicited a few boos; then he announced that he too was without a job. You can imagine the cheering, clapping and stamping that followed *that* announcement.'

'Ha ha, serves him right. It's what happened to Merv so it's only fair.'

'Yeah, I thought you'd enjoy that. Seems he *has* been stringing Bev along for years, pretending he had a wife and kids in Leeds, but also telling her that if things were different…'

'Really?'

'So rumour has it.'

'Where are you getting this from?'

'I couldn't possibly say,' Gen says, following it with a loud hiccup. Then I remember her good friend in HR.

'Well it couldn't happen to a nicer man.'

'Yep.'

Gen rattles on about the party after her revelation and while it's good to hear the gossip and know that several of my team have already secured themselves new jobs I find myself yawning through the detail and staring into George's sweet little face.

He looks more like my memory of his father every day and not at all like Elaine's gawky teenager.

Seventeen

November comes and goes and every day is a treat with George. He smiles and gurgles and coos and his eyes follow me around the room when he's sat in his bouncer.

I am the luckiest woman in the world. He's placid and sweet natured but at the same time alert and knowing. The health visitor says he is hitting all his milestones. He is, to me, just perfect.

He sleeps all night, going to bed at ten pm and sleeping right through until six – something Mum says neither Joe nor I did until we were nearly two. He's still sleeping in the crib beside my bed and I anticipate that he'll continue to do this for as long as possible. This, according to Mum will be the day he sits up unaided, which, fortunately, is a while off. When he wakes up in the morning he is so happy to see me his little face lights up, and even though he must be starving he treats me to a big gummy smile.

Elaine engineers the need to visit us or bump into us in the park at least twice a week. I don't mind, she's kind and caring and I feel I owe her. Had she not been there to deliver George I don't know what would have happened. Mum may have had two babies of her own but, as she says herself, she wasn't down the *business end* and wouldn't have a clue what to do.

George has grown out of the little cardigan Elaine

made him but she has knitted more; they are gorgeous and he wears them all.

As Christmas approaches and with it, New Year, I've thought a lot about Zippy. Is he still in Australia? Does he ever think about me? Does he even remember me? Given how much wine we consumed that night, it's possible he doesn't.

Gen has asked me again if I will consider Facebook to trace him; I've given her an emphatic no. Who knows how long anything posted on the internet will be there? I wouldn't want George, when he is old enough, to discover I used Facebook to try to find his dad. It's too horrible and, as I've still heard nothing from my old neighbours, I'm not holding out much hope that they can track him down either.

Gen's pressed me on using a private detective again, has even managed to find one who sounds a lot better than the agency I spoke to. I've told her I'm still giving it some thought. I know she means well, I know she thinks that a child deserves a father, but who's to say that Zippy will want to be a father even if he finds out?

Then I look at George; how could anyone not fall in love with him?

As we rattle through December the days grow shorter and colder. I've never noticed the seasons like I do now that I am outside so much. In the winter, before George, I rushed to work and home again in the dark. Now, I go out with my baby in his pram – aka travel system – at every opportunity, filling his lungs and mine with sweet, fresh air. As it's turned out I'm so glad we're not in London, the air is so much sweeter here in Wiltshire.

I love my annex – no one dares call it the granny

annex now. It's home; safe and sound and clean and quiet. It's my little haven where I can do as I please with help, support and love on the other side of the door. I am so grateful to Mum and Dad, and all my years of living in London, in the lovely flat that I called home for so long, are fading into insignificance. This place is my nest, my cocoon where I can hide away from the world.

I am happy.

George is asleep in his crib in my room and I am sitting in my own sitting room, my feet on the Moroccan pouffe knitting. Mum has taught me and it has been an arduous task for her. I'm attempting to make a cardigan for George; we agreed that I would knit a size bigger than he currently needs so that by the time I've finished it should fit him. I've been knitting it for weeks and I'm wondering if I should have gone two sizes up. Mum and Dad are out Christmas shopping again and I am enjoying peace, quiet and concentrating.

I've just got to a particularly tricky part which requires all my attention when I hear the crunch of tyres on the drive. It's not Mum and Dad because they've only been gone about twenty minutes. I carefully lay my knitting down and glance out of the window to see Elaine's car. I jump up before she rings the doorbell in case it wakes George.

'Hello,' she says, smiling. 'I didn't even ring.'

'No, George is asleep and I didn't want you to wake him.'

'Ah. I won't disturb you both then.' She offers me a smile that seems to want me to force her to come in; I consider it for a second then smile back.

'Better not, he's sound asleep.'

'Yes. Right. Well, I take it your mum's not in either.'

'Christmas shopping.' I roll my eyes. 'Again.'

'Oh yes, it's all go.' She hands me a large wrapped present. I know instantly from the paper that's it's for George and now I feel mean. 'I just wanted to drop this round before the big day. I won't have time to see you all over Christmas, we're very busy with family.' She beams at me. 'I expect you are too.'

'Yes, my brother and his lot.' I try to make my voice light but I'm feeling so mean about not inviting her in. Can I backtrack now? No, it will look even worse.

'You're looking lovely and slim, by the way.' She points at my smallest jeans which I've managed to squeeze into for the first time today and I do look thinner than in my usual leggings and baggy tops.

'Thank you. Can't breathe too well though,' I joke, although that's not actually true, I've been pleasantly surprised by how comfortable they are.

'Have a lovely Christmas and maybe I'll see you all in the new year.' Elaine turns to walk back to her car.

'Definitely, definitely. In the park, no doubt. Or here,' I add to her retreating form. Shit, I feel evil now. Why didn't I just invite her in?

I return to my knitting but I don't have the enthusiasm for it anymore and as I flop onto my sofa George wakes and starts an uncharacteristic yell. Damn it, Elaine can barely have got out of the street. I really should have invited her in.

'Elaine called round,' I tell Mum when her and Dad come back. 'She bought a present for George.

'Oh yes, she texted me.' Mum smiles at me and I

wonder if Elaine's text mentioned what an ungrateful cow I was and how I wouldn't let her in to see George. 'She's invited us over for New Year's Eve.'

'That'll be nice for you.'

'All of us,' Mum adds. 'You and George, Joe and his lot. She's got family coming too so it should be fun.'

'Right.'

Mum stops unpacking her shopping and turns to me. 'You don't have anything else planned, do you?'

'No.' I shake my head. 'No.'

'Good. I said you'd be there.' Mum turns back to her bags.

'I don't really want to go.' I tell Gen about the New Year's Eve get together when she rings a few days later to tell me about her new job. She's starting after Christmas and it's more money and better perks than she was getting before. Gen's delighted and I couldn't be happier for her.

'Why, what else have you got planned? I don't suppose you're organising your usual fancy dress piss up this year.'

'No. Of course not. Maybe I could cry off at the last minute.'

'Why? What else are you going to do? Sit at home and wallow? Remember last year and wish things were different?'

'I don't wish things were different. I love being a mum.'

'There you are then, no need to hide away on New Year's Eve, is there? Who knows you might meet a nice man who wants a ready-made family.'

'I knew you'd understand.' I make no attempt to

hide the sarcasm in my voice.

'Well, you can't hide away in that annex for ever.'

'I'm not.'

'Prove it then and get along to a party when you're invited.'

'It's not really a party, just families meeting.'

'Even less excuse not to go. Thought any more about finding Zippy?'

'I plan to give it some more thought in the New Year.'

'Good. I think you should.'

We say goodbye and I'm left with a bitter feeling, Gen has made it so obvious she thinks that Zippy should know about his son.

Suddenly it's Christmas Eve and we're getting ready for the arrival of Joe, Marlene, Benjy and Kiki. They're due late this afternoon. Mum is busy in the kitchen icing the cake she made months ago; she says she hadn't intended to leave it so late but time has just crept up on her. I'm sitting on the small sofa in the dining area giving George his bottle before he goes for his nap. We've got the small TV in the kitchen on and Mum and I are half watching the film *Casablanca*.

'This was your gran's favourite,' Mum says, wistfully.

'I know. She made me watch it with her often enough whenever I stayed there as a kid.' We both laugh together remembering Granny Suze. Christmas does that; makes you think of the people you've lost, forces bittersweet memories to the front.

'Damn,' Mum says, deliberately breaking the mood. 'I didn't get any parsnips. Sainsbury's were sold out and I meant to try Iceland, although

Sainsbury's might have restocked since last night.' She glances up at the clock and then down at the cake she's half-way through. 'I'll go after this,' she says to herself. 'But I need to get the mince pies in when the sausage rolls come out.'

We always have mince pies for Christmas Eve tea, it's part of our family tradition, not that the children particularly like them, and I can't say I'm fond either. Herman liked them though.

'I could go. George is going down for a nap soon, so I could pop out in the car. And you'd be here anyway, if he wakes up.'

'Would you? That would be so helpful. You'll need to go soon though, in case they close early. Get fresh if you can. And while you're at it could you get another carton of double cream, actually, make that two.'

Half an hour later George is sound asleep in his crib and I'm parking the car in the high street before scuttling along to Iceland. There seem to be a lot of people dodging about getting last minute necessities with that look of panic on their faces because the shops will be closed for a whole day. I've already tried Sainsbury's and have managed to get two cartons of double cream although one of them is brandy flavoured, so we need to ensure that the children don't have that one. I've also bought a fresh cream gateau to go with the mince pies Mum is probably doing now – for those of us who don't like mince pies. I message to let her know. She messages back a big smiley face and a thumbs-up.

It's bitterly cold and I can see my breath, there's been the usual forecast of snow which will probably come to nothing. All I know is that my feet are almost numb, and so are my fingers. I'm clutching my bag-for-life and watching my footing as there are patches of black ice on the pavement.

I think back to this time last year when I was on my way down here on the train from London. What a difference a year makes. I wonder how Yan and CeCe are getting on in the newly revamped flat, although I have to admit I've not given it, or my former flatmates, much thought. Other than exchanging texts when George was born I haven't heard from them, nor they from me. It's funny how you can live with people for over a year and yet never be truly friends with them. It's ironic that I thought they weren't friends either when in fact they had become lovers right under my nose. I remember how annoyed and betrayed I felt, now I wish them nothing but well. Good luck to them.

I've resigned myself to going to Elaine's for the New Year's Eve get together – Mum says it is definitely not a party, or at least not what I would call a party. I suppose she's thinking back to last year's party and the result of it – our darling George.

I step into Iceland and make straight for the fresh veg section but I have to pass the frozen veg section first so I check the parsnip situation there. There are none left, just a big sign advertising packs of honey glazed parsnips for only one pound. No wonder they are all gone.

I go around to the fresh veg but I don't hold out much hope, if the frozen are all gone, so will the fresh be. Then I spy it, a single pack of parsnips languishing on the shelf and waiting just for me. I march purposely towards the parsnip bag and hope that no one beats me to it.

Got it, my hand is on the bag.

But my hand is also on top of someone else's hand.

Are we going to have a tussle in the middle of Iceland over a bag of parsnips?

'Um,' I say, realising that the hand I am gripping is a man's.

'Ah,' a male voice says.

Neither of us looks at the other because eye contact will create some kind of bond, some kind of empathy where each suggests that the other take the parsnip bag, even though we both know we both want it.

'I think I saw it first,' I say. Well this could be true, equally it could not.

'Bungle? Is that you?'

Bungle? Bungle? Did this stranger just call me Bungle? Surely, I misheard. I don't answer. I don't know what to say. I don't know what to think. I turn my head away.

'Bungle. It is you. Charlie, isn't it?'

'Um, yes.'

We're still both gripping the parsnip bag and I am still half gripping his hand. My mind is running through a thousand possibilities and the one it's settled on is that I am having some sort of seizure.

'Charlie, do you remember me?'

I turn towards the speaker. Do I remember him? How could I not?

Then I think I do have an actual seizure because my knees start to buckle, the air starts to fizz and I let go of the damn parsnip bag.

He catches me – in his arms – as though I'm some silly swooning girly. He smiles right into my face.

'Are you okay? Don't worry, I've got you.'

He's nice and I have been remembering what he looks like correctly, but then I have been seeing a tiny version of his face every minute of every day for almost three months.

'Hello Zippy.'

Eighteen

'Oliver,' he corrects, smiling.

'Yeah.'

'Are you okay?'

'Yes,' I say, straightening myself up and smoothing down my coat. 'It's hot in here after being outside.'

He smiles, a great big lovely smile that fills his face and makes little crinkles on either side of his eyes.

'This is a weird coincidence.'

'Yes,' I mutter.

'Of all the freezer shops in all the towns you walk into mine.'

'What?'

He looks a bit embarrassed. 'Sorry, I'm misquoting from Casablanca, the film, you know, of all the gin joints…'

'Yes. I saw a bit of it earlier.'

'Me too. So, what are you doing here?'

'Staying with my family,' I say, which is true, if not exactly accurate. 'What about you?'

'Same.' He smiles and shakes his head. 'I can't quite believe this, we're from the same town?'

'No. My parents moved here after I went to London.'

'Still an amazing coincidence.'

'Isn't it?' I should tell him, shouldn't I? I should tell him he has a son, but I can't just blurt it out in the middle of Iceland in the fresh veg section, can I?

'You have them,' he says. 'I don't like them much anyway.'

'What?' I sound so stupid.

'The parsnips. You have them.' We turn to look at the shelf where the one remaining bag of parsnips in the whole of Aston Bassett sits waiting to be bought.

'Ah, perfect,' says a voice. A hand snakes in between Zippy and me and swipes the bag, pulling it back through the small space between us and hitting me on the hand.

'Ow,' I yelp but the perpetrator, a short, stout woman in sensible boots is oblivious as she marches down the aisle towards the check-outs.

'Now neither of us will have them,' Zippy says, laughing.

'No. How is your dad now?'

'He died.' Zippy looks down at his feet and I wished I hadn't asked. The flippant part of my brain wants to say, never mind, you've got a son instead. Inwardly, I slap myself.

'I'm sorry.'

'Thanks.' He looks up again, stares into my eyes. 'The good news is I'm back in the UK, probably for good.'

'Cool,' I mutter as my phone vibrates loudly in my pocket.

'Maybe we could meet up?' He sounds tentative. 'After Christmas, if you're still here?'

'Um yeah.' That'll be the time to tell him.

'Well, only if you want to.' He turns to walk away; I've put him off.

'I do. Yes, I do. Definitely.' My phone starts to ring.

He turns back to me and smiles. 'Do you want to

get that?'

'No, they'll leave a message.' The phone rings out and instantly vibrates with a message.

'Give me your number and I'll message you,' he says.

My phone starts to ring again.

'I'd better get it.' But the phone stops before I get it out of my pocket. I roll my eyes at Zippy. Then a message comes through from Mum: *They've arrived and they've brought bloody Fritz with them, he's just shit all over the living room carpet. Hurry up because George is awake now too.*

'I'll have to go. Emergency at home.'

I scuttle out of Iceland and race along the street to the car, jump in and roar home. It's only as I turn the corner that I realise I haven't given Zippy my phone number.

I can smell the stench as soon as I open the door. Instead of the sweet aroma of mince pies cooking, in its place, shit. Another Christmas marred by dog shit. At least I can't hear George crying.

'I thought you weren't bringing him.' Mum's voice sounds angry and harassed.

'We were let down at the last minute.' Joe sounds just as angry and harassed as Mum. 'It's not his fault, Mum, he was in the car for hours.'

'Then you should have walked him round the block when you got here, not let him bound in and do his business everywhere.' Mum gags. 'This is just disgusting.'

I tiptoe past the living room and see Mum and Joe on their hands and knees scrubbing the carpet, they're both wearing yellow rubber gloves. I fight the urge to laugh and creep on into the kitchen to find Marlene, Benjy and Kiki squeezed onto the small sofa and cuddling a gurgling baby George.

'Charlie,' Marlene yodels my name. 'He is lovely, your baby. So good.'

'Hello everyone.'

Benjy and Kiki jump up to hug me while Marlene jogs George up and down on her knee.

'This is a good workout for the abs and the thighs, Charlie. Do you do it?'

'Didn't take you long,' I say, and laugh. She's quite incorrigible, my sister-in-law. 'Where's Dad? And your naughty dog?'

'Grandad took him out for a walk,' Benjy says.

'Thanks Benjy, oops, sorry, Ben.'

'You can call me Benjy if you like.' Benjy gives me a shy smile. He's grown a lot since Easter; his shoulders are broader and so is his jaw. He's the double of my brother at that age.

'His girlfriend calls him Benjy, so it's all right now.' Marlene looks up to the ceiling.

'She's not my girlfriend, Mum, she's just a friend.'

Marlene, unusually, bites her tongue.

'Can we take George out in his pram?' Kiki says, jumping up and down like a puppy herself.

'Not today, it's a bit late and a bit cold.' I have a sudden horrible vision of bumping into Zippy. Oliver. 'But we definitely will.'

'Tomorrow then?'

'It's Christmas Day tomorrow; we might be a bit busy.' I laugh. Our usual Christmas comprises eating, presents, eating, presents and lying around watching crap TV.

Kiki's shoulders slump.

'You can help George unwrap his presents if you like, he won't be able to do it himself yet.'

Kiki's eyes light up. 'Oh yes,' she yells.

'How come you had to bring Fritz?'

'The dog sitter is ill, she has flu. Urgh. He doesn't usually do shits in the house. He was excited. He was in the car too long. Joe would not stop.'

It's good to know that Fritz's mishap isn't Marlene's fault. I smile and suppress a snigger.

Mum and Joe come through with a bucket of dirty water and Joe carries it into the downstairs toilet while Mum lifts the lid and gags as Joe tips it away. She flushes the toilet several times while frowning at any and everybody. I take George from Marlene and make excuses about changing his nappy. I don't want to be involved in the recriminations when they start, or rather, continue.

I stay away for as long as I can, changing George and playing with him. I can't stop thinking about his father; I can't believe he's here, in this town, visiting his own family. I'm simultaneously shocked, petrified and delighted. How do I tell him? How do I bring it up? How do I contact him without his phone number and he without mine? I kick myself for not waiting and giving it to him. I blame Fritz and his escapade for that.

I can't get Oliver's face out of my mind and, I can't help thinking how very attractive he is.

I think about ringing Gen, she's the only person I can really talk to about this. But it's Christmas Eve and her house will be as frantic as this one but without the dog mess.

In my kitchenette I make George a bottle and sit down to feed him, just as a tentative knock on the door reminds me that we have visitors.

'Hello,' Kiki's little voice calls. 'Can I come in?'

'Of course you can.'

Kiki sits down on the sofa next to me and strokes George's head.

'Would you like to feed him?'

She nods silently.

After jiggling and rearranging, Kiki sits feeding a contented George while I look on. He's happy with his cousin.

I hope he will be as happy with his dad.

'Nanny says tea will be ready at six,' Kiki tells me, as I show her how to burp George.

'We'd better go in a minute.' I take George from her and wipe his face. He beams up at me.

'He's so lovely, Auntie Charlie. Are you going to have another baby soon?'

I glance down at my stomach, which, until now, I thought was looking reasonably good and wonder what the hell comment Marlene has made that Kiki has overheard.

'No. I'm not.'

'Oh, that's a shame because it's nice to have a brother. Or a sister, like me,' she adds, getting up and twirling around. She's wearing a cute little flippy skirt over purple leggings.

'That's a lovely skirt. Come on, let's have our tea.'

'Has Nanny made mince pies?'

'Fraid so. But there's also cream cake.'

'Oh good.'

Fritz is nowhere to be seen when we go through to the kitchen but Dad has that ruddy faced look of someone who has been out in the cold for too long.

Over tea there's the usual chat and catch up with lots of questions about George but no one brings up his father. Mum must have primed them not to mention it. It must be killing Marlene for her not to say anything.

If only they knew that he's in this town, he could be in the same street for all I know.

Eventually I bring up the elephant in the room, or rather the dog. I have already made up my mind that Fritz will not be sleeping in the annex with me as Herman did last year. I have George now and he cannot be subjected to dog's mess and hair.

'He's in the garage,' Mum says, when I ask.

'It is too cold.' Marlene's tone is her best Germanic one, the one she uses to make fiction sound like fact – I once heard her telling Kiki that there is a tooth fairy because she, Marlene, had once been invited to take tea with her, at Buckingham Palace. I think Marlene was mixing up her royalty.

Joe sighs before he speaks. 'I've put his basket and blanket by the boiler, he'll be fine there. The garage is attached to the house; it's not separate like ours.'

'But he sleeps in the kitchen at home.'

'The princes' domain.' Mum's lips purse.

'What about the granny annex? He would be fine there.' Marlene isn't giving up easily.

'Not after last year,' I cut in. 'It's my home, my annex.'

'He'll be fine in the garage.' Joe reaches over and squeezes Marlene's hand.

Marlene scans the faces around the table and decides to let it go, before turning to me.

'I hope Charlie, that you have no unsuitable presents this year.'

My mouth drops open. This could escalate into a row where Marlene accuses me of killing Herman. But I'm not going to let that happen.

'Oh, it's getting late. It's George's bath time.' I stand up. 'Do you want to help me, Kiki?'

It's nearly midnight and George has been asleep for hours, Benjy, Kiki and Marlene are also asleep and Joe has just come back from taking Fritz out for his last walk before settling him in the garage.

'I hope he's done his business,' Mum says.

'He has, Mum. Don't worry. And I put it in the bin before I came in. Oh, and I've washed my hands, so we're all good.'

If looks could kill Joe would be dead and my mum would be up on a charge of murder.

'Anyone fancy a glass of port and a slice of cheese,' Dad offers.

'Oh, why not?' I don't even like port that much but the idea appeals to me and it might help me sleep because I can't stop thinking about Oliver and I know I'm in for a night of tossing and turning.

Mum fetches cheese and biscuits while Dad pours port into four bulbous glasses.

'M&S special offer,' Dad says, laughing. 'Theirs is always the best.'

I lift the glass to my mouth and take my first sip, it hits the back of my throat and I gasp.

Joe sniggers. 'You're useless, Charlie.'

'I prefer wine.'

'Would you like wine?' Dad asks.

'No. No. I'll stick with this.' The last thing I want is to be drunk in charge of a baby but if the wine comes out I might just use it to damp down my troubled thoughts. At least with the port I won't be tempted to drink too much. I help myself to a slice of cheese and hope it won't give me nightmares – if I do get any sleep.

'We've got George that Buckaroo thing,' Mum tells Joe.

'Jumperoo,' I correct as Joe and I giggle.

'He'll love that,' Joe says, pouring us all another glass.

'Hey, watch it.' I hadn't even realised I'd drunk the first one.

'To us,' Joe raises his glass. 'To all of us and to you Charlie, for having a beautiful baby and doing it on your own.'

'Cheers,' we say in unison as we clink our glasses.

'Not entirely on my own,' I add, nodding at Mum and Dad.

'You've heard from the father?' My mum is so bloody perceptive sometimes, it's scary.

I sit for a moment blinking at her.

'Don't cry, Charlie,' Joe says. 'You're doing great.'

I can tell from the look on his face he wishes he hadn't made the toast to me now.

I shake my head.

'It's not that, it's …' The words tumble out of me as Mum, Dad and Joe sit transfixed until I've finished telling them how I bumped into Zippy in Iceland.

'Well,' Mum says, 'that bloody Fritz has got a lot to answer for.'

We can't help laughing.

'You've no idea where his parents live?'

'No.'

'You definitely didn't give him your number?' Joe is clutching at straws.

'No, Mum was frantically messaging me. It all got a bit confused.' I shrug and try to make light of it.

'It'll work out,' Mum says, supping her third glass of port. 'These things do.' She sounds so confident I almost believe her until she continues. 'And if it doesn't then you're no worse off than you were this morning, are you?'

Now's she put it like that, it sounds reasonable. But it's not.

'I was already trying to find him.'

There's silence around the room and, for a few moments, all we can hear is the clock ticking, loud and insistent.

'Were you now?' Mum breaks the silence. 'How?'

'Gen tried to track him down through the costume hire shop but it had closed down because the owner died. I was thinking maybe of hiring a private detective.'

'You won't need to now. We have our first crafting session on 4th January, I'll put the word out. That bunch knows everything about everyone in this town, we'll track him down.'

'You make him sound like big game.' Joe winks at me.

'Err, thanks.' I try to make my voice sound grateful but all I can think about now is how everyone in this town will know *all* my business. Assuming that they don't already.

Christmas passes without mishaps. George loves his Jumperoo but only for about two minutes, but that's probably because he's a bit young for it at the moment. Benjy and Kiki love their presents, Fritz behaves himself and I don't receive any unsuitable gifts. By the day after Boxing Day we're all a bit stir crazy; the weather has been miserable over Christmas and we haven't been out at all.

'Are we going to the park?' Kiki asks, jumping up and down in front of me. 'It's not raining today.'

'Yes, let's go as soon as George finishes his bottle.'

By the time we're ready to go Mum and Benjy are accompanying us and so is Joe, with Fritz.

We amble around the park, all of us grateful for the opportunity to stretch our legs. Fritz sniffs every plant and post we pass and Benjy makes faces at George who beams back at him. I've let Kiki push the pram but she is supervised by Mum. Joe and I, and Fritz are dawdling along behind them.

'Are you looking for him?' Joe asks, catching me scanning the area.

'Is it that obvious?'

'Oh yes.'

'Yeah, well… I wouldn't want to bump into him and for him to find out this way. I need to at least prepare the way.'

'Yeah, maybe…'

'What? You think it would be better for him to be shocked into discovering he's a father?'

'No. No, I didn't mean that. But it's going to be a shock no matter how you tell him.'

'I know. I'm afraid to think about it and yet that's all I do.'

'It'll work out,' Joe shouts as he runs after Fritz who has chosen this moment to bolt off in front of us and jump up at George.

'He loves him,' Mum says when we catch up with her. 'Look at him smiling.'

'You'll have to get a dog, Charlie.' Joe gives me a

mischievous smirk.

'I don't think my princes will like that,' Mum says, killing any speculation that it might be a possibility.

'You said George loved him,' Joe says.

Mum gives Joe one of her best withering looks before urging Kiki to push a bit faster, soon we're trailing behind again.

'How would you react, Joe, to news like that?'

Joe laughs. 'Marlene would kill me.'

'You know what I mean. Hypothetically. Put yourself in Zippy's shoes. I mean Oliver.'

'I can't, Sis. It's just too…' His voice trails away.

'What?'

'I can't imagine. I do know I'd want to know. Even if…' He stops again.

'Even if you didn't want to know, so to speak.'

'Yes. I imagine so.'

'Thanks for that, that's really helped.' I laugh, I have to and Joe joins in.

'It'll work out,' he says, putting his arm around me and resting his head on top of mine. I love it that my brother is so much taller than me.

'You sound like Mum.'

'God help us. Come on; let's catch up with your baby before Kiki runs off with him.'

'Oh.'

'What?'

'It's okay. It's nothing. I just thought…'

'What?' Joe follows my stare. 'You thought you saw him?'

'Wishful thinking. Come on.'

That's all it could have been because we walk in the park every day after that and I don't imagine a glimpse of him again.

New Year's Eve arrives and what started out as Elaine's get together seems to have morphed into a full-scale party. Apparently, Elaine's sister and her husband and their children will be there as well as some neighbours and sundry others.

'I don't really want to go, Mum.'

'Just go for an hour. It's George she wants to see anyway.' Mum grins at me.

'I realise that but he'll be asleep in his pram.'

'Yes, but Elaine can look at him and tell her story, you know: *ex-pig farmer delivers baby and here he is. Just perfect.*'

'And I had nothing to do with it,' I say sulkily.

'Give her that moment of glory. She's genuinely in love with George, as much because he reminds her of her own son as because she delivered him.'

'Don't draw that comparison. He's a geeky, gawky teenager. George will never be like that.' I find myself folding my arms in defiance.

Mum laughs. 'Just keep telling yourself that and I'll remind you in fifteen years' time.'

'Benjy isn't like that. I don't remember Joe being like that.'

Mum raises one eyebrow. I'm impressed because I didn't know she could do that and momentarily it distracts me. She lets it drop slowly.

'Just come for an hour, you might even enjoy yourself.'

It's nearly seven and we're almost ready to leave. George is in his pram but he's not asleep, he's smiling up at the pattern on the hood and gurgling to himself.

I'm wearing the new dark jeans that Marlene and

Joe bought me for Christmas, teamed with the glitzy jumper from Mum and Dad. I feel good. I think I'm actually slimmer than I was this time last year. Gen says it's because I'm not knocking back a bottle of wine a night. I told her I never did that, only on Thursdays, Fridays and Saturdays and sometimes, Sunday lunchtime. She says I'm such a lightweight now. I've even had my hair cut, not too much, just reshaped so it looks like a style and it's short enough that I'm not tempted to scrape it back into a ponytail all the time.

I think back to this time last year when I was getting ready, wearing my tatty old sports underwear because it was the only thing cool enough under the Bungle costume.

My world has changed immeasurably in the past year and, if I'm honest, while I do miss some aspects of my former life, I'm happier now than ever. What was it that CeCe said to me when I sniped about her relationship with Yan? Love changes everything.

It certainly does, I think, as I look at my lovely boy in his pram, fighting sleep.

We're putting our coats on and loading wine bottles onto the bottom of the pram.

'Most inappropriate,' I say and I am not joking.

'Get over yourself.' Joe nudges me.

'What about poor Fritz?' Marlene's bottom lip comes out as though she is a child.

'Fed, watered and walked. He'll be fine.' Joe links arms with Marlene and urges her towards the front door.

We're walking to Elaine's as it's only a ten-minute walk and, according to Dad, easier than trying to park round there and anyway, who would want to drive home? That means, when I make my escape, I'll have to walk back alone, but, mercifully it's a dry night and it will be less disturbing for George.

As we walk down the road the children are excited because they will be allowed to stay up late, although Benjy doesn't think it's fair that Kiki can stay up as late as him. I've agreed that she can come back with me if she wants to. She says she won't want to.

Elaine and her family live in a dormer bungalow at the end of a narrow close. The front of the bungalow is brick paved and covered in cars; Dad is right, there is nowhere for us to park. Christmas lights adorn the front of the house.

'Cool,' Benjy says. 'Why don't you do that Grandad?'

'Um, next year, maybe.'

'He'll hold you to that.' Joe laughs.

The front door is yanked open before we even knock and Elaine's grinning face welcomes us into a spacious, square hall.

'Where's my favourite baby?' she calls, pushing her face into the pram.

George, despite the walk is still wide awake. Inwardly, I groan, because it means I have no excuse not to get him out.

Coats off, wine bottles removed and George out of his pram and we're ushered into a massive room, a sitting-dining-kitchen space that is not what I expected from the bungalow's kitsch exterior.

'This is nice,' I mutter to Dad.

'Yes.' He sighs. 'Don't say anything about it to Mum, this is what she wants to do in ours.'

'You should.' I nudge him. 'Nice little project for you, knock through a few walls.'

'Shush.' He nudges me back as Mum and Elaine approach with a tray of drinks.

We're introduced to a myriad of people whose names I instantly forget, if questioned I'll blame *babybrain*. There's no sign of Alistair which I'm relieved about, even if it does make me feel a bit mean.

'Where are the kids?' someone, who I think might be Elaine's sister, asks.

'Alistair has set up his games console upstairs. 'I think *both* of mine are up there.' Elaine mock rolls her eyes. 'And your two and Paul, Simon, Lulu and Elsbeth.'

'Both of yours?' Mum frowns. 'I didn't know you had more than one.'

'Long story. By my first marriage.' She rolls her eyes and skips off balancing a tray of samosas in one hand.

Hours fly by and George shows no sign of going to sleep. He's been shown off to every neighbour, friend and relative and the story of his birth has been retold, and embellished, several times.

I'm in the kitchen end warming his bottle when Elaine hands him back to me.

'Use my bedroom,' she says. 'It's too noisy down here. Left at the top of the stairs.'

I take George, his bottle and his changing bag and head upstairs. Along the landing I can hear the sound of a games console and fairly subdued shouting and cheering. At the far end of the landing a man of about twenty-five, who seems to be fending off the attention of a much younger girl, looks at me and smiles as though I have come to save him. Though obviously older, he's the double of Alastair, but his face and shoulders have filled out and he has a better haircut.

'Hi. You must be Alastair's brother.' I fumble for the handle to Elaine's bedroom door.

'No. Cousin. He's his brother.'

I follow his nod to see someone coming out of bathroom.

Our eyes meet. Our eyes lock. For a moment there is silence interrupted only by the sound of the games console.

'Charlie?'

'Zippy?'

'Oliver,' he corrects. 'So that *was* you I saw in the park the other day with your husband.'

'No, I…'

Right on cue George starts to wail, a great big loud yell that refuses to be ignored.

'Cute baby.' He nods at George. 'I'll leave you to it.' He skips down the stairs leaving me open mouthed and dumbfounded and holding a now screaming George.

Nineteen

George takes a long time to settle to his bottle; he's fractious and anxious. Is he picking up on my distress? Eventually he finishes it and then fills his nappy. I'm desperate to speak to Oliver but also relieved to be hiding up here with George.

I change him and cuddle him and settle him and eventually make my way downstairs. I search the faces – there seem to be more of them – looking for Oliver. But I can see him nowhere.

My brain is spinning. Oliver is Elaine's son. No wonder George reminded her of him. She didn't mean Alistair at all, she meant Oliver. How could this have happened?

Elaine is George's grandmother.

At least I know where to find him now.

In my arms George is whining, it's a soft little whine that means he needs to be asleep. I find Elaine and say goodbye. I find Mum and Dad and tell them I'm leaving. Dad offers to walk me home but I persuade him not to; I need some time alone to assimilate what has just happened. Kiki is enjoying herself and showing no sign of being tired so is not coming with me either.

In the hall I settle George into his pram, stuff my bags underneath and pull on my coat. I wrestle the pram outside and take a deep breath of air; it's cold and I hope it will cool and calm my brain.

I stand and wait for my heart to settle. I check on George, he's already sound asleep. In ten minutes I will be home and warm and away from here. I tell myself again that at least I now know where to find Oliver.

When I'm ready.

Up the brick paved drive, along the path and I'm faced with a man walking a small dog. He's silhouetted by the streetlight behind him. I ready myself to respond if he says hello, as so many dog walkers do.

'Hello Charlie.' It's Oliver.

I'm struck dumb.

'Where are you going?'

'Home,' I manage.

'Oh? Isn't your husband walking with you?' His tone sounds judgemental.

I exhale and watch as the long stream of warm air from my lungs shows white in the cold.

'That wasn't my husband, that was my brother. And just so there are no more misunderstandings I don't have a husband, boyfriend or any other man lurking about.'

'Oh?' Now his voice sounds hopeful or is that my imagination?

'When you have time, we need to talk.' Finally, I have found my voice, my strength.

'What are you doing now?'

'Going home.' I try to keep the annoyance from my voice.

'I'll walk with you. Can you just wait until I put my mum's dog back in the house? She's been hiding in the utility room; she really doesn't like the house so full of strangers.'

'I can wait.'

Three minutes later he's back. It's awkward and I don't know what to say. We walk on to the end of the street, the air crackling between us. Is this the right place to break the news? In the dark on a quiet street on New Year's Eve? I open my mouth to speak but don't know where to start and close it again.

'How old is your baby?'

He'll be three months in a few days.

He's silent. Is he working it out?

'He's called George,' I add.

'George,' he repeats.

'Yes.' Blurt it out, say it, I urge myself, but I can't.

'Any other names?'

'George Oliver Copeland.'

'Right.'

'Copeland is my surname.'

'Yes, of course.' He falls silent again.

He's working it out, he must be. He has to because we're running out of time, we've walked quickly and we're nearly home. As I approach the house he stays with me. I unlock the front door and tip the pram to get over the sill.

'Can I help?'

'I'm fine. Do it every day.' I wheel George into the hallway. Now what? 'Do you want to come in?'

'I think I'd better.'

He's worked it out.

We go through to Mum and Dad's kitchen and I put the kettle on.

'Coffee?'

'Please.'

I take my coat off and hang it up and he does the same. As I busy myself making coffee he stares into the pram but he doesn't speak.

I take our coffees over to the little sofa and wait for him to follow. As we both sit down, too close for comfort, I wish I'd sat us at the dining table.

'This isn't how I imagined it.'

'No?' He isn't going to make this easy, or maybe it's just the shock. Or, maybe, he *hasn't* worked it out.

'You have realised he's yours?' I blurt.

'Yes.' He nods slowly. 'Yes.'

'I tried to contact you, but the shop owner had died and the shop closed and no records and I wished I'd asked when I took your Zippy costume back but I didn't know then, obviously. And, anyway I was really annoyed with you because of the deposit thing; you got it, not me, after I trailed it all the way back. It was heavy too. Then it all got a bit complicated with work and the flat and then he came along and I didn't know how to find you and I was going to see about a private detective after Christmas.'

He looks at me with his mouth slightly open but he doesn't say anything, just searches my face with his eyes.

'And your mum delivered him.'

'Yes. I've heard.'

'I know it's a lot to take in, I know it's a shock. I'm not expecting anything from you. It's not like we even knew each other, is it? It's just I thought you might want to know.'

He nods slowly. 'Yeah.'

'I'm sorry.' I can feel tears pricking the back of my eyes. I don't know what I expected but it isn't this. Did I expect him to leap for joy, to declare undying love for us both? Maybe I did.

'Why?'

'Well,' I shrug, swallowing hard and breathing deeply through my nose. I am not going to cry. It will just make me look stupid. 'As I've said, I don't expect anything from you. You can walk away right now and no hard feelings.'

He blinks several times then picks up his coffee cup and takes a sip. I take the opportunity to do the same.

'And no one need know if you'd prefer it that way.'

George starts to snuffle in his pram and I jump at the chance to do something other than spout waffle at Oliver.

'I need to put him in his crib; he doesn't usually sleep in his pram at night.' I get up and go to George, carefully undoing the pram covers and lifting him out. As I turn I come face to face with Oliver.

'Sorry,' he mutters. 'I just…'

George is warm and contented in my arms.

'Would you like to hold him?'

Oliver nods slowly.

I pass George over, it's awkward and fumbling.

'Sorry,' Oliver says again.

George wriggles around until he is comfortable in his father's arms. A little windy smile escapes his mouth in his sleep. Then he opens his eyes and stares straight into Oliver's face.

'Wow,' Oliver says softly.

I watch his Adam's apple rise and fall as he swallows back his emotion.

'Would you like to sit down and hold him?'

'Yeah.' His voice sounds hoarse and croaky.

'Come through here.' I lead the way to my annex feeling strong and brave. 'More private in here and less likely to be disturbed when they all come thundering back in.'

'Who?'

'My parents, my brother and his family.'

'Ah.'

We sit on the sofa where George was born and Oliver stares into my baby's beautiful face and deep down inside me I hope and pray that this will all work out well.

'You okay if I just nip to the loo?'

'Sure,' he says.

As I zip my jeans back up I suddenly wonder if I should have left them alone. What if Oliver has run off with George? I wash my hands hurriedly and dash back out but they're still there, safe on the sofa.

'He's asleep.'

I smile and nod.

'He's beautiful.'

'I think so.'

'My mum's going to be hysterical when she finds out she's his granny. He's all she talks about anyway.'

'Really?'

'Oh yeah. She emailed me the day he was born. Said he reminded her of me as a baby.'

'Yeah she kept saying that to me only I thought she meant your little brother, Alistair.'

'Ginge.'

'Is that what you call him?'

'Only when I'm trying to wind him up. He's a good kid but he's so much younger than me I hardly know him, to be honest. Mum was very young when she had me, and quite old when she had him.' He smiles, then looks embarrassed as though he's just realised I must be *quite old* too, though probably not any older than him.

'So you're not annoyed?'

'Annoyed? God no. I'm shocked. But I'm also quite thrilled. I never thought I'd be a father.'

'Me neither. A mother, I mean. It was one hell of shock.'

'I'm sorry I wasn't there for you.'

'Would you have been?'

'I like to think so. If I'd known.'

'I couldn't get in touch with you.'

'No. I'm not …' he shrugs just as George stretches his arms above his head.

'He needs to be in his crib really.'

'Can I put him in it?'

We go through to my bedroom where George's crib is beside my bed and Oliver lays him down. George wriggles until he is comfortable then settles to sleep. I switch the baby monitor on before we leave.

'Would you like another coffee?'

'No, thanks.'

We sit side by side on my sofa, both of us studying the baby monitor and saying nothing. Eventually Oliver breaks the silence with a laugh.

'This is awkward.' He turns and smiles at me.

'Yes. It is.' I look down at my hands.

'It's eleven-thirty,' he says, looking at this watch. 'This time last year we hadn't even met.'

'No, it was midnight wasn't it? I got my head caught in your zip when we kissed.'

We both laugh at the memory and the innuendo, just as we had then.

'Then your friend had to cut us out.'

'Yan, yeah.'

'Zippy and Bungle,' he says. 'And you called our

baby George.'

I stop and look at him, it had never occurred to me. 'You're right. Not deliberately. I mean, I named him after my dad.'

He smiles. 'And you gave him my name as his middle name.'

'I did.'

'Thank you. Why?'

'I suppose I wanted him to have something of you. Even if I didn't really know you.'

'Thank you. I'm honoured.'

I frown.

'I mean it. I'm honoured that even though I wasn't there and you had no way on contacting me you named him after me. I can't thank you enough. Really.'

I nod. I feel the tears welling up again and, as I watch Oliver swallow making his Adam's apple bounce up and down again, I suspect he does too.

'What happens now?' My voice is quiet and a little squeaky.

'I'd like to get to know you both better. If that fits with you.'

I nod slowly and smile. 'Yes.'

'And, just so there's no misunderstanding when I said, as I left to catch the plane to Australia, that in different circumstances I'd like to see you again, I meant it.'

'Good.'

'Just as I meant it the other day, when we both grabbed for the parsnips. I like you, Charlie, for you. Not just because you're the mother of my son, he's just the cherry on the cake.'

'And I'm the cake?'

'You are.' He smiles and he looks shy and lovely and I really like him and I'm afraid.

'I can't rush into anything.'

'Absolutely not. We'll get to know each other slowly. But whatever happens I want to be in my son's life.'

'Yes. He should have a father.'

'Thank you, Charlie. You've made me a very happy man.'

This is the reaction I wanted. But I must not get carried away and yet I can't stop smiling and neither can Oliver. We're grinning inanely at each other.

The clock in Mum and Dad's hall strikes twelve.

'Happy New Year, Bungle.'

'Happy New Year, Zippy.'

'And thank you for George.' Oliver leans over and kisses me lightly on the lips. Nothing heavy, no intent there, not like this time last year.

'We should have a drink to toast in the New Year. What would you like?'

Oliver shrugs. 'What have you got?'

'Port.' I remember Dad's M&S special offer.

Oliver nods. 'Okay.'

I dash off to find the port and pour us both a glass, a rather generous glass. I find a tray and put the glasses on it together with the bottle. It's a third full so we can have more if we want.

We sip our port in silence, each contemplating the liquid in our glass as though it might have the answer, even supposing we knew what the question was.

'Another?' Oliver lifts up the bottle.

I nod my agreement. He fills our glasses almost to the top.

'Happy New Year, Charlie.' He raises his glass and

I realise that we didn't do this the first time, we were too intent on getting our fancy dress costumes off and knocking back wine.

'Happy New Year.' I clink my glass with his.

The port loosens our tongues and we start to talk. I tell him about my job, my run in with Bastard Bryan Smith, my best friend Gen. I tell him about the flat being updated, about Shilpa and Anand and CeCe and Yan. I tell him about the flat that got away and how I came to be living with Mum and Dad. He smiles when I tell him that.

'Lucky for me you are, otherwise we might not have met again.' He leans in and nudges me with his shoulder. 'I wish I could have been there for you. Seen you.'

'I was immense,' I say, wondering why I feel the need to tell him.

'I'm sure you weren't. You're so slim now.'

'I was.' I puff out my cheeks and mime myself as a barrel.

'No.' He shakes his head. 'Do you have many photos?'

'No. Not really. I'm not a big selfie taker. Oh God, there is a video on YouTube though.' Why am I telling him about the tap dancing video which even Gen has not been able to have removed?

He pulls his phone out and suddenly we're laughing over it together.

But the mood soon changes when he tells me about his dad, how he spent months going for chemotherapy until, in the end, his dad said no, enough and stopped all treatment. He cries when he tells me how his dad slipped away in his sleep and how that was the best option.

We finish the port and then I make us a tuna sandwich.

'Fish breath,' Oliver jokes as he bites into it.

'Oh well.'

We laugh together and then we fall asleep together on my sofa, the sofa where I gave birth to our son.

George wakes us before dawn. I jump up, despite the port I am a mother first and foremost.

'I should go,' Oliver says, checking the time on his phone.

'This has a familiar ring to it.' It's still dark outside and even though I meant it as a joke it doesn't sound like one, to either of us.

Oliver frowns and George yells out for attention. I rush off the fetch him and when I return Oliver is standing and waiting. He looks at his son with pure delight and George repays it with a great big beaming smile.

'Why don't you feed him?' I put George into Oliver's arms and busy myself making his bottle. A part of me is finding it hard to share George but a bigger part of me is delighted to.

George takes his bottle from Oliver easily, happily. I sit and watch my son with his father.

I want this to work out but I'm so afraid.

Afraid I'm going to have to share George no matter what happens between Oliver and me. Afraid we won't get on.

'How do you want to play this?' Oliver asks as he follows me through to George's room and watches me change his nappy. 'Us, I mean, telling people.' He half laughs. 'Telling my mum that not only is she a granny but she's a granny to her most favourite baby in the world.'

'Right. Um.' I reach for the tub of nappy cream. 'I think we should tell people together. I think I owe it to my parents to tell them first, they've been so good to me, stood by me, especially my mum.'

'Okay.' He nods his agreement.

'Then your mum and your family. But I think we need to do it soon.'

'Okay.'

'And I think we need to make it clear that we're not an item, that we're just getting to know each other. We don't want them jumping to the wrong conclusion.'

He doesn't speak for a moment, he's thinking about what I've said. 'Okay,' he says finally. 'When?'

'Joe and Marlene and the kids go home later today. I'd like them to meet you. So, it has to be today.'

'I'll be back at eleven,' he says. He leans down and kisses George's forehead; George gurgles his approval. 'I'll see you soon.' He leans in and kisses me lightly on the cheek, just once.

'I've got someone coming round at eleven,' I tell them all as they sit around the table in their pyjamas. Even Mum and Dad aren't dressed.

'Who?' Mum immediately starts to pick up dishes off the table.

'Someone I want you all to meet. It's important.'

No one asks but looks are exchanged across the table.

'Oh Gott,' Marlene mutters and jumps up. 'Come children, let's get dressed before Auntie Charlie's friend arrives. Kiki, Benjy and Joe jump up and disappear, quickly followed by Dad.

Mum carries on clearing up breakfast.

'You go, Mum, I'll do this. Did you have a good night?'

'Yes, but it ended much later than I expected.' She rolls her eyes as if her hangover isn't her responsibility.

This time last year I was the one with the hellish hangover; how things have changed.

At eleven on the dot there's a knock on the door and my entire family – who are now sitting prim and proper in the living room – look at me to answer it.

I feel nervous, anxious almost, and excited as, holding George, I answer the door.

Oliver smiles at me, he too looks nervous. He tickles George under the chin, George gives him a gummy grin.

'Okay?' he asks as he shrugs his coat off. It's still frosty outside and I can smell the cold air on him.

'Yes,' I whisper, because I'm keenly aware that the living room door is open and not a sound is coming from within.

We shuffle into the room together.

'Hello everyone,' Oliver says, his voice strong and confident.

'Hello Oliver,' Mum replies, half sighing. She glances at the clock.

'Hey, Oliver,' Joe says as though they are old friends.

'You know Oliver?'

'Yes, he pushed my car last Christmas when it wouldn't start,' Joe says.

'And you bought me a pint or two later as a thank you.'

'Yes, and you bought me one or two back.' Joe laughs.

'Ah, I remember,' says Marlene though she doesn't look particularly happy about it.

'You didn't say?' I turn to Oliver, I'm annoyed he didn't tell me he already knew my family.

'I didn't realise. Not fully.' He makes a face that seems to apologise. 'I wasn't really thinking straight last night.'

At the mention of last night Mum's ears suddenly prick up, her shoulders rise.

'Is this who you wanted us to meet? I thought Oliver had been sent round by Elaine to return the punch bowl I lent her.'

'No,' Oliver says at the same time as I say 'Yes.'

Mum looks between us for clarification. I look at Oliver and wait.

'I don't have the punch bowl, sorry.' Now he looks at me.

'Yes, this is who I wanted you to meet.'

Out of the corner of my eye I can see Benjy playing with the remote control. He doesn't know what's going on and isn't really interested; he'd far rather watch TV. Kiki, however, is staring intently at me.

With the exception of Benjy all faces now look at me with expectation in their eyes.

'I want you all to meet, or *remeet* apparently, George's father, Oliver.'

There's silence. Even Benjy is intrigued now.

'How?' Marlene asks eventually.

'The usual way,' Oliver says, glancing at Kiki and Benjy.

'I know that,' Marlene snaps. 'I mean...' Her voice trails away.

'As you already know we met at my New Year's

Eve party last year; I was Bungle, Oliver was Zippy.'

Marlene opens her mouth to say something but Oliver gets in first.

'And we lost touch because I had to dash off to Australia because my Dad was dying.'

Marlene snaps her mouth shut. Whatever judgement she was about to make must now seem churlish.

'And I only came back recently. And here I am.'

Joe jumps up and shakes hands with Oliver. Then Dad does the same. The three men are grinning at each other in that matey way that men do when they talk about their favourite football team.

Or is it embarrassment?

'Can I be your bridesmaid, Charlie?' Kiki asks as Benjy, suddenly very clued in, punches her in the arm. 'Ow, you bully,' Kiki yelps.

'Go upstairs,' Marlene spits at her children. 'This is adult talk.'

'He started it. He hit me.'

'Go.' Marlene stands up and closes the door behind them.

'We came across each other recently for the first time since then. Oliver didn't know about George.'

'I want to play a part in George's life. I want to be a father to my son.' There's a little emotional edge to Oliver's voice. 'I hope you'll accept me as that. I know it's a shock. I'm still in shock and so is Charlie.'

'That means Elaine is his granny. How ironic.' Mum half smiles. I'm not sure if it's a smile of pleasure or not. 'What does she think of that?'

'She doesn't know yet,' Oliver says. 'My family is next. They're expecting us at one. I'm confident she'll be ecstatic.'

'Yes,' Mum muses.

'I'll make tea.' Marlene rises from her seat and we all stare as she leaves the room.

'That's a first.' Dad catches Mum's eye.

Even Joe sniggers. 'Don't get too excited, you haven't tasted it yet.'

'And what about you two?' Mum waggles her finger between us.

'We don't know yet, Mum. We've only just met properly.'

'We like each other. We liked each other last New Year's Eve. We're seeing how it goes.' Oliver gives me a shy smile.

'Fair enough.' Mum nods her approval and gets up. 'Shall we see if Marlene has worked out how to put the kettle on yet?'

We all laugh. Laughter is a great reliever of tension.

Elaine cries when we tell her. Her face crumples into a hundred lines and she howls with joy, so much so that George follows suit. When they've finished and Elaine has composed herself and George has nodded off to sleep, tired from his exertion, she smiles the biggest, broadest smile.

'I knew I was there for a reason. It was fate.'

'Yes, I think it was.'

'What does Penny want to be called? Nana, Nanny, Granny?'

'She's Nanny.'

Elaine gives me a sideways glance. 'I think I want to be Granma,' she says.

'Granma, it is.'

'Excellent. Shall we celebrate with a cup of tea?'

'I'd rather have coffee,' Oliver says, giving his

mum a quick hug. 'I've had enough tea.'

'Me too,' I add, thinking of Marlene's dense tea. I really don't know how she managed to make it so thick.

'And what about you two?' Elaine echoes Mum's question and Oliver repeats what he told Mum.

Who knows what the future brings?

All I know is that the future is where I'm headed and I don't intend to look back.

Twenty

Two years later

'Where's George's shoe? I can't find the left one,' Mum calls out from George's bedroom.

'He had it last night. Look under his cot-bed.' I feel that combination of excitement and irritation. Today is the day we move into our own house.

'Got it,' Mum calls. 'Now he says he doesn't like it.'

'George,' I yell. 'Put that shoe on if you want to ride in the big van. You need to be ready when it gets here.'

I didn't think we had much to move really, we're not taking much furniture, just my bed, a vintage wardrobe I've recently bought, my chaise, my old sideboard, mainly just the stuff I brought with me from the flat. Much as I love the sofa here we've chosen others for the house and they arrived yesterday, just hours after the carpets were laid.

'Ready.' George appears in front of me as I'm struggling to stuff some clothes into a weird zip up bag that Mum has found. It's neither a shopping bag nor a suitcase, but I wouldn't call it a holdall either.

'Good boy, just stand there a minute.'

George flumps down onto the floor. 'Ready,' he says again.

'Are they back yet?' Mum appears in the doorway,

it's only nine in the morning and she already looks flustered, but we have all been up since six.

'No. I hope the van's not too big to manoeuvre.'

'Ready. Where's Grandy?' George says again sounding a little desperate.

Mum and I exchange glances.

'I should have taken him out for the day,' Mum says, not for the first time. I don't answer. 'Or he could have gone to Elaine's.'

Outside we hear the sounds of a big engine and tyres on the gravel.

George jumps up from the floor, climbs up onto the sofa and grapples with the curtains at the window. 'Ready, ready. Here it is,' he calls as he leaps up and down.

'Get down off there,' Mum says to him.

'George, you know you don't jump on the sofa.'

George gets down and runs towards the door just as Dad comes in.

Then Oliver appears, my heart flips, he looks so lovely. He sweeps George up into his arms.

'Van okay?' I ask, tentatively.

'Yeah, no problem. I just need to put the car seat in it for George.' Oliver leans over and kisses me while still holding George.

'Don't like it, car seat.'

'You have to sit in the car seat if you want to ride in the big van.'

George looks between me and Oliver, then Mum and Dad. He holds his arms out to Dad. 'Grandy?' he calls, looking for an alternative answer.

'You have to sit in the car seat,' Dad affirms.

George pauses for a moment. 'Okay.'

That little act from George explains exactly why it

will be so good to be in our own house. George is bright, he is mischievous, he is a child and he tries to play us off against each other. It's not his fault.

Oliver moved into the annex with us just ten months ago. We'd played the dating/not dating game for over a year and it was getting silly. I was so afraid of making a mistake. Oliver and George have developed a good relationship but, in his house, Dad is still the alpha male – and quite rightly too.

Within weeks of Oliver moving in we started the house hunt…

'I know it's a big house in a great location but look at it.'

'Just needs a bit of imagination.' Oliver had squeezed me tightly as we stood in the middle of the living room.

'It stinks,' I said, and I didn't mean metaphorically. The smell of damp was so strong it was quite nauseating.

'Yeah, but think of the potential. Four big bedrooms, plenty of room to grow.' He nudged me in the ribs, it was playful; I nudged him back, it was not.

'It's awful.'

'It's close to both our families, it has a great garden. It's perfect.' He wasn't going to be deterred.

'We can't afford it.'

'We can offer below the asking price, well below; it's been on for months.'

'Do you think?' I liked the location, I liked the size but I couldn't envisage how it might look. To me, it was a smelly, crumbling dump.

'It doesn't have to be too modern, I know you like old stuff. I remember that London flat you lived in and loved.' He put his arm around my shoulder. 'You can choose whatever you want, have it exactly how you like.'

I stepped away from him. He was winning me over. Could I even dare to believe that this house could be my home? I'd never had the home ownership dream, but then I'd never had the having a child dream either.

'Even if we can afford it we couldn't live in it like this, could we? And I don't think our budget will stretch to having it renovated.'

Oliver had stepped back further from me and frowned. He looked affronted.

'Thanks for the vote of confidence.'

'You're an electrician,' I said. 'You can't do everything.' I hadn't even known that Oliver was a qualified electrician; he was soon up to date with all the current regulations and was certified too. Once settled back in the UK getting work had been easy for him.

'I can do a lot. A lot more than you know about. And, whatever I can't do myself I know someone who can. If money becomes a problem then I can trade trades.'

'What?'

'I'll do work for them in return for work for us. Paul wants his place rewired, so there's a good start for the plumbing.'

How ironic that Oliver and Paul often found themselves working together. Paul had heartily approved of my finding Oliver and telling him about George, not that I needed anyone's approval, but he'd let me know he was pleased anyway.

'Yeah, but what about all the...' I waved my arms

about, 'stuff.'

'Stuff?' Oliver laughed.

'You know, damp, roof, kitchen, everything. Stuff.'

'All doable.'

I didn't say anything. I was thinking about all the money we'd be investing. I still had a sizeable chunk of my redundancy pay left and Oliver had a respectable legacy from his Dad's estate. I wasn't sure I wanted to move; living at Mum and Dad's was cheap and convenient. They babysat George when I worked two days a week in Sainsbury's and whenever we wanted to go out. Mum loved having all the babies over when it was my turn to host the get together from the antenatal classes. I was comfortable at Mum and Dad's, but Oliver wasn't. He said we needed a home of our own. On our own. Just us.

'We'll do the numbers when we get home,' Oliver said, seeing my face, reading my thoughts.

'Okay, but that doesn't mean we're definitely going ahead.'

He laughed at me and kissed me hard on the lips, right in the middle of the damp, smelly living room with its crooked wooden bay window and soggy floorboards.

'I think, behind that hideous boarded-up bit.' He pointed to the weird boxy chimney breast. 'There is probably a great Victorian fireplace.'

'Or a dangerous, ropey gas fire.'

'Or that.' He laughed again. He had a light in his eyes, he was in love with this house but it was only the third house we'd viewed.

'We need to see more houses.'

'Okay,' he agreed, a bit too quickly, a bit too glibly.

We did the numbers; we looked at ten other

houses, some brand new. We even ventured over to Swindon, looked at neat new estates with the promise of new primary schools, but even I had to agree that nothing compared to the size and the location of the dump he wanted.

I allowed myself to be convinced, persuaded.

Once the decision was made it all happened so quickly. The surveyor's report knocked me for six but Oliver just shrugged. It needed rewiring – we already knew that, he laughed when he saw the detail. It needed replumbing – no problem, Paul was onboard. It needed reroofing – Oliver had already done a deal with mate, trading trades. It needed a damp proof course and replastering – hardly a surprise. It was structurally sound and that was all that mattered.

'It's going to be an amazing home,' he said the day we got the keys.

'Better be.' I thought of the massive deposit we'd put down and the mortgage we were committed to for the next twenty-five years.

But that was the least of it, I'm not sure either of us had considered how little we would see of each other while the work went on. Oliver worked all day at his job – he had to, to pay the mortgage. Then worked every evening and weekend on our house, or someone else's when he traded trades. We hardly saw him; no wonder George looked to Grandy as his male role model, since Oliver had moved in with us, we'd seen him less than when we lived apart.

At first, I went to the house every few days, marvelling at progress as hideous old fixtures and fittings were removed and gems discovered underneath. Then progress seemed to stop, nothing changed, nothing improved, but Oliver was still working every hour of every day.

'It's all underneath,' he said. 'You'll see.'

I stopped going, I found it too depressing. I thought we'd made a huge mistake. But Oliver was undaunted, he was cheerful and optimistic, but he was also exhausted. We were growing apart already when we'd hardly had time to grow together.

It was Dad's comments that shook me, delivered one damp Saturday in November when Oliver, as usual, wasn't at home with us.

'You need to support that lad.'

'Lad?' I scoffed.

'Man then. Whatever you want to call him. He needs your support. He's building you a fantastic home, quite literally building it with his own hands. Get round there and show him you're grateful.'

I was shocked, Dad never said very much at all, it was always Mum who voiced the opinions in our family.

I went to appease Dad; I just turned up, leaving George at home with Mum. I walked up the drive – there was one now where previously there had been bramble-overgrown garden. But the drive was just gravel and for the builders' vans and lorries that were parked haphazardly on it. I had mud on my boots by the time I reached the wedged-open front door.

'Hello,' a stranger said as he humped a long plank of wood past my head. 'You all right?'

'Yes, thanks.' I felt stupid. This was supposed to be my home yet I felt like an intruder. 'I'm looking for Oliver.' It suddenly occurred to me that he might not even be there; he might be trading trades somewhere else.

'Charlie,' Oliver beamed, appearing at the top of

the stairs. 'Come up, come up.' He stood and waited for me.

I picked my way through dollops of plaster on the stairs and when I finally reached the top Oliver hugged me.

'Come and see George's room. I've built him a bed.' He grabbed my hand and pulled me towards a room. As we stepped in I stood with my mouth open; I was speechless. 'If you don't like the colour I can change it.'

I looked around the room, a brilliant white ceiling, bright blue walls, satin-polished floorboards, a smart fitted line of wardrobes. In an alcove by the chimney breast was a hand-built bed in the shape of a racing car, painted royal blue with white stripes and the number nine on it.

'I, I love it,' I finally managed to stutter. 'You built the bed?'

'Yep.'

'From a kit?'

'No. It's all my own work.'

'It's amazing.'

'Do you think he'll be okay sleeping in it?'

I examined the bed, estimated that it wasn't much higher than his cot bed; we'd already removed the sides from that because he had managed to climb over them. 'He'll be fine in it and he'll love it.'

'Cool. Is the colour okay?'

'It's perfect.' I felt mean and annoyed with myself for not being there to make these decisions with him. 'What's the nine mean?'

'It's our house number.'

'Is it?' I hadn't even noticed.

'Is the bed okay?' He asked again, needing

reassurance.

'Absolutely perfect.'

'Phew.' He mimed wiping sweat from his brow.

'I didn't realise you'd got this far.'

He didn't say anything, just looked at me briefly, his eyes betraying him just for a second, then he smiled. 'I hope you like the other rooms.' He pulled me into the two spare bedrooms, painted neutrally, fitted wardrobes, polished floorboards. Then the bathroom – better than anything I'd ever dreamed of.

'And this one.' He put my hand on the door. 'You open it.' He stood back and looked nervous.

I pushed the door open and stepped onto the same lovely floorboards as before. The room was enormous, even bigger than my bedroom in the Covent Garden flat. He'd painted the walls a perfect shade of cream, warm and bright and clean. Elegant fitted wardrobes filled the spaces on either side of a beautiful Victorian fireplace. I pointed at it, agog.

'It was here,' he said, hugging me around the shoulder. 'Hidden and just waiting for us.'

I spun around the room, imagining my bed in it, my own things. I felt myself welling up.

'I don't know what to say.' I gulped back the tears.

'Just say you like it.' He grinned at me. 'Please.'

'Like it. I adore it. It's so exactly what I wanted.'

'Thank God for that. I hoped I'd win you round.'

'You have. I'm sorry I lost interest. I'm really sorry.'

'Doesn't matter now. Come on.' He grabbed my hand and pulled me towards a door that I'm sure hadn't been there before. 'En-suite.' He flung the door open. It was beautiful.

I started crying then. Tears of joy.

'We should be in by Christmas,' he said.
'But that's next month. Will it be finished?'
'Pretty much.'

I left him to his work; I had a stack of paint charts and kitchen brochures and spent the afternoon marking my choices. When he came home he explained what would fit in our kitchen and what wouldn't. We chose the kitchen together and I got exactly what I wanted.

I visited frequently after that, marvelling at progress and falling as much in love with the house as Oliver had. I spent days in Ikea choosing rugs and accessories. I visited every furniture shop in Swindon and Bristol. I dragged Oliver to DFS where we spent two hours trying out sofas while attempting to prevent George from jumping all over them.

The drive was laid in the week running up to Christmas; we were lucky that the weather was so mild.

Mum had looked crestfallen when I'd first told her we'd probably move before Christmas. She didn't say anything, but her face spoke volumes. In the end we decided to wait; the living room carpet couldn't be laid until January anyway.

We had Christmas with Mum and Dad, Joe and Marlene, Benjy and Kiki, Elaine, her husband Alan, and Alastair. George jumped all over everyone and rode on Fritz's back whenever he thought no one was looking. Just after New Year we had his second birthday party which was almost a repeat of Christmas.

Gen and her family visited between Christmas and New Year and Oliver bonded with Ralph in a way I never thought possible – they both love watercolour painting. I had no idea.

I realise that there is so much about Oliver that I have yet to find out and he says the same of me.

So here we are, the middle of January, moving day.

'Where have all these bags come from?' Oliver frowns as he looks around the room. 'What's in them?'

'Clothes mostly. And the rest of George's toys.'

'I thought we'd taken most of the clothes over already. I didn't realise you had quite so many.'

'I don't. Some are yours and some are George's.'

Oliver doesn't answer me, just turns to Dad and suggests the furniture goes in first. I watch them lug my bed outside – it's the end of an era, the bed is going in the guest bedroom, we've chosen a new, bigger, better bed for our own room. Mum and Dad and Elaine and Alan have paid for a new bed for us for Christmas. It's very generous of them though I think they might have spent more than they anticipated.

There's a big space in the hall where our lovely old wardrobe will fit and serve as a coat and shoe cupboard. It was Elaine's idea and I love it. My skip-find sideboard will fit perfectly in the dining area of our large kitchen-diner. We don't have a table yet but Oliver has promised to build me one out of scaffolding planks – just like the one Yan made for the flat – only better.

I had a Christmas card from CeCe and Yan, they're married now and expecting their first baby. I'm going to mark them down as another success in my unofficial role as reluctant matchmaker.

'Ready,' George calls, as he sits in his car seat in the van. 'Steady, let's go.'

'Okay, George,' Oliver calls back as he starts the engine and Mum and I wave goodbye. We'll be following in Mum's car with a few odds and ends that won't fit in the van.

Elaine and Alan are waiting at the house. She's been cleaning the kitchen cupboards and has helped me fit in my new dinner service – Ikea's best – and my few pots and pans. There's so much space it seems ridiculous but Mum and Elaine have both assured me that soon my cupboards will be fit to burst – that's how it goes, apparently. I've never really been a kitchen person, certainly not a cook, I've always preferred M&S treats and ready meals. Oliver, however, likes to experiment in the kitchen and I'm happy to give him free rein.

George runs and jumps at Elaine while Alan goes out to the van to help empty it. Between the three of them it doesn't take very long. Mum helps me unpack the bags of clothes and fit them into the wardrobes.

Within two hours we're finished and all congregating in the kitchen. An exhausted George is asleep in his new bed upstairs. Elaine, with a flourish worthy of a magician, has produced six champagne glasses and set them up on the worktop.

'Ooo,' Mum says, 'what's this?' It sounds so rehearsed it's hard not to laugh.

'Well, we can't let this go uncelebrated, can we?' Elaine flings open the fridge – my big American fridge, I remind myself, which I chose – and points to a magnum of Moet inside.

'Wow, thanks Mum, thanks Alan.' Oliver kisses his mum and shakes his stepfather's hand, before yanking the bottle from the fridge and peeling back the foil.

'To Oliver and Charlie and most of all, George,' Elaine says, raising her glass to toast us.

'To all of us,' Oliver says, taking charge. 'Thank you for all your help and support. We couldn't have done it without you.'

I take a little sip of my champagne and feel the bubbles going up my nose.

'Something else for you,' Mum says, disappearing into the utility room. She comes back with a giant bouquet of pink roses in an elaborate vase.

'Where did you manage to get those at this time of year?' Elaine smiles her approval. 'They're just magnificent.' She winks at Mum.

'Wow, thanks Mum, thanks Dad,' I say, aware that I am just echoing what Oliver said to his family. 'Roses and champagne, what could be better?'

Later, Dad takes the van back to the rental place, Mum takes her car home, Elaine and Alan go home too. It's just me and Oliver alone in the house and George still asleep upstairs.

'There's still some champagne left. Fancy another.' Oliver shakes the bottle at me and smiles.

I shake my head and slide my glass across the worktop; it's still almost full.

'Hey, when did you get a refill?'

'I didn't. That's my first.'

'Well, knock it back, there's plenty left in this giant bottle.'

'I'd rather have fizzy water. I think there's some in the fridge.'

'Is there?' He opens the fridge and peers in. 'Oh yeah. What's wrong, I thought you liked champagne.'

'I was just thinking, this day three years ago I was

lugging your Zippy costume along the road and hunting out that weird costume hire shop you got it from.'

'Were you?'

'Yes, cos I thought I was going to get the deposit and I was a bit short of cash.'

Oliver laughs and gets a clean glass out to pour my water into. He sets the glass down next to the vase of pink roses.

'Then,' I continue, 'I find out that the deposit will be refunded to your credit card.'

He laughs again. 'Are you ever going to let me forget it?'

'Probably not.'

He hands me my drink and clinks glasses with me. 'To us,' he says, 'and to our son and our new home and our future.'

'I'll drink to that.' I take a swig and put my glass down next to the vase of roses. I stroke a petal, velvet soft and so perfect. 'Let's hope our future can be as perfect as these roses.'

'It can be with me,' Oliver says, leaning in for a kiss.

'I hope so.'

'We should get married,' he says, quite casually.

'Is that a proposal or the champagne talking?'

He laughs and starts opening the drawers in the kitchen. Pulling one out, closing it, pulling out another.

'Ah.' He pulls something out of a drawer, he has his back to me so I can't see it. He turns around drops down onto one knee. 'Charlie, will you do me the honour of being my wife?'

'What?' I wasn't expecting this.

'Will you marry me?' He proffers a ring box, balancing it on his hand and flipping the lid open. He looks anxious, there's fear in his eyes.

I blink. I don't know what to say but at the same time I know what the answer is and I know I want to say it.

'Yes,' I finally manage.

'Thank God for that.' He jumps up, yanks the ring from its box and grabs my hand. 'If you don't like it we can change it.'

'I love it.' I do. The diamond sparkles at me, it seems to wink.

'From the moment I met you, you've made me happy. I love you, Bungle.'

'Me too, Zippy,' I mutter into his shoulder as we hug and kiss. 'Except when I was lugging that damn costume around.'

'Urgh,' he groans.

'Champagne now?' He grins and pushes my still full glass towards me.

'No. Can't stand the smell of it, never mind the taste.'

'It's okay isn't it? Not off?' He sniffs the bottle.

'No, it's fine.' He pulls his phone from his pocket. 'I'm going to message them all now and tell them.'

'Ha ha, did they know you were going to ask me?' I tilt my hand and marvel at the ring.

'God no. What if you had said no? I'd look a right chump.'

'Did you think I would say no?'

He shrugs.

'But we live together, we have a son together, why would I say no?'

'I thought you'd gone off me, I thought you were

angry with me over the house.'

'I was, but I'm so over that. And I'm so grateful to you for pushing on even when I didn't really want to. I'm sorry I was so miserable and unsupportive.'

He grins again, he looks like a kid, he looks like George. He turns his attention back to his phone again. I push my hand across it, stopping his fingers from stabbing at the screen.

'Before you do that I have something to say.'

'Okay.' He looks almost as anxious as he did just now when he proposed.

'We're having another baby.'

He blinks. He can't take it in. Finally, he manages to speak. 'Really?'

Now it's my turn to grin. 'Yes, really. And this time you are going to be involved at every stage.'

'Yes, yes,' he agrees, still in shock as we hug again. 'I hope it's a girl,' he whispers into my hair. 'So she can be just like you.'

We hear a thud upstairs.

'George,' we say together, pulling apart and grinning at each other.

'I'll get him,' Oliver says, heading out of the kitchen and up the stairs.

As I watch him I marvel at how my life has changed beyond recognition. I think again of CeCe and what she said about her relationship with Yan: love changes everything.

She's right, it certainly does.

THE END

One last thing…

Thank you so much for reading this book. I really do appreciate it. I am an Indie Author, not backed by a big publishing company, so every time a reader downloads one of my books, I am genuinely thrilled. I've worked hard to eliminate any typos and errors, but if you spot any, please let me know: cjmorrowauthor@gmail.com.

If you have enjoyed this book please leave a review on Amazon and/or Goodreads, and if you think your friends would enjoy reading it, please share it with them.

Many thanks
CJ

Email: cjmorrowauthor@gmail.com
Blog: cjmorrow13.wordpress.com
Twitter: @cjmorrowauthor
Facebook: facebook.com/cjmorrowauthor

About CJ Morrow

I am a writer, word weaver, lover of things curious, unseen and unexplainable, as well as a general wordy person. I'm always watching, listening and laughing – mostly at myself.

I love to write about everyday life as though viewed side on – I like to catch the object that moves in the corner or your eye then vanishes when you turn. I'm fascinated by the ordinary man, or woman, who isn't quite what they seem. I see magic or mystery in every situation and relationship. I adore synchronicity – I see it everywhere. Life intrigues me and in my experience, it is often stranger than fiction.

I write across several genres: romantic comedy, psychological thriller and fantasy.

When I don't like what's going on in the world, I write another one. Join me.

Printed in Great Britain
by Amazon